The Hindsight Project

The Hindsight Project

Jeff Welch

THE HINDSIGHT PROJECT

© 2022 Jeff Welch

ISBN 978-1-7333289-8-2

Table of Contents

Acknowledgement

Many thanks to Sherry Johnson for her painstaking and patient editing of this book. Her expertise and insight made *The Hindsight Project* a story readers will enjoy.

Chapter 1 - Recruitment

"Why did you ask me if you weren't going to listen to what I think?" David's frustrated wife asked. Katy glanced at the oven timer as she stirred the sauce she was heating. Not yet a proficient cook, she was trying to make sure everything was ready at the same time.

"I am listening," David insisted.

"But you've already signed a contract?"

"It's non-binding. They just needed to know if I am interested. I can back out, no problem."

"Are you going to?"

"Going to what?"

"Back out."

David paused before answering. He wondered what he could have done differently in broaching the subject of taking the Hindsight job. "Perhaps I shouldn't have brought it up while she's busy cooking," he thought. "Maybe I should have emphasized the benefits first. I could have—oh, it doesn't matter. She would be against it no matter what I did."

This was as heated as arguments usually got in the Hall's household. Harsh disagreements were rare. Both spouses were naturally mild-mannered, but more importantly, they took Bible principles of life and godliness seriously. Most observers considered their marriage to be as close to perfect as it gets. They weren't entirely wrong. The Halls had a good marriage—just not perfect.

The two had met at church where he taught a junior boy's class which included Katy's younger brother, Patrick. Her family moved to David's area right after she graduated from high school, but he didn't take much notice of her until she finished community college. He used Patrick as an excuse to visit the Burns' home until the boy entered the youth group. That's when he finally had to fess up to the family that he was really interested in Katy (as if they didn't know).

Katy waited for a response. Every second her husband delayed his answer added to her frustration. How could he just up and decide they should move away from family and friends? She did not consider David manipulative, but he had a way of convincing her he was right—usually. She wasn't about to let that happen on a subject this serious.

David never claimed his biblical role as the leader of the home to get his way, but Katy felt like he often used their age difference against her. She frowned. "I'm not a child," she thought as she stirred the sauce more vigorously. It's true that, after spending two years with male college students, she was drawn to the calm and confident maturity of this man five years her senior. That was two years ago, and she wasn't in awe of him any longer. She loved and respected him but didn't bend to his will as easily as she used to.

The housewife blew back strands of straight blond hair that fell in front of her eyes. "Supper's almost ready. Can we talk about this later? Will you check on Reese, please?"

David was happy about the reprieve. He went to their six-month-old son's bedroom. His little hand grasping a pacifier, Reese was stirring, but not awake. David gently pulled the *paci* from the child's grip and touched it to his puckered lips. The infant sucked on it contentedly before falling back into a deep sleep. The room's dim lighting reminded David of the business trip he took that led to the couple's current disagreement. Maybe going to that orientation was a mistake. He thought back to just a few days before.

* * *

"Make history by revealing the past!" So read the banner.

David Hall was a bit amused by the attempt to create buzz among scientists with such a lame catchphrase. Still, there he was, in the drab meeting room of an outdated military base in Arkansas. He looked around at the others who accepted the same invitation to "learn about an incredible breakthrough." The lights dimmed before the room darkened completely.

Blackness was interrupted by a projector lamp shining a simple image on a portable movie screen, the kind used in schools during the sixties. Muffled conversations abruptly ended as more than a hundred eyes stared curiously at the projection of a stone.

"A rock?" David wondered. "Why did they bring an engineer all the way here to look at a rock?" The thirty-one-year-old man was purposely ignoring his background in astronomy as the likely reason for his invitation.

Besides sporting a maroon hue, nothing seemed particularly unusual about the item. The object's dimensions were displayed at the bottom of the screen in inches and centimeters. After a few seconds of silence, a man's voice boomed over the decades-old PA system.

"In March of 1952, this meteorite was discovered in a New Mexico desert. In case you cannot read the ruler, it was approximately thirteen by eight by five inches and weighed over forty pounds. Not long afterward, seven siblings were uncovered within a three-mile radius."

A voice in the dark interrupted, "Did you say forty pounds or fourteen?"

"I said forty—four, zero. It is incredibly dense."

The next image showed eight meteorites. All of them had the same tint that seemed more rust-colored on this slide. The first one shown was the largest, with the smallest being less than half its size. The rocks had the same basic features.

"You can see that the regmaglypts on these meteorites are not particularly pronounced."

Dim lighting from the projector revealed several raised hands. Anticipating the question, the speaker explained, "Regmaglypts are indentations on the object. Imagine pressing your thumb multiple times into a ball of soft clay. Some meteorites display very deep impressions. These do not."

A series of images showing various types of meteorites graced the screen while the speaker drew attention to their distinct features. This exercise was hurried, leaving the impression that the information was peripheral, at best. The display ended and ceiling lights brightened the room, revealing a lone figure at a podium near the front right corner.

Dr. Jacob Knab was a tall, fit man in his early-to-mid fifties. His love for science began as a child. Unfortunately, he lacked the acumen for any particular scientific discipline. His natural bent was in administration. Jacob used his education and skillset to stay on the fringes of science, ever hopeful of being involved in some significant development or discovery. Now this disciplined, but pleasant leader's dream was coming to fruition. The director continued his monologue.

"There are basically three types of meteorites: stone, iron, and a mix of those two ingredients. The eight we have been working with do not fit into any of those categories. While they are metallic, their properties do not appear on the periodic table. We've invited you here hoping you will appreciate the uniqueness of these eight gifts from space. They've been subjected to decades of study. Finally, like so many scientific advancements, we have stumbled upon the unexpected. Today, we are at the threshold of what could be one of mankind's greatest discoveries.

"That is why you are here. You represent some of the greatest minds in your fields. The metal in these meteorites possesses a property that can revolutionize the future by revealing the past. We invite you to join us on a two-year mission to exploit that property to its maximum potential. With that, I give you Dr. Carl Gordman."

An unassuming, middle-aged man stood, left his front-row seat, and awkwardly made his way to the lectern. The smattering of applause ended quickly as embarrassed participants felt conspicuous. No one in the room seemed to know what was expected of the audience.

Carl Gordman was at least seven inches shorter than Knab's six-two stature. His salt and pepper Van Dyke beard was poorly groomed, and his clothes were a bit disheveled. While not obese, Gordman could stand to lose thirty (or forty) pounds. His appearance was in stark contrast to the first speaker's trim physique, tailored suit, and shaved face.

"Thank you, Dr. Knab," Carl began, his high-pitched voice cracking with nervousness. He laid a single sheet of a typed page on the podium and never looked up as he read it.

"You have the opportunity to make history…by discovering history." He paused. Even with his head bowed, the front half of the audience could see his pursed lips, an indication that he, too, found the catchphrase uninspiring. After a deep breath, the reluctant speaker continued.

"The skill sets represented in this room will help us in the final stages of a scientific breakthrough beyond imagination. Each of you will receive a folder that includes a proposed contract for your employment should you choose to join us." Carl's upper body began to rock forward and back noticeably, and he raised a hand to the center of his chest. He moved his fingers up and down as if scratching an itch in slow-motion.

Dr. Knab returned to the lectern, placing his right hand on Carl's back to calm him. "Thank you, Dr. Gordman. I'll take it from here." Everyone watched as the dismissed speaker stepped toward the door. After a brief hesitation, Carl exited with labored breathing, still looking at the floor.

Jacob continued without any reference to what just occurred. "I realize you have been kept in the dark about our project. This could make it difficult for you to decide whether or not to commit yourselves to this endeavor. Let me assure you that this is not just a once-in-a-lifetime offer. This is a once-in-forever opportunity.

"In truth, we need fewer than half of you. We will choose our team from those who desire to join us after this orientation. Only the most qualified people in each field will be selected. We would love to involve all of you, but we do have budgetary constraints."

"Director Knab," an audience member interrupted. "I signed a *Do Not Disclose* agreement to attend this presentation. I assume we all have, but you haven't told us anything worth disclosing. Is this all there is? Are you really asking us to commit two years to a secret project with no specifics? I'm sorry, but your assurance that it will 'all be worth it' is not adequate."

"We are not employing *cloak and dagger* to create intrigue," Jacob insisted. "This project, more than seven decades in the making, must necessarily remain under wraps as much as possible. However, we understand your need for more information. Because hints about revealing history are not sufficient, let me bluntly state the crux of the matter. We have the means to witness past events. The unique metal in these meteorites somehow displays shadows of past activity.

"We hope to discover why this is and how we might replicate it. In the meantime, we need to take advantage of this discovery. Your task is to help us fine-tune the process so we can zero in on the history we want to observe.

Please understand that those who agree to work with us will not be doing us a favor. We arc offering you the greatest privilege of your professional career.

"Now that the cat is peeking out of the bag, let's go to dinner. Afterward, we will return and open that bag more completely." The director hurried out the door to check on Dr. Gordman, who was leaning against a wall, still rocking. "You okay?"

"I'm sorry," Carl mumbled.

"Hey, don't worry about it. I understand that speaking to a crowd of strangers is not your thing. I'm sorry I had to insist you do it. If you are going to be my second in command, I need you to step out of your comfort zone more than ever before."

Carl didn't respond, so Jacob continued, "Look, you've come a long way. And you're the most brilliant scientist that I know. If you would rather just work in the lab, that's fine, but I'd like you to take a leadership role. What do you think?"

Drs. Knab and Gordman had been colleagues and friends for more than a dozen years while working at Wentsome Industries. Carl was a scientist extraordinaire, which was what drew Jacob to him. Knab loved to listen to Gordman expound on his theories and discoveries. In return, Jacob and his wife helped this socially awkward friend navigate the challenges of human interaction.

When Jacob was asked to oversee this new project, he immediately invited Carl to serve as his chief scientist. Except for their mutual love of science, the two men were nothing alike. Still, they worked seamlessly together. That work had resulted in an amazing breakthrough.

"Let's get out of this hallway," Knab suggested. "Trina will be bringing the crowd out any time."

***

Trina Benson, Knab's executive assistant, gave the attendees instructions concerning dinner before leading them out of the room. The procession meandered through the bunker-like hallway. Reinforced doors were outfitted with two sensors: one read the magnetic strip on ID cards, and the other appeared to be positioned for retina scans. Every door was identified by a letter and number, and each had a milky white glass panel that visitors assumed allowed occupants of the room to see through.

At the end of the hall, visitors turned right and advanced another forty feet before entering the dining area. The kitchen staff had just finished setting up extra tables after feeding the project's current skeleton crew an early dinner. Each of the eight folding tables had four chairs on either side. The meal was served cafeteria-style where guests quickly moved through the line, choosing between ham and turkey. A small variety of sides followed the meat selection. Dessert items and beverages were on a separate counter.

As guests chose their seats, a few larger men (and one woman) moved a chair from the side of their table to the end for more elbow room. Few of the visitors knew others in the group personally, but many of them recognized those who were considered experts in particular fields. Forty-four men and eighteen women, who were practically strangers, began to carry on casual conversations which quickly morphed into discussions about Dr. Knab's quasi-revelation.

One of the youngest people in the group, Jonathan Daniels, was concerned about Carl and approached Trina to ask, "The second man who spoke in our meeting. He seemed to have some kind of anxiety attack. Is he okay?"

Reluctant to elaborate, the assistant simply offered, "He's fine."

"Does this happen often?" Daniels pressed. Despite his innocent expression, Trina suspected that the blue-eyed stranger was more interested in her than he was in Carl. She was wrong. She would come to learn that the computer programmer genuinely cared about people. For now, though, she misjudged the attractive blonde as just another guy hitting on her. She was not interested in the man whose stubbled face was either evidence of lazy grooming or an attempt to channel some celebrity.

Someone who overheard his query jumped at the chance to enlighten the twenty-six-year-old. "Don't you know who Dr. Gordman is?" the incredulous eavesdropper questioned. "The walking calculator who developed the Gretham principle? He's won more science awards than any other American —twice nominated for the Nobel Prize."

"Thanks," Jonathan answered as he looked to escape the interaction. Aggressive conversationalists made him nervous, especially in a setting of scientists.

The stranger continued, "He was robbed both times of the big prize because he suffers from some kind of emotional or personality disorder."

Daniels looked to Trina for assistance, but she just walked away. Jonathan thanked the enlightener in an effort to end the encounter, but the loose-lipped stranger continued talking as he followed his audience of one around the room. Daniels finally made his way back to a seat next to his colleague, David. Taking the hint, the informant walked away in search of another person in need of his insight.

David Hall and Jonathan Daniels worked for the Sycra Foundation. Sycra and Wentsome Industries were the two entities already involved with the project. At first, Sycra just provided funding. Now that the project was growing legs, they offered to loan some specialized equipment. Jonathan was best suited to operate it. That is why he was invited to the orientation.

While working at Sycra, the two men discovered they shared a common faith and had become good friends. Bible-believing Christians are not common in secular fields of science, so they were both grateful to God for a like-minded coworker. Jonathan felt particularly blessed to find a mentor and confidant in the workplace.

* * *

Following dinner, visitors returned to the meeting room. Some of them tried (unsuccessfully) to peer through the white glass to see what was in the rooms they passed on the way. As they reentered the meeting hall, everyone was handed a large manila folder with his or her name on a label. Director Knab took a microphone from the podium and stood to the side so as not to block the audience's view of the screen.

"First of all, the uniqueness of these meteorites cannot be overstated. Over several decades, these stones have been studied to the nth degree. Because there was so little of this interstellar material available, very little was used for each test. Interest in this study has been intermittent, depending upon each administration's priorities. The longest hiatus lasted about twenty-seven years.

"Almost a year ago, some material was successfully melted. This was no easy task, by the way. Metals melt at differing degrees. Red brass melts at 1,710 degrees Fahrenheit. Tungsten won't melt until it is subjected to 5,400 degrees. It took almost 7,000 degrees Fahrenheit to melt the metal from these rocks. In fact, developing a mold that could withstand that high temperature of liquid metal was a feat in itself. After cooling, the metal was less than 1/16 inch thick and somewhat translucent.

"One of the latest experiments conducted was to determine if this small sheet of space metal would block X-rays and possibly Gamma rays even though it was semi-transparent. A technician put a small bone under the plate, then took and developed several X-rays. In normal light, the bone could be vaguely seen through the thin metal. Not so, in the X-rays.

"The resulting images showed that the material was too dense to reveal items behind it via X-ray, but something curious struck the technician. She called in two colleagues to witness and confirm what she thought she had seen. Again, she took several images. Her associates agreed with her stated findings. At each release of the rays, the metal appeared to show an image as if looking through a hole in the floor. Because exposure time was so short, the image inside the window was hard to discern. It looked like weeds.

"These technicians obtained permission to have the equipment adjusted so that it could release X-rays for bursts up to thirty seconds. They taped the metal to a wall so that they could see the images better. Protecting themselves behind appropriate shielding with a larger-than-usual viewing window, they made the discovery of their lifetimes. While the equipment ran, that small plate of metal revealed a field of high grass waving in the breeze.

In the background were some trees. And further back, there appeared to be mountains. The visual had a slight rust tint like that produced by a camera filter lens. Otherwise, the image was quite clear.

"Upon being informed of this development, I instructed the team to repeat the procedure while recording the image. And now, I present to you that video. Lights, please."

The four or five seconds of darkness seemed longer as the crowd waited for the video to begin. The camera's zoom feature caused the unusual metal rectangle to fill three-quarters of the screen. The back wall of the room created uneven margins for the shot. The metal plate was just six inches tall and ten inches wide, which made positioning the X-ray equipment and camera challenging. After a minor camera readjustment, a voice was heard, "Ready? Here goes."

Suddenly, a grassy field appeared in the area of the frame filled with the metal. The wind was more boisterous than in the earlier description, bending the greenery violently. The trees and mountains that were described could be seen in the background. While this scene only appeared within the metal, most viewers noticed that the X-rays also revealed a stud in the wall surrounding the metal sheet.

Voices could be heard on the audio track, but only the occasional exclamation was loud enough to be clearly understood. After twenty-one seconds, the image reverted to the original scene as the X-raying was discontinued.

The meeting room's ceiling lights flickered to squinting eyes as the projection ceased. An unidentified voice spoke out, "Looks like you've discovered Hollywood special effects."

Someone else chimed in, "Why do you need real scientists when you have FX experts?"

Insolent comments continued to increasing laughter.

"Those weren't even particularly good effects."

"Looked fake to me."

Finally, one man stood and demanded, "Okay, Knab, what's this all about?"

Surprised by the reaction, Jacob looked around the room for some evidence of support. When he saw David and Jonathan sitting silently in the second row, he took heart that not everyone in the room was mocking him. David took a deep breath and stood to face the audience.

"Excuse me. EXCUSE ME!" Hall's booming voice cut through the noise. All eyes fixed on David as he continued. "I doubt that Dr. Knab invited us here to insult our intelligence. I can't imagine what he spent to bring such a respected group of scientists together. Perhaps we could stifle our adolescent behavior long enough for our host to address our concerns."

He turned to direct his next comments to the director. "Sir, you have a room full of noted and notable men and women of science. Surely, you can appreciate their skepticism. Is it possible to provide a live demonstration to alleviate their concerns?"

For the answer, Jacob looked at Carl, who shrugged his shoulders thoughtfully before nodding.

"In the morning?" Gordman half suggested and half asked.

"Very well," Knab answered. "I understand that most of you plan to leave shortly after breakfast. Those who wish to stay a bit longer can see Hindsight in action tomorrow.

Chapter 2 - Demonstration

When David Hall entered his quarters that night, he tossed his heavy folder on the small desk and sat on the room's only chair, an old metal folding one with a little rust. He stared at the 9x12 envelope that mocked his presence at this reveal. Even though he encouraged the attendees to give Dr. Knab a chance, David was almost as cynical as the rest were. His desire to emulate Christ motivated his supportive speech more than his belief that the project was worthwhile.

He reached for the package, then withdrew his hand. He looked to the ceiling and shook his head in disbelief. "What am I doing here?" he asked himself. Glancing back at the packet, Hall read his name on the label. Again, he reached for the envelope. This time, he took hold of it and broke the seal. He pulled out the contents, consisting of documentation of what he learned at the orientation. The most significant item in the packet was the three-page letter that defined his would-be role and compensation. The job description was fairly general but provided enough specificity for David to make an informed decision.

The position of a double bed, dresser, and desk with chair allowed only one straight path from the door to the opposite wall. David paced the ten-by-ten-foot room while looking over the contents of the folder two more times. The proposed pay was not impressive, but it was higher than his current job. He finally sat on the edge of his bed, bowed his head, and closed his eyes.

"Well, Lord, this is nuts," he began to pray. "Here I am fretting about what to do when I know full-well Katy will be against this. I can't imagine You want me to uproot my family for some pipe dream. Sycra seems to want me to come. What if saying no costs me that job? But then, what if this *is* legit? What if this is an opportunity of a lifetime?"

Without realizing it, David slipped from praying to thinking. "Assuming that the undertaking is as far along as described (which is doubtful), how could anyone ignore an offer to participate in the Hindsight Project?"

Again, the engineer/astronomer read the program synopsis, job description, proposed compensation, and contract of employment still to be signed. Unfortunately, contact with the outside was not allowed, so David couldn't seek advice. He decided to wait until the morning demonstration before making any decision. Then he took out his Bible and read for a few minutes. Normally he would have called his wife, but phones had been confiscated upon arrival.

This scenario repeated itself (minus Bible reading and prayer) throughout the compound with remarkably little variation. Every guest read a personalized proposal. Each specialist questioned the validity of the project. All of them weighed the pros and cons of participating. Few went to sleep confident about making the right decision.

* * *

Career-minded Trina stood at the small cafeteria's entrance, welcoming guests as they arrived for breakfast. She proved her mettle as an intern at Wentsome Industries and joined Jacob's staff a year before he transitioned to Hindsight. Like Dr. Gordman, she followed him to the new venture. Trina's attractive features and pleasant disposition kept her in the crosshairs of hopeful suiters—all of whom suffered gentle rejections.

Once everyone arrived and ate, she called attention to the change in the morning's schedule. "We want to thank you all for joining our project orientation. Dr. Gordman and his team have prepared the equipment so that you can see Hindsight for yourselves. If you plan to participate in this morning's live demonstration, please remain here until the others have left. Complete this form to help me arrange changes to your flight schedules if you have early flights planned. Those who choose not to stay will meet me back here at 10:00 with your overnight bags. As a reminder, you may not take anything from this compound that you did not bring."

Someone raised his hand, "Excuse me, but if we don't stay for the demonstration, are we disqualified from consideration?"

"Oh, no. Thank you for asking. My mistake. If you wish to be considered for a position at Hindsight, but you are not staying for the demo, please leave your signed contract with me when we meet back here at ten. For those who are staying, you can wait until after the demonstration to decide whether or not to sign your contract. Now if you chose not to remain, please gather your things and be back here in forty minutes."

As Trina laid the stack of forms for airline change requests on a table, over half of the guests stood to leave, some quickly, others somewhat reluctantly. Those declining to stay included thirteen of the eighteen women, most of whom cited other responsibilities as the reason they could not participate. Twenty men joined the exodus, leaving twenty-nine people to witness the promised demonstration. Of those who remained, few could understand why so many declined.

Once those leaving had gone, the committed and curious went to their rooms to retrieve all the documents they were given, then reconvened. The meeting room that was full of people the previous night did not seem as empty as one might expect. Most of the unneeded chairs were removed and the remaining ones spread further apart. The revised room arrangement gave the impression that the reduced number of attendees was appropriate and expected. Neither of the project's leaders seemed disheartened by the low number of guests who remained.

* * *

At ten o'clock, Dr. Knab was standing at the podium, with Dr. Gordman positioned behind his left shoulder, barely visible. Before a word could be uttered, a member of the security detail rushed it and whispered in Knab's ear. With a look of disgust, Jacob motioned for Carl to take over as he left the room with security. The duo quickly headed back to the dining room where those leaving were gathered with their belongings.

Dr. Gordman reluctantly took the podium, after his colleague's hasty exit from the room. He reached into his back pocket for a handkerchief to wipe the sweat from his suddenly porous forehead. He closed his eyes and sighed in disappointment when he found the pocket empty. It was all he could do to speak to the group in the reassuring presence of his boss. Left alone, he could sense anxiety building within him as he forced a few words through his lips.

"Thank you for staying," he said as if addressing the vinyl tile floor. A smattering of nervous laughter escaped the audience. Referring to four assistants present, Carl said, "These people will take you to see Hindsight." He stepped aside and wiped his forehead with a sleeve.

One of the assistants took the cue that Gordman was done speaking and jumped in to explain that only six people could observe the demonstration at a time. "Otherwise, you may not have a good view," he explained. Then he called out six names and instructed them to follow him. Just seven minutes later, another assistant called for six more.

* * *

A man in his early forties was seated alone at a table with two security guards standing behind him. The contents of his overnight bag were spread out in front of him. Miss Benson handed Dr. Knab a small plastic camera. "We found this in a hidden compartment of his bag," she said.

Jacob took the item, shaking his head in disbelief. After a brief examination, he handed the camera to the guard who came for him. Slowly, Dr. Knab looked around the room, peering into each set of eyes as if he could see their very souls. While most of the men and women met his gaze unflinchingly, a few looked away almost immediately. Jacob's lecture that followed seemed more suited for junior high students than accomplished scientists.

"I don't know most of you personally. You were invited here because of your reputations and upon the recommendation of people whose judgment I trust. The guidelines that came with your invitation were not ambiguous. They made clear that no information shared here was to be revealed outside of this facility. No images, reproductions, or descriptions are allowed. You were given a list of approved items you could bring to this overnight conclave. Not only were cameras disallowed, but so were writing utensils and note pads. That should have told you something.

"Your signature on a DND permits us to aggressively prosecute any digression. Because we are a government entity, non-compliance is a federal offense, punishable by fines *and* jail time. With a federal conviction on your record, you can kiss your precious careers goodbye.

"Now, I don't want the headache of doing paperwork necessary to prosecute offenders. So, I will give you one last chance to come clean. If you try to leave with any of the materials in your packet, or with images or notes of this meeting, you will not be heading home today. Is that clear enough?"

While security escorted the offender out, three men quickly opened their bags to retrieve hidden contraband. Several other men and women sheepishly sifted through their belongings just in case they had *inadvertently* stashed something they should not have. Once everyone finished policing themselves, security guards began going through their personal effects again.

Leaving his disconcerted assistant in charge of final instructions and departures, Dr. Knab was anxious to return to those gathered for the meeting he abruptly departed. Before her boss could get away, Trina asked, "Even if we confiscate everything we should, what will keep them from talking about this?"

"Fear," Jacob asserted. "Just fear."

* * *

Meanwhile, scientists followed their aides like ducklings do their mother, politely staying in the order in which they were called. They headed down a hallway that was off limits earlier. The building structure was the same cream-colored cinder blocks. Some of the florescent lights flickered above, giving a strobe-like effect to those at the back of the line.

The leader paused as a guard scanned her badge and took a paper from her. She stood to the side as her charges walked past the guard. He compared their name tags to the list, then handed the paper back to the aide. They continued, making two left turns before approaching a heavily reinforced metal door, manned by another guard.

Security was well aware of the plan to bring civilians into the restricted lab, but they still followed protocol. This included some redundancies. After checking the aide's list against name tags, the guard pulled a laminated card from his back pocket that was tethered to a belt anchor with a retractable cord. After sliding the card through a reader, he motioned for the group's leader to take the next step.

She positioned her right eye in front of a retinal scanner. When it beeped, she punched in seven single-digit numbers. The door clicked and she pushed it open with her shoulder. She stepped inside to hold the heavy door in place as her followers entered cautiously.

The large room looked pretty much like an X-ray technician's lab, minus a bed. A small metal plate was suspended from the ceiling a couple of feet from one wall. It was five feet above the floor. Just three feet in front of it was a protective wall with a window large enough for four people to look through, standing shoulder to shoulder. A photograph was dangling from the ceiling just inches in front of and facing the metal rectangle.

"Please, do not touch anything, especially the plate," the aide admonished. "We will walk behind it, so you can see the back, then position ourselves behind the protective barrier, so that everyone has a view."

As advertised, the plate appeared to be both metallic and translucent. The group observed that the picture hanging in front could be seen through the plate with a slight reddish tint. As the observers made their way past the object, one man instinctively reached for it. A woman grabbed his arm at the same time the technician ordered, "Stop!"

The almost-offender quickly pulled his hands back, palms facing forward with a surprised expression on his face. "Sorry," he said timidly. He then pocketed his hands for safe keeping.

The group stood behind the barrier with the three tallest men staggered behind the others so that all could see through the window. The hanging photo was removed, and equipment positioned to avoid obstructing anyone's view. Everyone was handed earplugs and opera glasses to use if they wished.

"We will bombard the plate with X-rays for about fifteen seconds," the technician said. "It will get rather loud, so I suggest you protect your ears."

The lights were dimmed, and the machine engaged. Instantly, the metal plate looked more like a high-definition video screen. The scene was an empty field with tall weeds gently bowing to the wind. What appeared to be a bird flew overhead. Those who weren't already peering through magnifying glasses hastily raised them to their eyes. The equipment continued to grow louder until the machine was turned off.

Earplugs and opera glasses were collected, and the visitors were escorted, first to a snack room to collect their choice of refreshment, then back to the meeting room. By the time the fourth group was called, the first assistant had returned to collect the last five guests. It took less than eighty minutes for everyone to observe the phenomena. All in all, each group was in the room for less than ten minutes, but that was enough time to make a strong impression.

* * *

Jacob returned to the meeting room while the third group was out. A couple of skeptics remained, but almost everyone was convinced that the agency had made a previously unimaginable discovery. The director enjoyed listening to spirited conversations among those who enjoyed seeing Hindsight in action. The atmosphere was entirely different from the night before. Discussions among the group evidenced a change from general doubt to exciting optimism. Most expressed interest in joining the team. Some even asked if they could revise their resume to bolster their chances of being chosen.

Knab took the lectern with renewed enthusiasm. Not wanting to appear giddy, he forced himself to subdue a broad smile. He could not, however, dim his beaming eyes. He was excited that the small crowd was finally eager to learn more.

"This is what we think we have discovered. Time is linear, but it leaves a type of shadow or residual effect. Something in the meteoric metal acts as a window to those shadows. What we see on the screen—a "screen" is what some of us call it—what we see, is that shadow. When we bombard the metal screen with X-rays, the image that appears is from some time in the past. We know this because the scene is similar but clearly different than the landscape and weather today.

"It gets even more interesting. As many of you know, X-rays have wavelengths between 0.01 and 10 nanometers. When we expose the screen to different frequencies of X-rays, the image changes significantly. We surmise that the various wavelengths present different periods of time.

"A few of you are experts in gamma radiation. We are enlisting you to help us discover if gamma rays produce similar or additional effects. There is much work to be done. We need to determine exactly how far back in time each frequency exposes and if that result is consistent. We need to extract and melt more of the material to create a larger screen with which to work. We need to build a portable structure in which to house and transport all of the necessary equipment. Such a structure must be able to withstand the rigors of intense exposure to X-rays, and perhaps gamma rays."

"This is still pretty unbelievable," Darren Oats blurted out. Darren was not a scientist in the traditional sense. He and a couple of others were invited because of their production capabilities. It didn't bother him to be just one of two African Americans in the room. He felt more out of place because he was a simple builder seated among world-class scientists. He had no idea how important his skills would be to the project.

"I understand your skepticism," the director confessed. "I've been involved with this project for so long that I've forgotten how unbelievable it is to the uninitiated." He glanced at his watch. The time reminded him that some of the visitors needed to leave shortly. Trina arrived just as he started to dismiss the group. She waved a piece of paper to get his attention. Jacob quickly realized what she was reminding him of.

"We need to collect your signed contracts before we go any further," He explained. "I must remind you that no one is guaranteed a position at this time. We have a limited number of opportunities. So, we will match the best candidate with each position that needs filling. However, we will keep your contract options handy in case we can offer additional positions or need to replace someone in the future."

Renowned scientists and other experts departed from the compound shortly after a hastily produced lunch. Each person wondered if he or she would be chosen to take part in future experiments that could make studying the past a precise science. Jonathan and David had time to spare since their scheduled flight was later. The director asked to speak to Hall privately.

"You come highly recommended by Sycra," Knab began. "I'm glad you decided to sign a contract—"

"Of course, this is contingent upon my wife not divorcing me," David interrupted with a smile.

"I understand," Jacob responded. "I wanted to personally tell you how much you are needed here. Between your knowledge of astronomy and your skill as an engineer and team leader, you'll make a perfect fit."

"Thank you. I appreciate your confidence in me."

* * *

Trina was tasked with seeing guests off. As she shook Jonathan's hand, he gently cupped hers with his free one. "Thank you for an enlightening experience," he said. "I hope to see you again."

She half expected him to pull the back of her hand to his lips, to impress her with debonair charm. That didn't happen. Instead, he just let go, smiled, and picked up his overnight bag. He did look back at her once as he passed through the front door. What Trina imagined to be a lame pick-up line, Jonathan simply meant as a pleasant goodbye—albeit, to a pretty girl.

Drs. Knab and Gordman started perusing previously compiled resumes and double-checking signed contracts. Budget constraints created minor conflicts between the director and his associate as they debated over leadership choices. The department could afford only one expert and one key assistant in each of the five fields. Those leaders would end up vying for necessary resources and additional support staff. Despite some difficult decisions, chosen recruits were receiving confirmation of employment within two weeks.

Chapter 3 - Satisfied

The baby's hard sucking sound brought David's attention back to the present. Pushing the memory of orientation out of his mind, David made his way downstairs. He knew an opportunity like the Hindsight project would never come to him again, but he also knew it might be impossible to convince his wife. He regretted not being able to share any details of the job.

"What took so long?" Katy asked. "Is Reese all right?"

"He's fine. I was just thinking."

Dinner was on the table in the small dining room. "Smells good," he said as he sat. Katy sat at her place opposite him with her hands on her lap. He reached an upturned hand toward her, resting it on the table. She finally made eye contact and with a slight resigned smile laid her hand in his. They both bowed their heads.

"Father, thank you for this food. We ask you to bless it to our bodies' needs." David's prayer felt wooden. They were the same words he often spoke before a meal. Because they were always sincerely said, he never considered it vain repetition. This time he did.

He squeezed Katy's hand affectionately before continuing. "Lord, we need your mind on this matter. I don't want to be stupid or stubborn or selfish. I want what's best for my fam…uh, our family, whatever that is. Give us the wisdom to know your will and peace to follow it."

David released Katy's hand and grabbed his fork. Katy dabbed one eye with a napkin. David took a bite and smiled.

"Tastes even better than it smells."

"So, tell me about this job," she said with a sigh.

"That's just it—I can't. It's a secret government job."

"Do you even know what you'd be doing?"

"Kind of. The director singled me out and gave me some more details in private."

Just three bites in, Reese started crying. Katy laid her fork down and pushed her chair back to stand up. They rarely ate a quiet meal together, and tonight was no exception.

"Want me to get him?" David asked.

"I'm sure he's hungry. You gonna feed him too?"

"Sorry, not equipped. I'll put your plate in the oven to keep it warm."

After feeding and changing her son, Katy brought him to David, who had finished his meal. Dad played with Reese while Mom ate. There was no more talk about the government job until bedtime. Even then, there was not much

David could tell his wife. After sleeping on it, Katy voiced some additional concerns at breakfast.

"Arkansas is farther from both our parents," she said, informing more than complaining. "Would family even be allowed to visit us at this secret base?"

"I really don't know," David admitted. "It never crossed my mind to ask about stuff like that. Honestly, before I got home, I wasn't yet convinced I should pursue it."

"What convinced you…to pursue it, I mean?"

"Intrigue, I guess—mostly," he answered as he finished his bowl of cereal.

"You'd be leaving a lot of friends here. I don't have that many, but there are some girls I would miss. And who is going to teach the boys' Sunday school class?" David's look told her she was grasping at straws for excuses. She continued anyway.

"Will we have a house or apartment? Would it be furnished? What will we do with our furniture? If you are in a secret place, how will I get ahold of you in an emergency? How close is the hospital? How good are the schools?"

"It's a two-year contract. I know Reese is smart, but he won't be in school before age three."

This set Katy on a whole new line of questions. "What will you do when the two years are up? What if you can't find another job? What if—"

"Sweetheart, stop," David said, half asking, half demanding. "You're right. There are a lot of unanswered questions. Why don't we take a trip down there and check things out as best we can?"

Katy took a deep breath and let it out slowly, Lamaze style. As she watched her belly shrink with the exhale, she wondered if she would ever lose the rest of her "baby fat." David never said anything about her added weight, but he hadn't complimented her appearance in a long time either.

She tried to ignore a stain on her blouse that wouldn't come out in the wash. She had precious few clothes that fit anymore. Her maternity outfits were too big and embarrassing. Her pre-pregnancy clothes were too small, bottoms and tops. The couple certainly weren't poor, but she didn't think they had money to spare since she left the workforce almost a year ago.

"Can we do that?" Katy finally asked. "I thought the place was top-secret."

"I'll check," David answered. "If they want me bad enough, we should be able to work out something. Surely, they've run into these concerns with other people."

* * *

David talked to his boss at Sycra, then to Dr. Knab. A long weekend survey trip was approved, and the Halls made the seven-hour drive. Grandma Crisp offered to keep Reese, but Katy couldn't imagine leaving him for so long. When her mother pressed the issue, Katy used breastfeeding as her argument for taking the baby with them.

They prearranged lodging at the motel closest to the base. Katy found it hard to believe the place was the same as advertised on the website. David quickly understood why the price was so reasonable.

"Well, it's not much, but at least it's clean," Katy commented as they stepped into the dimly lit room. David opened the curtains to let in more light.

"It looks cleaner in the dark," he laughed. "Are you sure you wouldn't rather stay in Decatur? They have nicer hotels."

"But it's almost an hour away," Katy answered. "We're here now. Let's stay the night. We can change places tomorrow if we want to."

David brought in the luggage, then made a phone call. "Dr. Knab? It's David Hall…Fine. I just wanted to let you know we are in town…at the Budget Motel…All three of us…No, really, it's not that bad…Tomorrow morning at nine would be great…See you there."

Upon ending the call, he informed his wife, "We're meeting the director at the Huddle House for breakfast tomorrow."

* * *

Saturday morning couldn't come soon enough. The bed was hard, and the roll-away crib was rickety. Katy chuckled when David came out of the shower with a towel wrapped around his waist. "Looks like he hasn't lost his baby fat either," she thought to herself.

Deciding to change accommodations, David checked out of the motel before driving his family to the restaurant. Dr. Knab and his wife were already in a booth with a high chair at one end. He waved until David saw him and stood when the family approached. He offered his hand as they greeted.

"You must be Katy. It is so good to meet you. This is my wife, Kathleen." A series of hellos were exchanged.

"And who is this treasure?" Mrs. Knab asked.

"This is Reese," Katy announced proudly. Kathleen's radiant smile instantly put Katy at ease. "He's almost eight months old."

Bringing his wife was the smartest thing the director could have done to win Katy over. The ladies talked for almost an hour as the men just listened. Since there was a strict prohibition against shop talk in public, the guys had little to say to each other.

Occasionally, Katy asked a question only the director could answer, but Kathleen was the main source of important information about the cost of living, shopping venues, restaurant options, nearby entertainment, crime rate, and child safety.

When Katy asked, "Where would we live?" Kathleen deferred to her husband.

"On the base," he quickly answered. "We've been upgrading the facilities to accommodate all the families."

"I think she needs to know more than that," Kathleen chided.

The director nodded. "Why don't we go for a ride?" he suggested. When he saw Katy give David a look of concern about the baby, he added, "Our car is large enough for both of you and a car seat in the back."

"Couldn't we just drive ourselves?" David asked.

"It would be hard to explain things and answer questions in separate vehicles," Knab explained. So, they both drove to the base entrance where they were met by security. After checking in, a sergeant told David where to park his vehicle. The car seat was secured in the middle of the Knab's back seat, leaving plenty of room for Mom and Dad.

"This is a big car," David commented.

"We raised three daughters," Kathleen said. "Even after they were gone, we could never bring ourselves to downsize."

"*She* could never bring herself to downsize," Jacob corrected.

"They could still visit," she argued. With that, Jacob began the guided tour by pointing out his open window.

"The first buildings we pass are maintenance and storage areas. That there was the commissary and PX. We will use the space for a convenience store, so you don't have to go off base for everything."

"But we can go off base, right?" Katy asked, seeking reassurance.

"Of course," Kathleen promised. "Despite David's work, you will live a pretty normal life here."

Jacob cleared his throat to warn his wife not to venture any further on the subject of work. "There's the park with a playground. You will have a small backyard, but I think Reed will enjoy the park when he is a bit older."

"Reese," Kathleen corrected quietly through clenched teeth.

"Reese, that is. I'm sorry," Knab said.

"No problem," David responded, glancing at Katy, who rolled her eyes at Jacob's faux pas. She looked back at her husband and offered a pretentious grin.

"Here is where one of three sections of housing begins. We expect to only need this one area for the number of families we will be housing." He pulled into an empty parking spot and took a single key from his cupholder.

Everyone exited the vehicle. David offered to carry Reese, but Katy held on to him like a security blanket.

"No front yard to speak of," Kathleen stated before either visitor could. "But the inside is pretty roomy."

Katy had never seen a townhouse with eight attached dwellings. Each residence had a single-car garage, but a large enough driveway to park two vehicles. Jacob unlocked the front door and motioned for Katy to step in first. She was barely inside when she stepped aside to let David lead. The others followed, but stayed behind, letting the couple explore on their own.

Passing the stairway, they visited the living room and adjoining dining area. Making a horseshoe turn, they entered the fully-equipped kitchen, followed by a small family room and half-bath. They glanced in the cupboards and three downstairs closets before checking out the garage. David took Reese before heading upstairs. They passed two small bedrooms that shared a Jack and Jill bathroom before entering the master bedroom with an ensuite and walk-in closet.

"This is enormous," Katy said, pleasantly surprised. "But it has three bedrooms. Would ours be much different?"

"This is yours," Jacob said with a smile, as he and Kathleen joined the couple upstairs. "The extra bedroom is just-in-case."

"Let's go see the back!" Katy said excitedly. She hurried down the stairs to a sliding glass door that opened onto a small patio and backyard. Privacy fences separated the neighbors and a chain-link fence at the end of the yard would keep pet dogs and small children safely inside. When David finally arrived with Reese, Katy turned and gave him the *I love it* look.

With the house tour being a resounding success, the rest of the base held little interest for Katy. They spent the last hour continuing their visit at the Knab's residence before Jacob took the Halls back to their car and saw them off. Their drive to the "big" city to find better sleeping arrangements was full of conversation.

"That house is twice as big as ours," Katy observed.

"Well, almost."

"And a fenced-in yard would be perfect once Reese is running around."

"Yup."

"You really can't talk about the work at all?" she asked, hoping for just a hint.

"I really can't. You saw how he shut Kathleen down when she just said the word *work*."

"She's a sweetheart."

"Kathleen? Yeah, she seems nice." David was careful about complimenting other women, even this one, twenty years his senior. He wouldn't call Katy the jealous type, but she did seem sensitive whenever he mentioned a woman from work or even church. It never seemed to be an issue before Reese came along. He just learned to avoid the subject as much as possible.

Realizing there might be a wrinkle in their plan, Katy's mood mellowed slightly. "What about church?" she asked. "Pastor always says, 'before making a move, be sure there is a good church to be a part of.'"

"I know. I did a little internet research before we came. We'll check out Calvary Bible Church in the morning and, if necessary, Fellowship Baptist Church in the evening."

"During the afternoon, can we drive around the town?"

"Sure, but what about Reese's nap?"

"We'll manage," Katy responded. "I think we need to be as thorough as possible with this visit. Check out everything we can."

After the Halls checked into a Holiday Inn, they went out for supper. Both of them seemed to have used up their daily supply of words, so the evening went by quietly, followed by early retirement.

* * *

On Sunday morning, the comfortable bed made getting up difficult. A crying baby made staying in bed impossible. Opting to skip the Sunday school hour, the couple didn't bother hurrying to get ready. After a leisurely breakfast, they made the almost hour-long trek back to Wentsville.

"Welcome," a greeter said, handing each of the visitors a bulletin. "Would you like to make use of our nursery? It's well-staffed."

"Thank you," David answered, "but we'd prefer to keep him with us if that's all right."

"That's fine, but it might be best if you sit near the back in case you need to slip out with the little one."

"No problem."

"Pastor likes to meet visitors after the service for just a moment if you have time."

"We'd like that. We are looking for a church home."

"Great! I'll tell him. His office is just down that hall."

Once the family was seated, several ladies approached and fawned over the baby. The service began on time and concluded before anyone but the children were weary. The greeter who met them at the door quickly approached and offered to lead them to the pastor's office. They stood outside the door for a few minutes waiting for him to arrive after greeting attendees.

"Hello, I'm Pastor Jeff," he said enthusiastically, shaking David's hand and giving a nod to Katy. "And who have we here?"

"Our son, Reese."

"Well, come on in."

The usual pleasantries ended abruptly when the pastor asked, "Are you two believers?"

Katy thought it was an unusual question to ask people who came to church. She didn't have long to think about it before Jeff explained, "I ask because a lot of people come to church who have never come to Christ. Do you know what I mean?"

"Certainly. I grew up in a Christian home and trusted Christ when I was eight." After about three minutes of telling his tale, David looked at his wife. "Katy…well, I'll let her tell you."

Katy was not embarrassed about her testimony, but she was a little afraid she might express it poorly. She wasn't as fluid as David, so she was rather succinct. "I got saved at camp when I was fifteen."

The three talked (well, mostly the men) for quite a little while, even delving into some theological issues. Eventually, there was a knock on the door that indicated Jeff's family was anxious to leave. "I'm sorry to have kept you so long," the pastor said. "That knock means lunch is probably burning." As they stood to shake hands he added, "Please, come visit again."

"I'm sure we will," David promised.

Once in the car, Katy asked, "Well, what did you think?"

"I liked it—and him."

"Me too. Do we even need to go to the Baptist church?"

"I guess not."

After a fast-food bite, the pair drove around town to get the lay of the land. By two-thirty that afternoon, they were ready to head back to the hotel for some rest. That evening they checked out the "big" city for a couple of hours, then headed home after a comfortable night's sleep.

* * *

Sycra's commitment to rehire David once his tenure with Hindsight was completed brought great relief to Katy. The Halls could see God's hand behind most of the pieces falling into place for their move. It was two months before the Halls were able to relocate into the refurbished housing at the obsolete Army base in Arkansas.

Only employees knew what advanced equipment was housed inside the nondescript facilities. To the outside community, it appeared that the Army base had simply reopened with a very small contingent. Military police provided security, including manning the sole entrance.

More than half of the committed experts were already in place when David arrived. Judging from the name tags he read, David was one of just a few who didn't have some type of doctoral degree. In reality, that was only true among the team leaders.

Dr. Knab conducted his introduction at a specially called meeting. "You will see a new face around here," he began. "This is David Hall. He is the man who will make sense of the data we are collecting."

Suddenly, David felt uneasy. It was becoming apparent that he wasn't just another employee—or team leader. Dr. Knab expected him to play a pivotal role. Jacob had tried to make that clear at private meetings, but David just brushed aside the *we really need you* speech as buttering him up.

"He will schedule meetings with each department head next week. You can bring him up to speed then. Don't bother him now. Let's give him a chance to get oriented to his role and acclimated to his environment."

David did meet with the human resources department to complete paperwork and learn more about his benefits. Since security was provided by the Army, Captain Bucks was tasked with explaining protocols and procedures. That took most of Thursday. What time he had left was spent touring the restricted areas of the base. David returned home exhausted.

Chapter 4 - Acclimation

"I love this new stovetop," Katy said when she heard him close the front door. "The oven even has a convection setting." Her back was turned, so she didn't observe his body language as he walked past her to sit at the table. She did notice that he didn't respond or even kiss her. So, she looked in his direction.

For a while, he stared straight ahead. When he closed his eyes and sighed deeply, she walked over and placed her hands on his shoulders. After glancing at Reese in his playpen, Katy turned her attention back to her husband. "What is it? What's wrong?"

"I may have gotten myself in too deep."

"What do you mean?"

"I can't talk about it," he sighed. "I wish I could."

Katy leaned over and whispered, "Who would know?"

David turned his head to make eye contact and smiled, "God." He looked around the room, pretending to suspect it was bugged with surveillance equipment. "Who knows who else?"

Katy straightened and went back to the kitchen. She opened the oven to check on the chicken before stirring the vegetables on the stove. Then she went into the family room and interrupted her son's playing by picking him up.

David sensed she was not amused by his silly remark. He used to talk about his work at Sycra all the time. Secrets made her uncomfortable, even good ones like surprise parties and trips. She just didn't like feeling ignorant. David tried to mend the fence.

"Seriously, sweetheart. I do appreciate your wanting to show support. And I feel worse than you do not being able to tell you about work. I've just got to honor my commitment. Understand?"

She answered without looking in his direction. "I guess, but if you can't talk about it, maybe you should leave your complaints at the office too."

He wanted to argue but didn't. Instead, the good daddy put on his happy face and took Reese so Katy could finish fixing supper. A few minutes of playing on the floor turned out to be good therapy. When supper was ready, David placed the child in his highchair and secured the plastic belt. The parents sat and each took one of Reese's hands. They held each other's free hand, reaching across the table, and Daddy prayed.

David loaded his plate but hadn't taken his first bite before he recoiled in disgust at a putrid odor. "Oh, Reese!" he exclaimed.

"It's not Reese," Katy contradicted with a laugh. "It's these pureed peas." She pressed the baby food jar toward her husband's nose. "It's awful. Smell it."

With knee-jerk reaction in full force, David pushed against the table to distance himself from the offending odor. Since the chair legs didn't move, he found himself tipping backward, landing with a thud. Reese's eyes widened at the spectacle.

"Are you all right?" Katy asked, suddenly regretting her action. Having gotten over the shock, Reese began to laugh hysterically. The sound of his cackling was too much to ignore. Soon, all three were tickled.

"I'm fine," David finally said, catching his breath between chortles. "I think I'll just eat down here where it's safer."

David did make it back up to the table. The rest of the meal was uneventful, although the mood was uncommonly lighthearted. After dinner, David helped with the dishes while Reese entertained himself. There was scarcely a thought about work for the next four hours. After putting the baby to bed, the couple cuddled on the couch and watched a chick-flick.

When he went to bed, David purposed to get up a bit early and spend extra time in prayer and Bible reading—especially prayer. Unfortunately, Friday morning came too early, and the *rubber* of good intentions met the *road* of oversleeping. Skipping morning nourishment, both physical and spiritual, the engineer hurried off to work.

* * *

"I can't believe I'm going to be late to work my first week," he fumed while driving. He pulled into the parking lot with a bit of a tire squeal that caught the attention of a couple of pedestrians. Once parked, he unbuckled and reached behind his seat for his briefcase. Nothing. He was just starting to panic when he realized he hadn't taken a briefcase home. Next, he touched his chest to make sure he had his name badge.

"Thank you, Lord."

The man who exited the car wasn't any calmer than the one who entered it mere minutes prior. As salaried staff, David didn't punch a time card, but his arrival time was forever archived in the computer when he scanned his badge—08:37. He went straight to his office to find a tower of folders on the corner of his desk. David picked the top folder up and opened it slowly. He was reading the second paragraph when a Trina poked her head through the open door.

"Mr. Hall? I'm sorry to interrupt, but Dr. Knab wanted to see you as soon as you arrived."

"Thank you, Miss Benson."

"Please, call me Trina. And you're welcome." She disappeared, and David closed the folder and laid it back on top of the pile. He made his way to the director's office, taking two wrong turns in his haste. He knocked on the closed door and waited to be invited in.

"David!" Jacob's pleasant greeting was tainted with a hint of concern. "I tried to call." David touched his empty shirt pocket, then all four pant pockets.

"I'm sorry, I must have left it at home," the embarrassed employee confessed. "I woke up late and got here as quick as I could. Never thought about my phone."

"Rough first day?"

"Not really," David paused, then corrected himself. "Well…yes. It was a bit overwhelming."

"I understand. Coffee?"

"Please."

Jacob poured them each a cup from the in-office coffee maker and sat at his desk as he motioned for his new hire to take one of the two chairs in front of him. David briefly described his Thursday and his plans for today. Jacob encouraged him to take things at a reasonable pace.

"Trina will schedule meetings with the department heads for you. On your way back to your office, stop by and let her know of any time you need to be blocked off. It will probably take you all day to weed through the reports. I want you to meet with Dr. Gordman and me first thing Monday morning before you see anyone else."

"Yes, sir."

"Oh, and by the way, you don't have to wear a tie here—not unless we are hosting visitors. Nice one, though."

"Thanks," David replied as he loosened the noose around his neck. "I'm liking this place more already."

* * *

"You wanted to see me?" David asked as he entered Dr. Gordman's office. Carl was reading some technical data, so he didn't answer right away. David bided his time by glancing around the room. He was surprised that there were no pictures on the wall, just framed diplomas and some certificates of achievement.

Gordman had two desks. His working desk was against the back wall and could be hidden by accordion doors. He didn't usually bother concealing the messy stacks of papers and books. While Dr. Knab encouraged his assistant director to keep the office desk free of clutter, it was almost as unkempt as the back one. Carl's chair was positioned between the desks so he could pivot between the two. Gordman finally looked up.

"I understand you are an astronomer," Carl said straight away.

"I do have a degree in…"

"That is one of two reasons Dr. Knab and I wanted you on this project."

David was curious. "I thought you hired me for my engineering expertise."

"That was the other reason," Carl answered. "That's an unusual combination."

"It is," Hall agreed, then explained. "I studied engineering as a career path, but I've always enjoyed studying the cosmos. I was able to pursue a double major without much difficulty."

"So, you are smart," acknowledged Carl.

"I do alright, but I'm sure I'm no match for all the PhDs around here."

"Probably not, but your skills are just what the doctor ordered." Gordman was referring to Dr. Knab, not the idiom, so he was surprised when David chuckled at the pun. "Is something funny?"

Straightening his face, David answered, "No, I'm sorry. I just thought of something unrelated. What did you want to see me about?"

"As you know, each X-ray wavelength causes Hindsight to reveal different images. We postulate that those images are from different times in history. We need you to determine the exact distance in time each wavelength represents."

David's mouth fell open as he stared in bewilderment. "How…how am I supposed to do that?"

"That's your job."

"I don't even know the wavelength range of X-rays," Hall commented.

"Most range between ten picometers to ten nanometers," Gordman said. "Our expert in the field will answer all your questions. You should take an image of the night sky at various frequencies and compare the star formations."

David interrupted to show he followed the thinking. "Determine when in history the images represent and determine if the ascending wavelengths have consistent time differences. We can then program the equipment accordingly."

"Precisely."

"That will be interesting and enjoyable work," David commented.

"If you say so," Carl answered. "I don't mind pouring over mounds of data, but staring at pictures of the sky doesn't appeal to me."

"I'm looking forward to it. After all, the heavens declare the glory of God."

"Excuse me?"

"I enjoy studying the heavens because they are so awe-inspiring. They demonstrate how big God is and how small we are."

"I've never given much thought to the concept of higher life forms," Carl confessed. "I believe they are possible. I just don't see much use in spending time on something unknowable. I prefer to work on real science."

David decided to leave the subject for now. Letting Dr. Gordman know his belief in God was sufficient witness for the time being. He confirmed who the expert on X-rays was and took his leave to visit that department. Afterward, David returned to his office, and perused the folders full of documentation, explanation, and analysis. The proverbial fish-out-of-water found himself googling unfamiliar words and terms all day long, but by four o'clock he had a reasonably firm grasp of what he was evaluating. More significantly, he understood why he was chosen for the job.

* * *

"Mr. Hall! Hey, Mr. Hall," a voice called out as David made his way through the parking lot. "The Missus wanted to know if you and your family could come over Sunday for lunch." David recognized the man from orientation several months earlier.

"That would be great. Let me check with Katy, my wife. Can I get your phone number and call you later?"

"Sure. By the way, the name's Darren, Darren Oats."

"I remember meeting you at—" David suddenly remembered that work discussions were not allowed outside the secured facilities. "I mean...good to meet you. I'm David, by the way. Mr. Hall is my dad."

"I hear you." Darren's family of five was the largest on base. His wife was great about welcoming new arrivals. Darren called out his cell number as David punched it into his phone. He pushed "call," and Darren's phone rang.

"Now you have my number too," David said. "If I don't call you by nine, holler at me. I don't want to leave you hanging."

"Sure thing. See you Sunday—I hope." Darren got into his Toyota Tundra and drove past David's Hyundai Elantra with a smile and a wave. The full-sized truck dwarfed Hall's small sedan, leaving him feeling a little belittled.

* * *

At dinner, David brought up the invitation, which was met with enthusiasm. So, he made the phone call. Darren was a little surprised that the Halls responded positively, so quickly. After reporting the news to his wife, he offered details.

"Destiny says we will eat a little after noon, but you all can come over as early as eleven. Our address is 149 Roosevelt."

"I don't think we can get there until after twelve. I'm not sure what time church will get out."

"Oh, church…no problem. Just get here when you can. I'll fire up the grill but wait till you get here before putting the meat on. Ribs okay?"

"Ribs are great, thanks." David ended the call a little amused by the awkward response to his revelation of going to church. "May as well let the news get out early," he thought to himself.

* * *

Saturday was a day to relax with a visit to the base children's park and lunch at a local diner. They made it to Sunday school the next morning where David was asked to introduce his family and give a short version of his testimony. Since the pastor was teaching, he knew David would have no problem sharing a few words. After the morning service, the Halls followed GPS directions to the Oats residence, which turned out to be less than a two-minute drive from their house.

The Oats' three children were playing near the front door, waiting for their guests. Their son had the same dark complexion as his dad, but the two girls were a far lighter shade of brown. The oldest daughter ran inside to announce the arrival while the boy watched the youngest daughter approach the Halls as they unloaded.

"Ooo, you have a baby," the nine-year-old said.

"Yup, this is Reese." Katy removed the face-covering blanket to reveal a sleeping child. "And who are you?"

"I'm Deana, and Drake's my brother. And that's Keisha. She's thirteen."

The teenager returned just in time for the introduction. "A baby!" she exclaimed as she rushed over for a look-see.

"You all can come in," Drake announced. Just then, Darren showed up and motioned the family to enter. "You kids come inside too."

Everyone followed the man of the house to the kitchen where Destiny was taste-testing her delectables. During introductions, she washed her hands and dried them on her colorful apron so she could shake David's hand. She then took Reese from his mother's arms and placed him in David's. The nearly six-foot-tall woman then embraced her guest.

"I'm so glad you came," she said.

The shocked hug recipient barely moved during the experience. She did manage to reply, "Me too."

After a little while, Destiny stood at the screen door to observe her husband's progress before speaking. "You said twelve-thirty. It's twelve-forty and everything is on the table except your ribs."

"The ribs will be ready when they are ready," the self-imagined BBQ king replied. "Right now I'm showing our guest how to barbecue properly."

"You have to know it to show it," Destiny teased.

His next statement was to David, but for his wife's benefit. "You have to treat them just right, with a loving, but firm hand—like a woman."

"Like you know how to treat a woman," she mocked.

"I'll treat you later," he said.

"Mmm hmmm, we'll see."

By this time all the adults were laughing, and the girls were doing their imaginary gagging. Drake just kept looking at the ground, waiting for the embarrassing episode to end. Judging from the children's reactions, this kind of bantering happened a lot—a whole lot.

A few minutes later, when everyone was seated, Destiny used her sweet voice with Darren. "Honey, do you want to say grace?" Taken aback, the man of the house lowered his eyebrows in disapproval. "These folks came from church, remember?" she said.

While he frowned, her attention veered to the guests. She informed them, "We used to go to church regular before we moved here." She looked back at her husband, who had composed himself enough to ask David to say the blessing. He happily complied.

"Father, thank you for new friends and this food they are sharing with us. Bless them all, I pray in Jesus' name."

"A-men!" The mother and youngest daughter said in unison.

"Oh…mmm…oh! These ribs are fabulous," David raved when they finally began eating.

"Everything is," Katy added.

During dinner conversation, Katy mentioned, "I'm curious about your children's education. Where do they go to school?"

"In town," Destiny answered. "Children on base are bussed to the local schools."

"They allow buses in here without supervision?" David asked.

"Sure," Darren answered. "Visitors are allowed on base with proper permission and identification."

The Halls were beginning to understand that the powers that be wanted the facility to appear less restrictive than it was. Hidden in plain sight, Hindsight activities were conducted in high-tech labs disguised as simple barracks, garages, and office buildings.

"We're just not allowed to talk about Dad's job or education," Keisha chimed in.

She was right. Team members' families and friends were not welcome near the laboratories, and discussions about the project were strictly forbidden outside the workplace. Even those with high-security clearance were not allowed to speak about work amongst themselves when outside secured areas.

The visit turned out to be very informative. Thanks to the Oats family and the Knabs, Katy was growing very comfortable in her new home. They made it back to their place at about four o'clock, and after a relaxing evening, David was ready for the challenges of the next week.

* * *

Monday morning was spent with Drs. Knab and Gordman further clarifying David's role and answering what seemed like dozens of questions. On Tuesday and Wednesday, he met with the department heads whose reports he had read the previous week. He went to work on Thursday a new man, with a plan to meet, if not exceed, his employer's expectations. That plan included someone he had not seen on campus.

Friday morning, David met with Dr. Knab to discuss his need. "There was a computer programmer at your original orientation, Jonathan Daniels."

"Yes, I remember him," Jacob answered, anticipating David's next statement.

"I need him."

"We asked him to join us. He signed a tentative contract, but when we called to confirm, he said he was happy where he was. Didn't you two work together at Sycra?"

"Not together, so much, but we saw enough of each other. I can't believe he turned this down."

"What did he say when you told him you were coming?" Jacob asked.

"I never did. We never talked about this project."

"I'm impressed that you took the DND so seriously—surprised, but impressed. I'm happy to bring him on board if you can get him to come."

"I can call him?"

"Sure, but you will have to convince him to come without offering any additional details about the project."

* * *

David knew Jonathan rarely took personal calls while at work, so he phoned his friend's office line. Jonathan was happily surprised to hear from David.

"How is it?" Jonathan asked, knowing his friend couldn't really answer.

"Good. I'm surprised you didn't come too."

"I would have, especially if I knew you were taking the job."

"We weren't supposed to talk about it," said David. "Didn't you figure it out when I left Sycra?"

"By then, it was too late. Remember, you said Katy would never agree to a move. I didn't want to go alone, so I turned them down when they called. A week later I heard you were gone. What was I supposed to do?"

"I'm sorry, man. You're right, I didn't give you fair warning," David admitted. "But I have good news if you're interested."

"What's that?"

"You can still come. In fact, I really need you. I got permission to offer you ten percent more than the original starting salary."

"Really?"

"Yup. The leadership assumed you turned down the job because it didn't pay enough. When I told them I need you, they approved a higher offer. What do you say?"

"You need an answer right now?" Jonathan asked.

"No. You can pray about it first," David answered. "I'll wait."

The phone was silent for a moment before Jonathan understood his friend intended for him to pray right then, and give him an answer. Of course, David was teasing.

"Call me back tomorrow," Jonathan said. "I want to call my dad and get his advice."

"Be careful you don't tell him anything classified."

"I will," Jonathan promised.

Despite remaining ignorant of the proposed job's details, Jonathan's father offered some godly counsel. After praying about it himself, Jonathan felt comfortable about making the move. Seventeen days later, he was on site.

Chapter 5 - Results

Dr. Gordman stepped into the newly built lab as technicians positioned Hindsight to face straight up. The entrance area was like a foyer with a large window directly ahead and a door to the workspace on either side. All the walls of the much larger laboratory space were protected by a lead coating three times thicker than OSHA required. Carl watched as the team wearing protective gear prepared to take images of the sky.

Jonathan was too busy with his equipment to notice the assistant director's presence, but David saw him while surveying the room, watching the team work. He waved but Gordman didn't respond. After another quick glance around the room, Hall stepped into the observation area.

"Dr. Gordman, I'm glad you could come."

"This is an important step in the project," said the assistant director.

"Yes, it is," David agreed. "I was a little nervous at first, but I think this will work out well." When Carl didn't respond, he continued. "It would have been nice to work from a more traditional spot for stargazing."

"That would have offered more data to compare your results to?" Gordman asked.

"Exactly. I did find online sites that offer sky charts based upon zip codes."

"Will they be accurate enough?" Carl questioned.

"We'll see," came the uncommitted answer.

One of the technicians indicated the team was ready to begin, so David stepped back into the lab. An image of the stars from an unknown time soon filled the large screen made from the metal of several meteorites. Carl watched the activity for about forty minutes, then left. That was a long time,, considering he did not have a good view of the screen.

With David's help, Jonathan had programmed the computer to manipulate the X-ray machine so it would change the wavelength by ten nanometers at a time. When the view wasn't a night scene, the team had to wait several hours and check again. This gave the equipment time to rest. Each image was recorded digitally with pertinent information included in its file.

The exercise took almost a week. Then the process was repeated four times, moving Hindsight to the four corners of the room to obtain additional views. Finally, the multiple images for each wavelength were combined to provide the largest view of the night sky possible from the laboratory.

Once the data was accumulated, David shared it with Drs. Gordman and Knab. Carl offered to help, and his keen eye for discrepancy saved Hall and

Daniels a lot of time and effort. While the men could program a computer to do the necessary math, Gordman provided the formulas necessary to discover the desired information.

* * *

Most Hindsight employees signed contracts for two years of service. Within fourteen months of Jonathan's arrival, the team was experiencing advances at breakneck speed. Modern technology made progress with the necessary precision possible. After diligent research, testing and evaluation, a miracle was born or, at least, built.

Finally, it came time to unveil the Hindsight Project to senior government officials and the two corporate sponsors, Wentsome Industries and The Sycra Foundation. Dr. Knab was serving on the board of Wentsome when the company was tagged to renew research on the meteorites. His early involvement made Jacob the obvious choice as director back when the project became a separate entity. Jacob brought along some competent and trusted colleagues for the agency's inauguration. Wentsome Industries remained active, mostly in an advisory capacity, but occasionally lending employees to meet temporary needs.

The Sycra Foundation provided much of the specialized equipment needed for experimentation. It was also the source of hard-to-obtain scientific data. The only staff that came from Sycra were those needed to explain the data or operate the equipment. Only two of these ever became full-time employees of the agency, David Hall and Jonathan Daniels. These men were the foundation's way of remaining relevant to the project.

Others present at the unveiling were somehow associated with the federal government: General Pyle from the Joint Chiefs of Staff, Senator Cody from the Select Committee on Intelligence, an official from the Vice President's office, and the Assistant US Attorney General. They and their respective gaggle of attorneys and aides assembled at the base to learn what Hindsight could do. The gathering of such prominent leaders signaled high expectations.

Dr. Knab welcomed the attendees and began his introduction. "We can see the past—literally. We can watch what occurred on this spot a year ago, a decade ago, a century ago, and millennia past. Something we learned early on is that seeing is believing when it comes to something so revolutionary. So, before we hand out documentation and offer details and explanations, we want to show you the Hindsight Project in action. For your protection, we must insist that you wear protective suits."

Agency aides distributed silver outfits that looked like they came from a low-budget sci-fi movie costume closet. Though there was some rolling of eyes, no one complained about having to wear the protective coverings.

Following one team member's demonstration, they stepped into the one-piece suits, pulling them up to the waist. Agency employees went around, helping pull the heavy garments to the wearers' necks while participants forced their hands into attached gloves. Once the zippers were raised and overlapping flaps were secured by Velcro, headgear was distributed.

Helmets were covered with the same material as the suits except for a large transparent shield in front of the eyes. The helmets were secured to the suits, and everyone was checked and double-checked to ensure they were properly covered.

While dressing, everyone noticed the stage curtains behind the director opening to reveal a fairly small platform raised just two steps higher than the ground floor. On the platform were several items: an X-ray machine, a gamma-ray emitter, two video recorders, and a sheet of metal that measured almost three feet high and four feet wide. The slightly red, semi-transparent metal was fastened to supports that kept it perpendicular to the floor. All the equipment was aimed toward the metal plate.

VIPs and their entourages were instructed to position themselves so that they could see the metal straight on or at a slight angle. Once everyone was in position, lights were dimmed and the equipment turned on. Immediately, the translucent metal became a *window*, and Dr. Knab described what they were seeing.

"This image is from one hundred and twenty years ago. This area was just an open field with high grass. Those mountains in the background look about the same in this image as they do today. You can see a small wooden structure in the distance. Can't tell for sure, but it might be a barn. You notice that the grass is waving as if we are watching in real-time. We are. What we are witnessing is from exactly 43,512 days ago—almost to the minute. And it stays that long ago from our current time. As our time elapses, we are witnessing time pass back then. Let's look back another hundred or so years."

The image suddenly changed. The mountain background seemed identical, but the trees were smaller and more spread out. The barn was gone. Everyone expressed delight as several deer appeared on the right side of the screen. The deer scurried off as if frightened. Then, to the crowd's amazement, two native Indians emerged from the trees. Every eye was glued to the scene.

"Wow, I wasn't expecting that," Knab exclaimed. "We always record these sessions so we can study what we've seen in more detail. You never know what you might witness."

Some of the guests noticed that the equipment hum was becoming more pronounced and asked about it. One of the technicians explained, "We try not to run the ray machines longer than twenty minutes at a time. We've not had a breakdown, but the noise tends to keep getting louder. Director, shall we move on?"

Jacob nodded and the scene changed again. "Have any idea when this took place?" he asked. After a few wild guesses, the director said, "This is how things looked just over a thousand years ago. Hard to believe it is the same place. Notice how barren it is. Quite the contrast."

After another excursion further into the past, the equipment was turned off and room lighting was restored. Employees assisted with removing their radiation shielding attire. Everyone was sweaty. Some were drenched. Director Knab offered a suggestion. "Why don't we all freshen up, change clothes, and meet back here in an hour?"

Although they were teeming with questions, nobody objected to the proposal. The adjournment was enough time to shower, dress, and get one's thoughts in order. Few took advantage of the full hour. Many had returned in barely half that time. Once they reconvened, Jacob introduced Dr. Gordman as the man to answer technical questions.

Carl never liked being the speaker, but he understood that his role required this of him. He was indeed the person most knowledgeable about the project. Despite all his practice and the encouragement from supportive staff, he doubted he could make it through without a panic attack. One speaking trick he had learned was focusing on one person at a time when speaking to a group. Carl fared much better in a one-to-one conversation. So, he planned to employ this technique.

Unfortunately, his audience suffered from divided attention, having returned with information packets that had been placed in their rooms. Everyone was reading the material, pointing out particular items of interest to each other. Instead of allowing Dr. Gordman to present information in an organized way, attendees began to bombard him with questions.

At first, Carl was frustrated that he couldn't present his well-planned speech. "What a waste of preparation time," he thought to himself. Then it dawned on him that going directly to questions was a reprieve from the thing he most hated, public speaking. Finally, he happily gave in to the pressure and agreed to go right to questions—one at a time—one person at a time.

Most of those who asked questions were not key figures themselves, but unidentified assistants or attorneys. Gordman recognized the first of several hands that were raised. "Why does the image have a red tint?"

Though the answer seemed obvious, Carl answered politely, "Well, as you can see, the plate has a slight rust hue. Though technically a metal, it looks somewhat like stained glass. We have discovered that a thinner plate has a reduced tint. This sheet is one millimeter thick, which is just over 1/32 inch. That is the thinnest we've been able to make it."

The next question was, "Can you zoom in to see what is further back? It would be nice to get a better view of that barn; or even better, those natives."

Carl responded, "What you see is what you get. The image is exactly what you would view if you were standing in the same spot as you are now, looking in the direction of the 'window' with the naked eye. Looking at the screen through binoculars, for example, gives you the same effect as looking at a television screen with magnification. The only way to see further back is to physically move all of this equipment in the desired direction."

Dr. Knab interrupted, "For example, if this equipment had been mobile, we could have turned it to follow the movement of those Indians—I mean, native Americans—we saw earlier. We could have followed them as long as our movement was unrestricted. Unfortunately, that would have only been to that wall twenty feet away."

A voice spoke out from the back, "So, open spaces are preferable."

"Exactly," Knab answered, "especially if we are trying to follow movement or if we are searching for something in particular." Jacob then nodded to Carl, who resumed his role.

"We do have a trailer that allows this whole assembly to be mobile, but it is only large enough to house the equipment, the technicians, and maybe two additional spectators."

Someone asked, "Is there any way to get sound?"

Carl paused to avoid sounding harsh. His initial thought was, "That's ridiculous." One condition of his disorder was difficulty in feeling empathy or seeing things from someone else's perspective. With Gordman, everything was black or white, right or wrong. With him, there was such a thing as a bad question, but he did his best to avoid referring to the inquiry as nonsensical. "As far as we can tell, obtaining audio will remain impossible. For one thing, sound dissipates quickly. More importantly, there is no microphone at the source to pick up any audio."

The natural follow-up question was, "You said, 'As far as we know.' Does that mean you are holding out hope for being able to obtain sound?"

"Not at all," Carl clarified, "I only use that qualifier because, until recently, I thought it would never be possible to see the past either. Now, here we are."

Finally, the dreaded question came, "Does this portend time travel?"

"Definitely not!" Carl stated emphatically. "As amazing as this discovery is, we are still dealing with real science, not science fiction. Despite the entertainment industry's obsession with time travel, it is unrealistic. Time is linear. What's past is past. Nothing can change that. Incredibly, we can now witness history, but we will never be able to go back into history."

"I'm afraid Einstein would disagree," came the follow-up. "His theory that time is relative has been scientifically proven, in case you were unaware."

There was a collective gasp among those who knew Dr. Gordman's reputation. While he, himself, would never presume to be in the company of Albert Einstein, many of his admirers believed his contributions to science would, one day, be considered just as important. Carl answered matter-of-factly.

"Time does move more quickly and slowly depending upon certain factors, such as gravity and an object's speed. But it always moves forward. There is no scientific evidence, only conjecture, that time, under any circumstances, moves backward."

Sensing the need to change the subject, a large man in the back asked, "Can we look through the 'window' from both sides?"

"No, the image only appears on the side being bombarded with rays. From the other side, the window looks like a dark red cloud. The backside isn't translucent while the front is being subjected to gamma or X-rays."

A related question was, "What happens if you view the window from an angle? Can you get a wider or fuller view?"

The weary scientist kept his impatience in check. "You get the best view by looking straight on. However, if you stand to the left, you can see a little more of what is to the right and vice versa. That is why we record with two cameras facing from opposite sides of the machinery. If you look from any angle more than thirty degrees off-center, the images become fuzzy and eventually unrecognizable."

"Since the metal is so thin, is it fragile?"

"We don't think it would shatter like glass, but it can break. At this thickness, it will bend easily, which distorts images. A bend that results in a crease messes things up. We learned this by manipulating our original small plate after fabricating this larger one." Carl glanced at the clock on the wall.

Finally, the most intelligent question came, "How do you know how far back in time we are witnessing?"

Carl recognized this opportunity to escape the limelight. "That has been the most tedious aspect of our experimentation. David, would you care to enlighten our group?"

Hall anticipated the likelihood of offering explanations at this gathering.

"Certainly," David replied as he stepped forward. "I was tasked with determining the exact timeframe of the images," Hall began. "I'm not sure how much detail you want."

"Just the basics…and in laymen's terms," Dr. Knab interjected.

"Um…okay," Hall answered, his mind racing to find an explanation that could be easily digested. "First of all, we discovered that revealed time frames were controlled by the frequency of the rays striking the plate created from the meteoric metal.

"Gamma rays and X-rays have different effects. Each ascending frequency of a gamma-ray only slightly changes the timeframe while each X-ray frequency alters the image by decades. So, we decided to begin with the more precise gamma rays.

"We found a digital clock, displaying both date and time, that had been on the same wall for several years. We took Hindsight to that location and aimed it at the clock, recording the date and time for each gamma-ray frequency. We were able to use that data to determine how much time elapses between frequencies. Higher frequencies went further back in time.

"When we used the lowest frequency of X-ray, the window showed no clock and no wall because it took us too far back in time. So, we aimed Hindsight at the night sky in several locations and recorded the results of ascending X-ray frequencies. Comparing that data with computer-generated star charts, we were able to determine general timeframes. We then discovered that bombarding the screen with both X-rays and gamma rays at the same time allowed us to adjust the image to precise periods of time.

"I then assisted Mr. Daniels with calibrating the equipment. He would be the best person to explain that process."

Jonathan, who was seated amongst the Hindsight equipment, looked up from his laptop. He glanced over at Dr. Gordman in a silent plea for help. While not as averse to public speaking as Carl was, Daniels had no desire to be in the spotlight. When Carl did not recognize the desperate cue, Jonathan looked to the director, hoping that a sympathetic leader might rescue him.

"That's a good idea," agreed Director Knab. "Jon, why don't you fill us in?"

Daniels swallowed hard. He looked down at his computer screen while mustering the courage to address the visitors. Still seated and facing downward, he began.

"I took the data David, uh…Mr. Hall gave me and wrote a computer program to interface with the Hindsight hardware. Software development was fairly easy because the amount of time between frequencies is pretty consistent. So now, once powered up, all of Hindsight's functions are controlled from this computer. All you have to do is input the number of years, days, and hours you want to go back. The program then informs the equipment as to what gamma and X-ray frequencies to use. That's about it.

Oh, um, I'm working on a software upgrade so that you just have to input the date and time you want to view. Almost done with that."

For the first time since questions began, no hands were in the air. The assembly sat dumbfounded. They understood the words that were spoken by the two last men but couldn't imagine the complexity of the task that Hall and Daniels had described so nonchalantly. After several silent seconds, the general asked a pertinent question. "How many machines do we have, and how many more can we make?"

Director Knab fielded the final question. "Unfortunately, we have used much of the meteoric metal for various experiments over time. It took half of the remaining material to create this plate. So, we can only make one more unless we find a way to duplicate the effect. So far, we have had no success with that."

After closing remarks, leaders and entourages gathered their things and prepared to leave. Before they left for their rooms, several of them approached various members of the Hindsight team to ask follow-up questions or to just chit-chat. Everyone left, trying to imagine the ramifications, significance, and potential of this new device.

Chapter 6 - Proposal

"So, you and Johnny, huh?" Carol Castle teased as she waggled her eyebrows repeatedly. "How long has that been going on?"

"What?" Trina asked innocently, but she couldn't restrain the escaping grin. Twenty-seven-year-old Trina Benson had a reputation for being all about business. Her two years at Hindsight left her with little time for herself. Besides, she had little interest in the single men at the project and even less for those who lived in town. Trina had resigned herself to staying single, at least until she moved on from this endeavor.

Her duties exposed her to a lot of interaction with several key players in the Hindsight Project, including Jonathan Daniels, the project's programmer and chief technician. Once the program was firmly on its feet, all the employees found themselves with less restrictive schedules. This lent itself to more socially focused interaction.

"Oh, it's nothing serious," Trina deflected. Then, realizing how lame the "We're just friends" answer was, she motioned for her friend to join her. Carol sat and leaned in for a hushed confession. "We've been seeing each other for a few months now."

"So? Details, please."

"We often ate lunch at the same time and occasionally ended up next to each other in the cafeteria line. Well, we kept bumping into each other in the cafeteria line. We'd talk while filling our trays, but then we'd go our separate ways. One day..." Trina blushed as her smile grew bigger. "One day, we just kept talking, and he followed me to my table. The next time, I joined him. Soon, we were eating together regularly."

"You know, I do remember you two sitting together once or twice, but you didn't look like an item." Carol commented. "It wasn't until Jessica from transportation saw you going into a movie theater forty miles away that the rumor mill began grinding. I was surprised to learn about you fine-arts patrons from the grapevine. I thought we were tight. Are you trying to keep it on the down-low?"

"Not necessarily," Trina answered. Then she corrected herself. "I guess... maybe."

"Is it serious?" her friend pressed.

"I'm not sure," Trina confessed. "I fix him supper about once a week, and we go out on Friday or Saturday every weekend."

"Do you go all the way to the city every weekend?" Carol pressed. "Sounds like you don't want anyone to know."

"That's not it at all," Trina insisted. "There is nothing in town we are interested in. Neither of us is a drinker, so the bars are out. The city just has more to offer."

Since Carol accepted the explanation, it was time to move on to a juicier subject. "Has he started spending the night yet?"

Unfazed by the intimate question, Trina answered matter-of-factly, "No, Jonathan's a real gentleman. He greets me with a simple kiss, and we hold hands on a date. Last weekend was the first time we really kissed before saying goodnight." She smiled. "It was nice.""

"That's kinda weird." Carol rolled her eyes and looked at her friend disapprovingly. "Is he just shy? I know he's religious and all, but maybe you need to be more aggressive."

"Well, actually, it's nice having a boyfriend who doesn't have sex on his mind all the time." Trina gazed off into the distance with a look of satisfaction. Her companion suddenly felt that sinking feeling in her stomach.

"You haven't gone all religious too, have you?" she asked in a tone that revealed both concern and disappointment. "I heard that Mr. Hall and your Jonathan are cut from the same cloth. I guess they aren't really scientists, but it does seem strange to have Bible-thumpers around here."

"They aren't Bible-thumpers. At least, Jonathan's not." Trina argued. "But he is a true believer."

"Did you know that they believe the earth is only a few thousand years old? If that's not crazy religion, I don't know what is."

"Jonathan told me that's what David believes, but he's not sure himself."

"Not sure!? Girl, he's sucking you in," Carol warned. "Look, I guess it's okay to take the Bible seriously, but don't take it literally."

"No…well…I told him I believed a lot of what he does. But truthfully, he puts way more faith in the Bible than I think I ever could. Still, when we do talk about that stuff, it sort of makes sense the way he explains it." After a brief pause, she confessed, "I promised that I would start going to church with him."

"Oh, girl. Please don't get caught up in some cult."

"I won't," Trina promised. "If it gets weird, I'll bail."

"Good," Carol said before switching gears with a mischievous grin. "I've got some news too."

"Oh? What's that?"

"I've got me a man too," Carol revealed. "I was at the office supply store getting toner and some stuff when this cute Asian guy asked if I knew anything about computer printers. He then pulled a printer off the shelf and asked, 'Is it better to get a cheap printer that requires more expensive ink, or spend more on the printer to get cheaper ink?'"

"Really? And you fell for that?" Trina chastised.

"Of course not, but he was cute, so I played along," Carol asserted. "We hit it off right away and discovered that we had a lot in common."

As she stood up to walk away, Carol wryly stated, "Carson is not as pure and patient as your guy. And I don't mind that a bit."

It didn't take long for other female employees to start giving Trina the "I know your secret" look when they crossed paths. The gossip wasn't restricted to women either. Jonathan got his fair share of joshing from the men. This small group of strangers became a close-knit family in short order.

* * *

At supper one evening, Katy could tell something was eating at her husband. He wasn't agitated or nervous, just distant. It was obvious something was weighing heavily upon his mind. She knew she couldn't ask about it since whatever happens at work stays at work. David was remarkably good at leaving his work troubles at the office. That's what made his mood so unusual.

After putting Reese to bed, the couple repeated their evening ritual of watching a bit of television. Once on the couch, Katy snuggled up to her distracted husband. Placing his arm around her, David finally opened up.

"I blew an opportunity today," he said. She pulled away just enough to see his face and waited for more. He looked her in the eyes briefly, then stared ahead as he recounted the event he was referring to.

"One of the assistants in…in one of the departments came to me today. She said, 'I know that you are a religious man. I was wondering if you would pray about something for me.' She explained that she doesn't know much about religion, but did believe God could be real. Anyway, her mother is seriously ill, and she thought it might help if I prayed for her."

"It's nice that she came to you about that. It allows you to share the faith with her."

"It should have, but I'm afraid that probably won't happen."

"Why? Did the mother die?"

"What?" David looked confused by the question. "What do you mean? It just happened today."

"Well, you seem so upset that I thought you might have prayed but the woman died anyway. I doubt that girl would be interested in your *religion* if your prayer didn't help."

"No, that's not it. When she asked me to pray, I should have done so right then with her. I said I would pray, but kind of left her hanging."

"Couldn't you have gotten in trouble if you prayed with her at work?"

"I doubt it, but maybe."

Katy thought for a moment. "Couldn't you just offer to pray with her tomorrow?"

"That would be pretty awkward," he answered.

"Not necessarily. I bet she would appreciate it if you ask about her mother, then offer to pray right then."

"That's a good idea," David said. The newly relaxed man wrapped his arm around his wife and pulled her close. He kissed her on the top of her head and asked the rhetorical question, "When did you become so wise?"

* * *

Director Knab and his wife Kathleen assumed their unspoken parental roles with grace. Jacob was adept at leading and correcting his staff in an amazingly unthreatening way. Kathleen claimed her Hispanic heritage suited her well for commanding large family group activities. She didn't mind the stereotype—she embraced it.

All three of the Knabs' daughters had married (one since divorced) and rarely made it to the base for visits. In the early months of the project, when Jacob was especially busy, Kathleen made frequent trips to visit her grandchildren. She had become more of a homebody lately and had developed close friendships with several of the other women, both employees, and spouses of employees.

As the assistant director, Dr. Gordman spent a lot of time with Dr. Knab, both at work and after hours. Though brilliant, Carl had always been quite backward socially, especially going into college. While there, another student took him on as a project and made some headway regarding his refinement, so much so that she married him. It didn't take but a few months for her to regret that life decision. Fortunately, there were no children to suffer from their separation.

When he wasn't hanging with the Knabs, Carl spent most of his time alone. He read a lot, technical journals mostly. He was most happy when working out the solution to a challenging math equation or science dilemma. He enjoyed playing chess on the computer. He did claim one other friend, Darren Oats. Carl was intrigued by Darren's ability to imagine and assemble useful things. Sometimes, he visited the transportation department just to watch the team build something.

Darren's crew was responsible for creating Hindsight's mobile platform as well as retrofitting the trucks to haul all the equipment. He and his wife had a reputation for hosting great parties. They never evidenced concern that their family made up a third of the African-American population on base. Their three children were well behaved and captured the hearts of almost everyone they met.

David Hall's wife Katy was sweet but bashful. When the couple attended social gatherings, she was more of a wallflower, while her husband was often the life of the party. One reason for Katy's shyness was her youth. David was several years her senior. Their only child was the youngest on base, so she often lost him to older mothers clamoring to hold him.

Another reason for her timidity was the couple's religious faith. Only a handful of employees went to church of any kind, but the Halls, along with Jonathan Daniels, were the only unapologetic Bible believers. This being the case, she felt looked down upon by the intellectuals as well as by the brutish. In reality, no one ever intentionally belittled her for her faith. While most of the experts thought the Halls were misguided when it came to religion, they respected David's skill and leadership enough to overlook that shortcoming.

There was no caste system at the base, especially at the Christmas party. Everyone from janitors to Ph. D.s attended. Even the security personnel and their families were included. Destiny helped Kathleen plan the get-together all three years. Usually scheduled about two weeks before Christmas, it was always well attended.

The base Christmas event was more family-oriented than typical business office parties. Santa showed up to give presents to the children. There was no live music or D.J. Instead, a couple of volunteers created a digital playlist with a variety of holiday fare. As the night grew on, the music became more adult-oriented. This cued parents to consider taking their children home. Even with just the adults, the party never became risqué. Kathleen saw to that.

Hindsight employees were allowed to invite one guest each to the activity. This year, there were a few. One of them was Carol's boyfriend, Carson. This was not his first time on base. He was a frequent visitor to Carol's quarters, and she had been introducing him around for weeks.

* * *

"So, it's Carson, right?" Darren shook his hand. "You and Carol were over to our place about a month back. I'm Darren."

"Yes, I remember. I appreciate the invite to your cookout," Carson said as he placed his newly freed hand on the small of his girlfriend's back. "Great burgers. Say, I forget, what do you do here again?"

"You didn't forget, Bro. I never told you." Then Darren turned the tables. "You didn't tell me much about yourself, either. Carol says that you test and review stuff. Is that a Consumer Reports kind of thing?"

"Yeah," Carol interrupted. "That's how I busted him. He played like, 'what printer should I buy?' and all the time, he is this expert on all things electronic."

"I confess. I just wanted to meet you." Carson responded before turning back to Darren. "To your question, I don't do it for the general public. I freelance for companies and flush individuals who want objective evaluations of expensive products they are considering."

"I see. Forgive me, but I'm not good at distinguishing Asians from each other. Are you Chinese?" Carson asked.

Carson nodded, "My family is from Hong Kong. I moved here as a kid."

That and other conversations were abruptly interrupted by the sound of silverware tapping on a ceramic coffee mug. Everyone looked toward the Knabs first, then to Darren and Destiny. Finally, their eyes found the source of the sound. Jonathan Daniels was standing with his arm around Trina's waist. His face beamed with excitement while hers blushed with embarrassment as he spoke.

"Can I have your attention, please? I have an announcement I'd like to make while everyone is still here. As most of you know, Trina and I have been seeing each other for a while." Her elbow nudging his side suggested that he move quickly to the announcement. "I, uh, well, I've asked Trina to marry me."

Instead of the anticipated cheers and congratulations, the news met a silence that seemed a bit rehearsed. Jonathan glanced around the room at stoic faces. After a few long seconds, someone asked, "Well, what did she say?"

"I said yes!" Trina proclaimed.

Then the cheering and congratulations began. Usual quips ensued from the men.

"What took you so long?"

"I hope you know what you are doing."

"When is the baby due?"

"I believe every man should get married. No one should be happy all his life."

"I hope you've got a good lawyer."

Meanwhile, the women gathered around Trina to admire the engagement ring that she had kept hidden under dress gloves. They were genuinely happy for the young lady who could keep a sweet spirit through almost any ordeal. Many administrative assistants rub people the wrong way as they carry out their duties and instructions. Trina was not one of them.

That she was marrying another favorite team member made the announcement all the more joyous. Jonathan was one of the most pleasant individuals on base. Despite his sometimes intense job and challenging deadlines, he never seemed flustered or angry. You could even count on him to make time to help someone in need.

Darren put his strong arm around Carson's shoulder and faked a sigh. "I wonder who will be next," he said with a smile. Carol gave him the evil eye, took her beau by the arm, and pulled him toward the refreshment table. Carson was just as happy to escape his awkward encounter with the big man.

Having been passed around from woman to woman most of the evening, young Reese started acting cranky. Even Katy couldn't console the toddler.

"I think we need to go," she told David.

Her husband looked at his watch and evidenced disappointment at leaving so early. "Okay, in a minute," he promised.

But the minute dragged on, and Reese was getting crankier. Finally, Katy reached into David's pants pocket for the car keys while he was talking.

"I'm going to the car," she declared.

Realizing he had broken his word, David responded, "Okay, I'm sorry. I'll be right there. Just need to finish this."

Katy sat in the back seat of the cold car for five minutes, cradling the youngster. Then, she laid him down long enough to lean forward and start the car. The engine's gentle hum and newly produced heat lulled the child to sleep in her arms. After ten minutes more, David got into the car.

"Sorry," he said. "You gonna put him in his car seat and come up here?"

"Just go," she insisted. Not another word was spoken between the two for the rest of the night.

Parents at the party took the hint when *Santa Baby* began to play and started gathering their children to head home. Jonathan took Trina's hand.

"I know it's still pretty early, but do you mind if I take you home now?" he asked.

"I noticed you left when the kids did last year. I figured you were concerned with how wild the party might get," his fiancée answered. "It does stay relatively calm."

She could tell that he was weighing his comfort level against her apparent desire to stay. Even though Trina had recently made a profession of faith in Christ, she struggled a bit with Jonathan's sensitivity to what she considered normal adult things like casinos, dance halls, and R-rated movies. She was growing in her faith, however, and in her love for him. So, instead of forcing Jonathan to make an uncomfortable decision, she backtracked.

"You know, it's fine. We don't need to stay. We won't miss anything, believe me."

As the couple slowly made their way to his car, they heard children call out their goodbyes. When they reached his vehicle, they stopped to soak in the moment. They were engaged, and now everyone knew it. Trina laid her head on his shoulder and sighed. They looked into the clear sky and silently admired the stars. Well, he did anyway. She mostly kept her eyes closed as he wrapped his arm around her.

Unconsciously, their bodies began to sway to the faint sound of music coming from inside. She reached up and gently caressed his cheek. They gradually turned to face each other with her arms around his neck and his hands placed carefully on her hips. Slowly, he slid his hands to her back and pulled her to himself. They shared one long, passionate kiss before he released his hold and allowed space between them. Trina was more reluctant to let go. She appreciated his commitment to celibacy until marriage. It endeared her even more to him, but she was determined to have a short engagement period. Jonathan, not surprisingly, hoped for the same.

In typical fashion, he opened her car door. They held hands while he drove the six blocks to her residence. It was the far-right dwelling of a quadplex. He walked her to the door. She pulled her keys from her small purse and handed them to him. He unlocked the door, then opened it. They gazed into each other's eyes for several seconds. Trina looked down at Jonathan's chest as she placed her hand flat over his heart. He placed two fingers under her chin and raised her head so that their eyes would meet again. This kiss was less lingering.

"Goodnight," he said softly. "I love you."

Trina smiled. "I love you too. I wish you knew how much."

Jonathan stepped back as Trina went inside and slowly closed the door, peeking through the crack as long as possible. Alone outside, the new fiancé looked heavenward and smiled.

Chapter 7 - FBI

Several months passed without a government official following up on the big reveal. Drs. Knab and Gordman were growing concerned that their pet project wasn't as well-received as expected. It was just after New Year's when Hindsight leadership assembled for a hastily called meeting. Everyone was surprised and a little confused about the presence of two visitors.

"These are Special Agents Griffin and Hines from the FBI," came Director Knab's introduction. "They are here on special assignment. The FBI's assistant director contacted me two days ago to request our cooperation."

Jacob's moderately-sized office seemed small when occupied by more than five people. Such was the case for this meeting. The standing-room-only crowd included Hindsight employees Carl Gordman, assistant director; David Hall, technical director; Darren Oats, mobile unit chief; Debra Minx, attorney, and Trina Benson, executive assistant.

The FBI special agents were less intimidating than one might expect. Both wore off-the-rack dark suits, but neither was particularly physically fit. Griffin was an older man. His shoulders rolled forward from years of hunching over a computer keyboard. Hines was a middle-aged black woman of average build. She seemed tense and poised to take action as if to compensate for her partner's apparent lack of physical prowess.

Agent Griffin spoke while Hines observed and interpreted the attendees' facial expressions and body language. "The agency has requested use of your machine."

"Our machine?" Debra asked, feigning ignorance.

"Really?!" Hines retorted.

Dr. Knab intervened. "Even though they were not involved in our demonstration last year, the FBI is well aware of Hindsight's existence, and needs our help."

"Hindsight—as you call it—may be our best hope of solving a serious crime," Griffin continued. "Someone is smuggling poison-laced drugs into the Southwest. At least forty-one deaths have been attributed to the deadly product."

Darren spoke up, "That doesn't make sense. Why would someone provide junk that kills? Wouldn't that reduce their clientele? I know drug dealers are wicked people, but killing your customers has got to be bad for business."

"We believe the product is being intercepted by a rival cartel," the agent explained. "They then lace the drugs to make them lethal. Once word gets around that the established supply line is dangerous, they can introduce themselves as the alternative."

"Wow, that's twisted," Trina muttered to Darren.

"Word," he responded.

"We believe we have found a place where the cartel worked," Griffin continued. "They are smart enough to avoid using the same location for very long, but if we can see into the recent past with your equipment, we might be able to identify some of the perpetrators, if not the leader.

"The FBI understands that your project is still a secret to the general public. We will not jeopardize that. All we need is the intel your machine might provide. The agency will then compile independent evidence to build a case. Your involvement will never be known. If this works, you will set us on the right path to solving this case more quickly."

"And save countless lives," Agent Hines added.

"I'm all for saving lives and stopping bad guys," Hall offered.

"I'm concerned about the legality of using Hindsight in a federal criminal case," the attorney cautioned. "I think we need to get some counsel before committing to anything."

"Me too," agreed Trina. "This is uncharted territory. We need to have proper authorization and clear instructions before we risk taking Hindsight thousands of miles away."

"Who will protect it while outside the base?" asked Darren. "Assuming Jonathan will run the equipment, who will he take orders from when we get there?"

"There are a lot of questions that need to be answered," acknowledged the director. "And I want everyone in this room to list issues and reservations that need to be addressed. We will meet again this afternoon, but let me be clear, we will cooperate with the FBI in this matter."

David nudged Dr. Gordman as they exited the room. "You didn't say anything in the meeting."

"Too many people," Carl explained.

"What do you think?" Hall asked.

"Not sure," came his unexpected answer. "It would be a good opportunity to test Hindsight's real-world application, but I'm not very comfortable about working with the FBI."

The government representatives agreed to return the following morning, allowing the Hindsight team time to problem solve and coordinate efforts. Project leaders met again after lunch to discuss plans. It took three hours to resolve the issues that came up and plan contingencies for the concerns that could not be dealt with completely. The last item of business was to determine who would be included in the travel team.

To avoid being any more conspicuous than necessary, only the most necessary employees were approved to participate with David. Darren, with three of his team, was in charge of loading and transporting Hindsight and the mobile platform he designed. Jonathan was the most proficient at running Hindsight, and the quickest at pinpointing the desired timeframe to view. With him were an assistant who could do the job if necessary and one other tech to man cameras (among other duties). The team attorney came along, just in case, as well as Miss Benson.

Director Knab decided to accompany his team, leaving Carl in charge of the lab. But with Hindsight off the premises, there was not much to be in charge of. Staffing had been reduced recently due to a combination of budgeting constraints and diminished need. With the Hindsight Project completed, there was less experimenting, data collecting, engineering and building to be done.

* * *

"Mom just called," Katy told her husband as he walked into the kitchen.

"Your mom?"

"Yes. She's upset with Patrick again."

"Now what's he done?" David asked.

"Got a tattoo."

"That's all?" he asked, shaking his head. "Your mom is too high-strung."

"She believes Christians should have high standards," Katy said defensively.

"That's fine. It's even good. But she can't force her standards on others, especially her adult children." David said as he washed his hands at the kitchen sink.

"She's just worried about him. He has made some bad decisions since going to college," Katy explained. "You know my mom has strong biblical convictions."

"She didn't seem to have a problem ignoring the Bible when she divorced your dad." The words were barely out of his mouth when he wished he had bit his tongue. Katy's moist eyes revealed the pain David's comment caused, but she didn't say anything right away. She just turned and opened the refrigerator even though she wasn't looking for anything.

"I'm sorry," the repentant man said. "I know that was a really hard time for all of you. It's just that your mother can't demand that others live by her simplistic and narrow-minded understanding of scripture."

She turned to face him. "Are you saying that tattoos are okay?" she asked.

"I wouldn't get one," David answered. "And I would discourage others if they asked my opinion. The Bible isn't as cut and dried about the subject as

52

some Christians believe. People tend to focus too much on the external, but God looks at the heart."

"Do you think Patrick's heart is right?" Katy asked pointedly.

David paused. He was aware of his brother-in-law's recent spiritual struggles. He leaned against the counter and folded his arms before saying, "Probably not. Considering all the choices he's made lately, it doesn't seem like the Lord is on his mind at all."

"See? I don't know why you argue with me when you really agree," the frustrated woman said. "Anyway, she was hoping you would call and talk to him since you were his Sunday school teacher and all."

"That was years ago when he was a kid," David argued. He tried to think of a good reason to avoid getting involved, but nothing came to mind. "Look, I'm not going to get in his face about any particular decision, but I'm willing to call to ask how he is doing spiritually and see where that leads."

"That would be good," the appreciative wife answered as she put her arms around his neck. He unfolded his arms and gave her a warm hug. "Thank you," she said, then whispered, "I love you."

* * *

The sun had not yet risen when the assembled team, along with four FBI agents, headed out of the base in two box trucks, a van, and two sedans. To avoid making it a two-day trip, the convoy completed the thousand-mile journey in seventeen hours, taking breaks only when necessary.

After speaking with the agents, Dr. Knab announced to his team, "That was a long trip, and it's late. We are going to meet for a late breakfast at nine-thirty so you can get plenty of rest."

The box trucks looked normal, but they were reinforced to protect the contents from would-be thieves and vandals. Even though the equipment was secure, FBI agents took shifts guarding the vehicles. Inside the motel rooms, few members slept in. Even still, not feeling rushed was appreciated. After breakfast at a local pancake shop, the team loaded into their vehicles.

The building to be examined was forty-five minutes from the motel, isolated behind a thick tree line and surrounded by overgrown brush. It took almost an hour to unload everything and securely mount the equipment on its mobile platform inside the small warehouse. Hindsight was moved to a distant corner of the only room large enough to have been the drug staging area. It was positioned to obtain the widest view possible. Generators were filled with gasoline and powered up. Once everyone had donned their protective gear, they were ready to begin.

Hindsight was engaged, and cameras began recording while two FBI agents watched the screens. Since the alleged activity was believed to have occurred between one and three months prior, only the gamma-ray emitter was required. Starting at the one-month mark and working backward, Daniels changed the time by three-hour intervals every two seconds. Within seven minutes, Hindsight was showing what had occurred in the warehouse two months earlier..

"Stop!" Griffin shouted, but Jonathan had already ended the sequence and had begun to *re-wind* the scene seven minutes at a time. When he reached the point where people first entered the building seventy-two days earlier, he let the scene play out in real-time.

"We're recording this, right?" one of the new agents asked. Everyone, including the Hindsight team, watched in awe as the event unfolded. Even though most of them knew what Hindsight could do, it was surreal to see it in action—watching people work who had no idea they were being spied upon (so to speak).

"Can we get a close-up of those two men?" Special Agent Hines had keyed in to who was likely in charge by reading body language (one of her specialties). "And we need to see the face of that one with his back to us."

The team moved Hindsight's platform close enough to the targets that only their heads and torsos fit on the screen. Once a clear image of the first man was recorded, the wheeled platform was turned around to face the opposite direction and record the other man's face.

"This is incredible," Agent Griffin exclaimed, then sighed, then chuckled. He looked at Dr. Knab and predicted, "Your invention will revolutionize law enforcement."

Once finished, a team of FBI agents left with the recordings to follow up on their case while the other duo escorted the Hindsight team back to the base. They made a special stop at a bar and grill where they ate a hearty, celebratory meal. Team leaders instinctively gathered at the same table while members of the support crew fended for themselves.

"Did you see the faces on those FBI agents when Hindsight solved their case?" Darren reflected. "That's the first time I've been around cops without worrying about getting arrested."

"You've been arrested?" the director asked, trying to hide his shock.

"No, man, but I've been stopped and questioned more times than I can count."

"Too bad Carl couldn't have been there to see it," David lamented. "Hindsight is really his baby. None of us would be here without him."

"For real," Oats agreed.

"That's true," Knabs added. "Maybe next time."

A few hours later, they stopped for a good night's rest. Before going to sleep, David called his wife. While he understood the need for secrecy, it continued to frustrate both of them that Katy couldn't know anything about his work.

"How did it go?" she asked politely.

"Great! Couldn't have gone better." David answered. "In fact, we are on our way home early. Should be there a little after lunchtime tomorrow."

"That's good. I miss you."

"Miss you too. Love you, bye." Even though he had his own in a suitcase, David pulled the Gideon Bible from the nightstand and thumbed through it for a few seconds. Once he settled in on a passage, he read for a little while. After returning the Bible to its drawer, he intertwined his fingers behind his head and laid back to stare at the ceiling. Soon, his eyes were closed.

Despite plenty of time to sleep, almost everyone seemed to drag the next morning. The recent excitement had drained their energy. Everyone except those driving slept while on the road. And few drivers lasted for more than two hours before asking for a reliever. Once the team was home safely, their grateful FBI beneficiaries left. No one at the base ever saw those agents again.

* * *

"Maybe I shouldn't ask this, but does Darren not talk about work at all?" Katy asked as Destiny poured baby blue paint into a tray.

"He really doesn't. David?"

"Not a word. They could be spies for all I know."

"Or in the mafia," Destiny suggested. "Darren's always trying to make me"—changing to her Italian gangster voice—"an offer I can't refuse." With that, she started painting the walls in Reese's room.

"I appreciate your help, Destiny, but I could do this myself."

"And how long have you been saying you need to paint this room?"

"It hasn't been a year yet," Katy laughed.

"Uh-huh. Girl, if you were going to do it, you would have already."

"I guess. It's not like I'm too busy."

Destiny added, "Besides, I need some adult conversation once in a while."

"Darren's home every night, isn't he?"

"Like I said…" Destiny hinted. They both laughed.

Reese played with some toys in the hall while the ladies talked. Katy stood in the doorway so she could see her son while talking with her painting friend. Destiny was finished in no time, and the three went downstairs for lunch. Their casual conversation turned more serious once Reese was down for his nap.

"Are you that concerned about your man's job?" Destiny asked.

"I don't know. I guess it's not the job that bothers me."

"What do you mean?"

"Well, I worry that David will get good at keeping secrets from me."

"Girl, your man is solid," Destiny asserted. "I mean, he is a legit Christian. Everyone says so."

"Really? People talk about it?"

Realizing she just opened a can of worms, Destiny tried to recover. "Not like all the time, but it's come up."

"What do they say?" Katy pressed.

"Look. All I should tell you is that most of the wives here envy you." The confidant paused to gather her thoughts. "Not just because of David. They... we envy you because of your faith. I'd say I'm a Christian too—raised in the Church of God, but my family is a mess."

"Oh Destiny, that's not true." Katy could see that her friend was about to lose it emotionally.

"My fourteen-year-old is sneaking around with a boyfriend. My son has been in detention four times this year. And my baby is back-talking me something fierce."

"I'm so sorry. I didn't know. You all look like you have it all together."

"It's breaking my heart, and all Darren will say is that they are going through a phase. I don't know what to do. I even suggested we start going to church again. Nobody wants to 'cept me."

Katy had never seen Destiny so distraught. Her friend's problems made hers seem so insignificant. Not knowing what else to suggest, Katy asked, "Have you considered counseling?"

"Are you kidding? Darren won't even go to church. Do you think he'll go to counseling?"

"I guess not." Katy was at a loss. She wanted desperately to help in some way. Finally, she took her friend by the hand and offered to pray with her.

"Father, Destiny needs help. Her family needs help, but they don't want it. Please, change their hearts and minds. Show them your love. Show them that your way is best." While praying, Katy realized that she needed what she was praying for her friend. "Show me too, Lord. Amen."

"Amen," Destiny whispered. She hugged Katy for a long while and thanked her for praying. "I better get going. The kids will be home soon. I'm sorry to dump all that on you. I came to help, and you ended up helping me."

"I'm here for you, girlfriend," Katy said, reassuringly.

* * *

That night, after dinner, David played with Reese until bedtime. Like most families, the Halls had established an unspoken routine. Mommy put their child to bed and Daddy turned on the television. Depending on his viewing choice, Katy either sat on the couch with her husband or in a nearby chair reading. This night, before carrying Reese upstairs, she told David, "Don't start watching anything yet, please. I need to talk to you about something when I get back."

The announcement seemed ominous, so David ignored the remote control while he tried to imagine what might be up. Katy returned with a box of tissues. "That's not a good sign," David thought to himself. His mind raced to remember something he had done (or hadn't done) that would bring his wife to tears.

"Destiny came over today," she began. As she told him about their conversation, David quickly realized that he wasn't in trouble—neither was their marriage. Newly relaxed, he listened with a sympathetic ear.

"I told her we would be praying for them," Katy informed him.

"Of course," he agreed. Realizing she was hoping he would pray right then, he walked over to her. They knelt by the sofa where he took her hand and prayed for the Oats family. While kneeling, the thought struck him that they had not prayed together like that in ages. Oh, they prayed at meals; that was routine. But really pray together? Not so much.

So, David prayed. And Katy felt peace.

Chapter 8 - Objection

"We have a problem," Jacob announced. David wondered why just he and the company lawyer were meeting with the director. Dr. Knab's blunt statement made him more nervous. Jacob continued.

"It didn't take long for the FBI to identify most of the people in the video we provided at their crime scene. It turned out that the sabotage was not cartel-related after all."

"I saw that on the news," Ms. Minx said. "Turns out some wealthy investment realtor had come up with the scheme to dry up the drug trade in his area."

"I haven't heard anything about this," David admitted.

"This Justin Moore guy, well, his business was suffering from low housing prices due to drugs and drug-related crime," Knab explained. "Apparently, he came up with this idea to discourage the drug trade in his area."

"Have they proven he's the one who intercepted and tainted the drugs?" Debra asked.

"The FBI says so. They say he reasoned that once word got out that the product was deadly, demand would decrease enough for dealers to just leave the area."

"What about the victims?" David asked.

"Maybe he figured those who died got what they deserved for participating in illegal activity," Debra surmised.

"Once they had the right target, the Feds were able to build a solid case against the businessman," Knab stated. "There was just one problem. Attorneys for the accused questioned the predication for investigating their client."

"Predication?" David repeated.

"There has to be justification for using certain investigative measures," the attorney explained. "A good reason to believe a person might be guilty of a crime is the predicate."

"I guess the prosecutors' attempt to produce that predicate without Hindsight's help was unsuccessful. There seemed to be no reason to suspect Mr. Moore of any crime, yet mountains of evidence somehow made its way into the Federal prosecutor's office."

"Okay, so why is that our problem?" David asked innocently.

"FBI higher-ups tried to convince the judge that the case was solid even though they could not reveal the missing predicate. When the case was clearly in doubt, someone leaked to the judge information about how Moore's involvement was discovered."

"Oh no," Minx and Hall groaned together.

"I'm sure that leak was intended to bolster the prosecution's position, but it had the opposite effect," Jacob said.

"I'm sure," Debra agreed. "That information would be considered dubious at best. Probably met with contempt."

"This made it necessary to show the video recording to the presiding judge," Knab went on. "She then ordered that it be included in discovery so the defendant's lawyers could have a copy."

"I imagine Moore's attorney quickly filed a motion for dismissal based upon the legal metaphor, *Fruit of the Poisonous Tree*," Minx stated.

"They did. They argued that their client was the victim of illegal search and seizure, and that the FBI had no legal right or authority to view or record past activities of the accused without his permission," Jacob explained. "Naturally, the Justice Department disagreed vehemently with that argument."

"I'm sure," the lawyer said. "It's not my field, but I'd say the government was on shaky ground."

"In desperation, the FBI called me to request our participation in an inquest that the judge is holding. Since this is unprecedented, she is trying to determine what action to take on the defense attorney's motion.

"I'm afraid I won't be able to answer technical questions satisfactorily. And I'm reluctant to send Dr. Gordman, despite his superior knowledge, especially since he wasn't involved at the site. So, I need to send you two."

Both parties knew that the exercise would be uncomfortable for Dr. Gordman; not to mention that Carl's idiosyncrasies could be off-putting to the judge. As the project's only attorney, Debra understood that she would have to be involved, no matter who else went, but David was not at all comfortable with the assignment.

"So, it will just be Ms. Minx and me?" he asked.

"Yes, unless you think someone else should go too."

Hall thought for a moment. He knew Katy would not be happy about him taking a business trip alone with another woman—especially an attractive redhead. Unfortunately, he couldn't think of a good reason to involve anyone else.

David headed home right after the meeting. He spent the entire four-minute drive thinking about how he would break the news to Katy. It was the only time he regretted having such a short commute. "I have another assignment that will take me out of town," he told Katy when he arrived home.

"Oh?" Katy responded as she handed the toddler to his father.

"I have to go back to...that place I was at a couple of months ago." David realized mid-sentence that where he had been was classified. It was even a mistake to offer what information he just had. "I think it will just be a couple of days."

"That's good," Katy answered. "Your last trip was shorter than we expected."

"Yup," he agreed. Katy had learned to avoid asking questions about work. She suspected that her husband sometimes said more than he should. She didn't want him to get in trouble, so she rarely prodded him for more information. That was emotionally difficult.

David needed to vent, so he tried to choose his words carefully. "I have to see a judge and answer questions about what we did there."

"Are you in trouble?!" Katy demanded, throwing caution to the wind. "Are you all doing something illegal?" Her sudden outburst startled their child, who began to cry and reach for his mother.

"Oh, no," David reassured her, handing the boy back to Katy. "I'm just providing technical information about some...uh...equipment we used."

Katy patted the calming child's back and stared at her husband, unconvinced. He sighed and lowered his shoulders in defeat. "I'm just nervous about the whole thing. You know how secretive this is. Now I have to decide on the spot what questions I should answer, and how."

"Are you going alone?" Katy asked, calmly.

"Just me and our lawyer," he said without hesitating. At this point, Hall was glad that it wasn't public knowledge the team's attorney was female. Even though everyone knew most everyone else on base, job titles and duties were never revealed to non-employees.

* * *

Ms. Minx prepped David as best she could before they met the judge. The trip was uneventful, and Hall was careful to avoid any appearance of impropriety. He even asked that their separate hotel rooms be on different floors of the building.

"Do you want to have dinner together?" Debra asked. The almost forty-year-old divorcee had no idea how concerned her partner was about them spending unnecessary time together. Her invitation was purely polite with no ulterior motive.

"You go on without me. I want to relax in my room for a while. I might order room service."

"Alright. See you in the morning."

The information David provided at the judge's one-day inquiry was of little help. She couldn't wrap her head around Hindsight's ground-breaking technology. That evening, David made his nightly phone call.

"Did you have your meeting?" Katy asked.

"Yeah," David answered, his tone of voice betraying how things went.

"Sorry it didn't go well," she consoled.

"It wasn't that bad. I just don't think I made a difference," he shared. "The good news is, we're coming home tomorrow."

"We?" Katy queried.

"Me and our lawyer," David clarified.

"Oh, yeah. I forgot about him." David didn't correct the pronoun. "I'm glad you're coming home soon. Reese misses you."

"Oh, did he tell you that?" David teased, knowing that their son wasn't yet putting three words together.

"Yes, yes he did," Katy answered jokingly. "See what you miss when you are away?"

After ending the call, David went through his usual nightly routine before going to bed. When he couldn't find a Gideon Bible, he pulled his own out from a briefcase. He didn't read long. He was exhausted after an emotionally challenging day.

David and Debra arrived back at the base in the late afternoon and briefed Drs. Knab and Gordman about the trip. David got home a little later than normal that night. Katy had his favorite meal ready at a candlelit table, with soft music playing. He was really glad to be home.

* * *

Judge Hurst didn't take long to form an opinion and render a verdict on the motion to dismiss. "We are in unprecedented territory. I'm not even sure if I believe how this video was obtained. I certainly cannot find a legal basis to allow it as evidence. It is incumbent upon the prosecution to present legally obtained evidence. While this new technology may have a place in jurisprudence, it is not within my purview to allow it in court. I believe this is a matter that Congress must address before judges can allow it. When the legislative and executive branches create a law that identifies and qualifies this type of evidence, only then will it be welcomed in my court—and I dare say, in any court. I, therefore, grant the defendant's motion to dismiss. Case dismissed. Mr. Moore, you are free to go."

The judge's decision to not allow Hindsight evidence was devastating even if it was well reasoned. To make matters worse, with the existence of the Hindsight Project being leaked, the trial made national news. This blindsided everyone involved in the program. The director spent hours on the phone trying to track down the leak, to no avail. Agency employees nervously waited for another shoe to drop. Now that Hindsight was no longer a secret, what would become of their jobs?

Finally, the US Assistant Attorney General returned Director Knab's calls. During the conversation, he offered a word of consolation. "While I understand how disconcerting this development is, it could have been much worse. Instead of just dismissing the case on merit, the judge might have required even more information. That could have jeopardized your location and other important information. At least you still have some anonymity."

This callous brush-off frustrated the director, but wisdom dictated a humble response, and Knab obliged. "We understand that you have no control over the judge's actions. I just hope this doesn't jeopardize our project."

"I'm sure it won't," the assistant AG responded. "What you have will revolutionize criminal investigations. Congress just has to act so we can avoid future disappointments."

The satisfaction of solving a heinous crime was short-lived. Members who worked on the case were particularly disappointed. "It makes me sick to my stomach to know that a creep who killed dozens of people to boost his bottom line is getting off scot-free," one person lamented. Everyone else agreed.

Everything was soon back to normal. That meant more lay-offs. The research and development department was the hardest hit. The project didn't have enough meteoric material to conduct further testing. Nor did they need to with Hindsight's value somewhat quantified. What was needed next was to determine practical—and legal—uses for the equipment.

* * *

"Did you know that Stacy left?" Carol asked Trina.

"Among others," she answered.

"Why didn't you tell me?"

"I can't share that information."

"I lent her my vacuum cleaner and never got it back."

"Maybe she left it at the house. I'll ask maintenance to check for you."

Carol's body language indicated that she had more to say, so Trina invited her.

"What's wrong, Carol?"

"I don't get Carson. Everything seemed great between us, and suddenly he's becoming distant."

"I'm sorry."

"We've been together almost as long as you and Jon, but he won't talk about marriage."

"Maybe he thinks you aren't interested."

"I wasn't, but I am now. He shuts me down every time I even hint at the subject."

"I hate to say it, but are you sure he isn't already married?"

"I've thought of that. I don't think that's the problem. If he was married, we probably couldn't spend so much time together. I feel like I meet his needs. I don't understand what his problem is."

"Maybe he's afraid of commitment. Or he figures why buy the cow when you get the milk for free?"

"That's a little harsh."

"I'm sorry. It's just that, most men are so selfish."

"Tell me about it," Carol agreed. "Johnny too?"

"Just the opposite," Trina professed. "He tries so hard to please me that I sometimes feel guilty. He says men are like coffee mugs, but women like me are fine china."

"Is that in the Bible?" Carol asked with a smile.

Trina laughed. "No…at least, I don't think so. I don't know what to tell you, Carol. I guess you'll just have to get Carson to open up to you."

* * *

"Are you ready for Sunday?" Jonathan asked his friend.

"Pretty much," David answered. "One nice thing about new church membership is I can use old material." They both laughed.

"You seemed to hit it off with the pastor."

David agreed, "Seems like it, but I was a bit surprised he asked me to substitute teach the adult class."

"Who else is he going to get while he's away on vacation?"

"You."

"Yeah, right."

David knew Jonathan did not enjoy public speaking. He was much more of a behind-the-scenes guy. Daniels would do anything—could do anything, except teach or preach. He knew the Bible well enough and could certainly follow a curriculum guide if it was available. But knowing there were others far more capable fed his lack of confidence in this one area.

David didn't attend seminary like most pastors do, but he grew up in church and consistently fed his appetite for God's Word. He was the natural choice to teach whenever there was a need.

"Changing the subject a bit," Jonathan said, rubbing his chin. "I read that book you gave me—about Creation?"

"Good. What did you think?"

"I didn't realize there was so much scientific argument against evolution."

"I know, right?"

"Still seems hard to believe that most of the modern world is wrong about the age of the earth. I just figured God used the evolutionary process as His way of creating the universe."

"But there are too many theological problems with that," David insisted.

"I guess. Maybe I'm too practical, but it just doesn't seem logical."

"Well, if you are willing, I've got some DVDs you can watch that might help you think it through."

"I'm game. Just don't call me a heretic if I don't end up agreeing with you."

"Never. I'll have to look through my stuff to find them. They are in a box we never unpacked."

* * *

Sunday school went well. The thirty-some adults in Sunday school seemed to enjoy David's presentation. Katy wasn't one to stroke her husband's ego, but even she said the lesson was pretty good. That evening, as usual, David watched the news before going to bed.

"Justin Moore, the real-estate investor recently released from prison on a technicality, was found dead this morning inside one of his rental properties," the broadcaster announced. "His criminal trial made national news when it was revealed that prosecutors used a so-called 'time machine' to witness his crimes after the fact."

The reporter paused and stared intently at the teleprompter. In a particularly unprofessional manner, he stepped out of character, "That's what it says folks—a time machine." After a brief smirk, the broadcaster continued. "His cause of death has been ruled a homicide. No suspects have been identified."

"Well, what do you know," David mused while watching the evening news.

"What's that?" Katy asked, stepping into the living room with a bowl and dishtowel in hand.

"Oh, nothing." He tried to disguise his interest in the broadcast. "Some guy who killed a bunch of druggies finally got his." Katy stepped back into the kitchen, a little confused about why that news had such meaning to her husband.

Before heading upstairs, she asked, "Did you ever talk to Patrick?"

"What?" David responded before remembering his promise. "Oh, not yet."

"Are you going to?"

"I said I would."

"That was weeks ago," Katy reminded him. Knowing he should bite his tongue, David bit his lip instead. "Whatever," she said and turned to climb the stairs.

David's first thought was to wait until morning to call his brother-in-law as promised, but the Lord wouldn't let him wait any longer. He picked up his cell phone and found Patrick's name in the contacts. Before pressing the button, he took a deep breath, then prayed, "Father, Katy's right about me procrastinating. I don't want to call Pat. I'm afraid I won't be any help, and it will just be a waste of time. I know that's just being selfish. If you can use me to minister to him, please do. For his sake, for Katy's peace of mind, and in Jesus' name."

The call was cordial but didn't result in a miraculous turnaround for Katy's brother. David just shared the family's concern, asked about the man's welfare and plans, and offered to pray with him. Ten minutes later, David was upstairs apologizing to his wife.

* * *

There was, among the Hindsight team, a communal sense of poetic justice as news of Moore's death circulated among staff. After missing for two days, he was found dead of gunshot wounds at one of his listed properties. Whether his murder was a random act of violence or the result of cartel revenge made little difference to most. Even the judge who felt forced to dismiss the case secretly believed that justice had been served by the assassination.

The FBI exercise did demonstrate great potential for the project if Congress would act accordingly. Soon other departments, agencies, and institutions began lobbying for access to Hindsight. In the meantime, investigative reporters from various news agencies began working to uncover all they could about the *time machine*, beginning with its location.

Chapter 9 - Tabloid

"You heard me right, folks. The government is not content to surveil you in real-time. Now, they're working on a plan to watch what you did yesterday, last month, last year, and last decade. The Nanny state is real, and it is dangerous." The cable news anchor's ominous message resonated with his conspiracy theorist viewers.

Tabloids and off-beat cable programs jumped on what little information about Hindsight they could. Few of them were content to publicize the limited truth available that there existed equipment capable of recording history as it actually happened. Terms like time-machine, reality-distorter, and history-modifier were somehow included in much of the reporting. Artists' renditions and "expert" analysis painted distinctly inaccurate pictures. Since the idea of viewing history like a cable TV program seemed ludicrous, the news cycle on the subject would not have lasted very long—if it hadn't been for the video.

"We have exclusive video of the secret government machine we've been telling you about," the cable host announced. "What you are about to see will shock you. This is evidence used against Justin Moore at his trial. Since there is no audio, I will explain what is going on as you watch. Roll the track.

"What you are seeing is the magic window our government has been hiding from you. There! See that? See how the image changed from an empty warehouse to a busy one? See how several tables and people appeared out of nowhere? "What just happened?" you ask. The machine is recording something that happened in that room months or even years before.

"See how it is focusing on that one person? Now it's turning to show the other man's face. My friends, this is outrageous. They can go anywhere and watch anything. Then, just like they did to Mr. Moore, they can use it against you in a kangaroo court."

Despite efforts to keep the FBI recording under wraps, the copy given to the late Mr. Moore's attorneys found its way into the light. The "exclusive" video was shown on multiple local and national news outlets. It was dissected and discussed ad nauseam on cable talk shows. The video was ridiculed and rejected for the most part, but somehow, conspiracy theories kept the subject alive and in the news.

"What are the chances this will blow over?" Carl asked his boss and friend.

"I don't know," Jacob answered. "I'm not sure it's such a bad thing."

"How can you say that?"

"What we can do is amazing, but all the dis-information out there exaggerates Hindsight's capability. If the public knew our limitations, the conspiracy people might not have such a gullible audience."

"I see, but wouldn't that put our project in jeopardy? If we are known to be the only ones able to see the past, won't we become targets of espionage or attack from jealous enemies?"

"Hmmm, you might be right," Jacob acknowledged. "Hopefully, interest will wane."

* * *

But interest didn't wane. Some investigative reporters made it to the small town in New Mexico where the drug warehouse in question was located. Several locals recalled the visit from an unusually large group a few months back. The motel manager was the most helpful. He recalled that there were twelve or fourteen travelers who rented six rooms total.

"I figured they was just mov'n cause they had a couple of box trucks," the manager recalled. "But I thought it was funny that some of them was wearing ties." He looked through the records and confirmed that most of the vehicles had Arkansas license plates.

A regular at the diner recalled, "We saw 'em leave town before lunch. Didn't think much of it. They headed west down the county road—a whole slew of 'em."

"Had themselves a convoy," the cook added to a round of laughter.

Not much to go on, but it was a start. There wasn't anyone particular to talk to about the abandoned warehouse. The video jogged a few people's minds, and they directed the visitors to the desired location. As investigators discovered the building's whereabouts, they let themselves in through any convenient means. Enough time had passed that tracks from the mobile platform and gasoline odors were no longer evident. There were no clues except a couple of empty water bottles. And there was no telling who left them or how long they had been there.

Some reporters gave up on their cold case. Other sleuths persevered. Determining and following the best routes from the warehouse to Arkansas, one of them came across the restaurant where the team had eaten on their way home. Sheri Curtis worked for what most would call a tabloid, but she had real skills. She spent the next two days calling every motel on every logical route to Arkansas in an effort to find one where the mysterious group might have stayed.

* * *

Meanwhile, pressure was building to make use of Hindsight in new ways. Every government agency that knew about the project envisioned how they could benefit from it. Leaders were lobbying hard to get some face time with the director to convince him that their cause was worthwhile.

Dr. Knab was well aware that his project was at a crossroad. At a leadership meeting, he announced, "Hindsight left the experimental stage almost a year ago. It's time for it to earn its keep."

"How do we do that?" David asked.

"I'm being hounded by government lobbyists to let them plead their cases for making use of Hindsight."

"I guess we aren't a secret project anymore," Carl demurred.

"I know I won't be the final decision maker," Jacob said. "But I presumed I'll have some say in what direction the project takes. Does anyone have any initial advice to offer?"

"Can you tell us who wants to use Hindsight?" Minx asked.

Jacob named several departments.

"Since viewing the past is the machine's sole usefulness, an agency with an emphasis on history is the logical first choice, in my opinion," Dr. Gordman suggested, "in order to use it to its full potential."

"Since it is so far useless to law enforcement, we should probably focus on less controversial applications," the attorney added.

Everyone agreed, but the director was unable to limit meetings to strictly history-minded lobbyists. For a supposedly secret project, a whole lot of government entities knew about it. Congress's legislative inaction did not mean members didn't talk about it otherwise. Loose lips and special privilege don't bode well for clandestine activities. So, the line of interested parties grew.

* * *

"Hindsight looks to be the perfect tool to debunk many conspiracy theories while discovering the truth about historically significant events," an agent from the Department of Education suggested. "With your help, we could make teaching history exciting again. America's educational system would offer the most accurate accounts of history, bolstered by videos of actual people and events.

"Can you imagine seeing Vesuvius erupt or the Titanic sink? What if we could catch Jack the Ripper in action? Not to watch his heinous crimes, but to discover who he was. We could learn so much and solve so many mysteries."

The Office of Science and Technology suggested, "Science would be greatly helped by being able to see how diseases and plagues began. We could look back millions of years and verify or correct scientific assumptions and theories, which would enable us to make more precise predictions. Earth sciences might benefit the most from examining the past. Being able to watch a family or clan of early humans would greatly inform archeologists and sociologists. Replacing artist renderings of prehistoric people, things, and events with actual images would be incredible."

General Pyle's office saw the potential for the armed forces as well. "While the military has other means (like satellites) of obtaining desirable information, there are many times when being able to see more precisely an enemy's past activities would provide valuable defense intelligence. This could save thousands of American lives."

Along with that same thinking, Homeland Security was confident that its effectiveness "would be greatly enhanced if we could zero in on a person or activity from the past, especially the recent past. Imagine being able to trace back the steps of a person of interest. There is no end to what help it would be to witness a spy or terrorist in action. We are not always fortunate enough to obtain video of an event, like seeing who plants a bomb or takes a shot."

Immigration and Customs Enforcement leadership made their pitch as well. The much-maligned agency couched its appeal in a plea for sympathy. "Much of the public does not realize how important our work is. Nor do they understand how necessary it is to protect our borders." The ICE representative was not specific about how they would utilize Hindsight. It wasn't even clear how the department knew about it, or how much it knew. He simply asserted, "Your equipment would help us fight the fight."

This, of course, led back to the FBI and their desire to use Hindsight for investigative purposes. Unfortunately, until Congress took some action, looking into the past of American citizens would not stand up in court.

The Central Intelligence Agency promoted the fact that it does not contend with that restriction. "Since the CIA conducts foreign intelligence and missions, laws protecting Americans' rights are not an issue. When US citizens are unintentionally caught up in a mission, there are protocols that the CIA follows."

Dr. Knab was not impressed with the agency's assurance. While he didn't say so to the representative, Jacob didn't have much confidence in the Department of Justice in general. What he told the agent was, "The main issue concerning CIA's use of Hindsight is the extensive international transport. Not only would it be difficult to safely and covertly move it around the world, but it would be even harder to use it in secret. I imagine that many of the rendezvous and exchanges that the agency would want to look back upon are held in public places.

"Another factor that limits Hindsight's value to law enforcement of any kind is the lack of audio. While lip-reading could partially resolve this limitation, isn't what's said during an encounter as important as any activity revealed?"

Even OSHA got in on the action, suggesting that the multi-million-dollar project was best put to use investigating workplace safety violations. Dr. Knab soon regretted not vetting lobbyists more carefully—something he rectified by assigning that task to his able executive assistant, Miss Benson.

With all the recent visitors invading the base, direct work with Hindsight ceased. Much of the staff weren't sure what they could or should do while the equipment was in lockdown. Fortunately, things settled down at the compound with Trina fielding calls. Carl's stress returned to its usual level—moderately high. And most activities returned to normal. That didn't change the fact that no one knew what the next step was or should be.

* * *

One morning, Jonathan caught David as he entered the building. He signaled his colleague to join him in one of the labs. Once alone, Daniels explained, "I was double-checking calibrations last week and decided to try a little experiment. So, I sent the techs out on an errand and set the timeframe for a million years back."

Knowing that Jonathan was strait-laced, Hall was surprised at his revelation. "You didn't get approval first?" he asked.

Jonathan shrugged sheepishly, unsure if the question indicated that his friend was going to berate him, or even report him. There was no concrete rule against the technician's actions. After all, it was in his job description to keep the equipment and software functioning properly. Still, Hindsight had only been run for strictly defined purposes with at least two or three people in attendance.

"Well, I was checking settings." came Jonathan's defense. David rolled his eyes as his friend continued. "We had never gone back more than a few thousand years. How would we know if the program settings were accurate for extreme time periods if we don't experiment?"

David relented and encouraged Jonathan to get to the point. "So, what did you discover?"

"Nothing," Jonathan said with a smile. "Nothing showed up at all. Before doing this, I checked the internet to see what I should expect. One million years ago was supposed to be the middle of the last ice age. That was the time of mastodons and mammoths in North America, as well as prehistoric horses."

"I'm not surprised you didn't see much if it was the middle of an ice age," David stated.

Jonathan argued, "Temperatures in the ice age were only about ten degrees colder than now. It wasn't like…uninhabitable. That's not the point. The screen was black. No ice, no ground, no sky, no sun, no stars—nothing at all. So, I checked 500,000 years ago, then 200,000 years ago, then 100,000 and 50,000 years ago. Nothing. I had to stop because my assistants were returning from their errand."

"Humph," David looked thoughtful. "Do you suppose that means Hindsight doesn't work that far back?"

Jonathan raised one eyebrow. "You mean to tell me you've been preaching about a young earth, and you aren't excited that Hindsight might confirm your theory?"

David lifted his head and belted out a hardy laugh, followed by a boisterous, "YES!"

"This is big!" David asserted. "Where's the video?"

"Um, I didn't record it," Jonathan responded, anticipating his partner's disappointment. "Since it wasn't a sanctioned experiment, I thought it best to do it incognito."

"That was probably wise," David admitted.

Religious beliefs were rare among this group of scientists. A few of them claimed a spiritual heritage that they insisted didn't influence their work. While this pair didn't see eye-to-eye on everything, David and Jonathan were soul mates, spiritually speaking. The biblical account of Creation was one area Jonathan struggled with. His experiment was not quite enough to convince him that David was right, but it was evidence in his friend's favor.

"I don't dare do another experiment without permission," Jonathan stated. "Try to get approval to work more on this."

"I will," David promised. "We can't tell anyone why though, or we'll get shut down for sure. "I love it when science confirms the Bible," he said as he left the lab grinning from ear to ear.

The two were not ashamed of the faith that their associates derided. Neither were they pugnacious or belligerent towards their detractors. They discussed religious subjects at work only when asked, which was rare. Because the men were so accomplished and respected in their respective fields, colleagues mostly overlooked their "superstitious" beliefs.

Daniels approached Carl about conducting tests. "We haven't tested Hindsight's accuracy beyond a few thousand years. Don't you think it makes sense to make sure it works properly further in the past? Especially since we don't know who will get to use it and how far back in history they will want to review."

"That's a good idea," Gordman responded. "Jacob is in Washington D.C. for meetings. When he returns, we can talk to him about more tests." David was antsy to see if Hindsight would, indeed, prove the earth is young. His disappointment about waiting was evident, even to Carl.

"It should only be a few days," the assistant director said.

* * *

The time came to decide what agency would get the next crack at the newest scientific marvel. Shortly after arriving in the nation's capital, Dr. Knab was called to the Director of National Intelligence's office. There, representatives from Sycra Foundation and Wentsome Technologies joined the core group of decision-makers, including the Vice President's chief of staff and the National Intelligence director himself. Also in attendance was a handful of attorneys and note-takers, as well as Debra Minx, Hindsight's attorney, who felt a little out of her depth.

Introductions were made and pleasantries extended. Then Carol Myers from Sycra and Caleb Trace from Wentsome waited patiently while the others discussed which government entity had made the most compelling case for using Hindsight. Once it became clear that there was no obvious frontrunner, Carol spoke up.

"As you know, the Sycra Foundation furnished most of the data and much of the equipment necessary to make this project a success. And Wentsome Industries provided the irreplaceable staff as well as significant seed money to get Hindsight off the ground. We have a suggestion."

Carol recognized Caleb, who also prefaced their proposal, "Both Sycra and Wentsome are proud to have participated in this extraordinary endeavor, but neither organization saw our involvement as purely philanthropical. We were assured that our participation would be rewarded should the results bear fruit. We believe this is the opportune time for the government to make good on its promises and provide for a return on our investments."

Carol took the baton, "Just as there are many departments in our government that would love to take advantage of Hindsight's unique ability, there are many nations around the world that would also. And some of those nations would pay handsomely for these services."

"We are not suggesting that our government relinquish Hindsight's benefits in favor of our allies," Caleb chimed in. "Just set aside a reasonable amount of time each year to rent Hindsight to trusted nations. Once they know what Hindsight can do, revenue from these extracurricular activities could easily finance the future of this department and produce a fair return on our investments."

Carol concluded their proposal with a question. "Wouldn't it be great to have a department in the US government that brought in money instead of just spending it?"

Facial expressions throughout the room indicated that the idea of the federal government making money off anyone besides its citizens had never been imagined, let alone considered. Since government employees and elected officials would not personally benefit from such activity, there was no motivation to pursue such a vision. However, flouting a new toy and provoking other nations to jealousy over it—now that was worth considering.

Chapter 10 - Congress

There was little interest in the U.S. Congress for writing legislation concerning the use of Hindsight intelligence. Of particular concern was the constitutionality of relying on such unverifiable evidence in cases before the court. Mostly out of curiosity, many elected officials insisted upon hearings to help them understand what Hindsight could do and how that related to jurisprudence.

There was still very little accurate information about Hindsight in the public domain; however, no shortage of conspiracy theories and misinformation was available. To expedite information gathering, a non-standing joint committee of congresspersons and senators was formed to conduct hearings. Due to the sensitive nature of information regarding the project, the committee agreed to hold its initial hearing behind closed doors.

After the typical introductions, Dr. Knab and Deputy Assistant Attorney General Kenneth Hensley were welcomed as the only planned witnesses. Jacob described the project in as few words as possible, followed by a video of Hindsight in action. When the questioning began, most of the inquiries were anticipated, and the answers were unchanged from those given in various orientations and demonstrations over the past two years. Then, an obvious question was posed for the first time.

"How do we know that the images are accurate?" Congresswoman Hardy enquired.

Jacob hesitated thoughtfully. "We have no reason to believe that Hindsight is revealing anything inaccurately."

"How have you verified that?" Hardy pressed.

"Everything we have seen matches what we would expect. How would you suggest we verify its accuracy any further?" Dr. Knab replied.

"I don't know. I would think that your scientists should have already considered and answered that question." The congresswoman was blunt in her disparagement.

Senator Abbot requested to be recognized so that he could offer a suggestion. "We have lots of news footage from decades ago. Could you not set your machine up where a camera was located and tune into the time frame of the recorded event? Perhaps you could determine where a camera was stationed at JFK's assassination and compare what your equipment shows with the actual recording."

"Or use it at Fenway Park to see if your miracle machine matches one of the earliest games recorded on film," interrupted Congressman Shemp.

"Better yet, see if it can change the outcome to improve the Red Sox's record," Congressman Buck cackled to a chorus of laughter.

"Order!" came the chairperson's command as she exercised her gavel. "As entertaining as all this is, we will observe proper decorum in this committee." The laughter and chatter subsided, but almost every face continued to sport a grin or smirk.

The director was accustomed to such negative initial responses to his project. While looking into the past had become commonplace to him, Jacob understood how bizarre the idea was to the uninitiated. The information Dr. Knab shared usually left listeners scratching their heads. Committee members who were not downright incredulous were at least uncertain about what to believe. Jacob answered questions for over an hour. Next came the deputy assistant's turn.

Mr. Hensley was an accomplished attorney and judge before joining the Department of Justice. He had been thoroughly briefed on Hindsight, including witnessing two demonstrations. His role in the hearing was to answer legal questions pertaining to Hindsight's value to the legal system, as well as its constitutionality in court proceedings. Questions posed to him were along those lines.

Congresswoman Chaplin began questioning with, "Exactly what kinds of crimes would this...uh...thing be used to investigate?"

"At this point, we don't foresee being able to build more than two units," Kenneth explained. "Therefore, Hindsight would only be used to aid in the most important cases after traditional means have been exhausted without satisfactory results. Certainly, Congress has the authority to set limitations; however, we hope you will allow as much leeway as possible. We never know what sort of cases may go unsolved because of overly strict rules."

Senator Martin asked, "How can law enforcement justify utilizing such an after-the-fact surveillance?"

Kenneth replied, "We believe that Hindsight should qualify as an enhanced senses tool. Flashlights illuminate what the natural eye cannot see in the dark. Vision enhancers like binoculars allow investigators to view objects and activities farther away than the naked eye can see. As you know, the Supreme Court has ruled that the use of such tools is acceptable."

"Looking into the past is a little different than using a flashlight or binoculars," Martin argued.

"Agreed," the deputy responded. "But we are not asking Congress to allow carte blanche use by investigators. On the contrary, a warrant should always be required before Hindsight is used and its findings allowed in court."

"Still, I find it hard to accept that having access to viewing the past should be considered reasonable search and seizure," Chaplin complained.

"Why should it be any different than a hidden surveillance camera?" Senator Chase interjected. "How many crimes are solved because of a recording that a violator did not even know existed?"

"I would like to get back to the subject of warrants." Senator Allen encouraged. "Warrants are only granted when a judge is satisfied that there is probable cause. If I understand correctly, Hindsight's value is to determine probable cause. How can you justify a warrant before probable cause is established?"

"Admittedly, justifying a traditional search warrant could be a sticky issue," Hensley confessed. "Perhaps the government should impanel and empower special judges like we have in the FISA court. These judges would understand the use and value of Hindsight and appreciate the need for a lower threshold for signing a warrant."

Congressman Hawn exclaimed, "Just what we need, another secret court."

Congresswoman Hardy let out an exaggerated sigh, "Here we go again."

"Order!" the chairperson shouted, slamming her gavel twice. "I've allowed committee members considerable latitude thus far, but you will direct your comments and questions to the witnesses, not to each other. Senator Chase, you have the floor."

Chase continued, "It seems to me that a compromise might be advisable. We could allow the use of this equipment to gain intelligence that aids investigators, but any case against the accused would have to be built with additional evidence. This machine can set law enforcement on the right path, but cannot, itself, be evidence in court."

"That's exactly what the FBI did that brought us to this place," the deputy countered. "The presiding judge deemed all of the evidence 'fruit of the poisonous tree' and tossed the case out."

Allen interrupted, "That is what our legislation would rectify. That judge had no legal standard for admitting evidence developed by your machine. A law that defines its limited use would provide judges with a proper basis for allowing evidence that is predicated upon your machine's findings."

"Respectfully," Hensley answered, "We prefer that you allow Hindsight's findings themselves as evidence in court. A video recording of a crime being committed would be most compelling. If the results from a Hindsight operation can lead to evidence gathering, why can't it be evidence itself?"

Questions to the deputy assumed that Hindsight could do what Dr. Knab had affirmed. Sadly, despite the spirited legal discussion, many elected officials still doubted the project's ability to truly reveal the past. The hearing continued with questions that were, by and large, repetitive. They diverged into political speeches that focused more on philosophical differences than finding common ground. Fortunately, there was not as much grandstanding among members as would have been in a public hearing. Finally, grumbling stomachs urged a recess.

Congressman Shemp suggested calling more witnesses from the project to verify the director's claims. Senator Abbot countered with a proposal that the committee see it for themselves. That recommendation resonated with most of the committee. Never shy to spend money or find a reason to leave the capital, the joint committee adjourned after instructing Dr. Knab to recommend a venue and time to demonstrate Hindsight.

* * *

Dr. Gordman, David, and Miss Benson were tasked with finding a suitable place to demonstrate Hindsight to the elected officials. The plan took four months to finalize. After several failed attempts to convince authorities that the use of gamma radiation would be safe, the search committee stopped mentioning gamma and X-rays altogether. Instead, they simply stated that a joint committee from Congress wanted to meet at a chosen location and asked for available dates.

Calendars and schedules were compared, and a date was set. Committee members were very surprised and a little confused when they were instructed to meet at Fort McHenry in Baltimore, Maryland, on the first Tuesday of October. As members arrived with their entourages, it became obvious that choosing a wide-open venue was a wise decision.

Jacob Knab welcomed officials as they arrived at the national monument. The historic shrine was closed to visitors that Monday and Tuesday for "routine maintenance and repairs." So, only some National Park Service officers were inside and around the fort when Hindsight was set up for the demonstration. Some legislators were a few minutes late, none more than twenty minutes.

Jacob stepped up to a microphone on a small portable stage and began by sharing some disappointing news. "Before we begin, I must ask everyone who is not a member of the joint committee to follow Miss Benson and security to a holding area we've set up for you."

No one moved except to look around at each other, wondering who Knab was referring to. The director then asked for all congresspeople and senators to raise their hands, which they did proudly.

"If you are not currently raising your hand, please follow Miss Benson," he restated.

There was some shuffling of feet, but no real movement. Staff members who looked to their bosses for direction received shrugged shoulders and raised eyebrows in response. Jacob tried again.

"Let me explain. First, this project is still considered secret."

Gordman whispered, "Barely," under his breath.

"But more importantly," Knab continued, "we have a limited number of protective suits for observers to wear. This exercise is completely safe, but we don't want to take any chances. So, we are requiring every participant to wear radiation protection.

Accompanying assistants and attorneys reluctantly followed park officers into a building and out of view, leaving just four security personnel with the committee members. Once adorned in radiation-safe garments, the group appeared like something between a hazmat clean-up crew and astronauts. The legislators took their places.

Knowing that Dr. Gordman despised speaking to groups, the director tasked David with narrating the presentation while Jonathan operated the equipment.

"As I'm sure you know, Fort McHenry was the site of a decisive battle in the War of 1812." David's impression of a tour guide was spot on. "After watching American soldiers successfully defend this fort from the British navy in September of 1814, Frances Scott Key wrote a poem that became our national anthem, 'The Star-Spangled Banner.' We chose this spot so we could demonstrate Hindsight in a most dramatic way."

David explained, "Hindsight is bolted to a mobile platform so we can rotate the equipment to provide a more panoramic view. This evening, we will take you back to that fateful night of bombs bursting in the air. You will see the battle as it was waged over two hundred years ago.

"We have added one item to our usual instruments—a giant monitor. On it, you can see what this camera is recording. Of course, you will want to watch the miracle screen at first, but it is quite small, and you must keep a safe distance. So, once you are convinced that Hindsight is truly presenting the Battle of Fort McHenry, you can get a better view by observing the big screen."

The team decided to wait until sunset to begin the demonstration. Participants would be able to see both screens more easily in the relative dark. Fortunately, the mild fall temperature kept the protective garb from becoming too uncomfortable. Plus, the team timed everything quite well, so no one was wearing the bulky suits more than fifteen minutes before showtime.

"Ladies and gentlemen," David's introduction engaged every attendee. "We give you September 13, 1814." With the equipment pointed toward the Patapsco River, an image of the ships in the distance appeared on the metal plate. Everyone squinted to see the Hindsight screen more clearly. They passed around a few opera glasses that Miss Benson had thought to bring. Michaels continued his narration.

"In the early morning, several British ships approached through the Chesapeake Bay. Just three weeks earlier, Washington D.C. had fallen, and several significant structures were burned down. The Presidential mansion and the Capitol building were among them. Our technician, Mr. Daniels, is going to present Hindsight's version of time-lapse. We spent all day yesterday finding the best times of the battle to show you. So, we will move through the entire battle in just a few minutes, pausing occasionally for short bursts of real-time action.

"As you can see, the British navy began bombarding the fort early in the day. You can't see their grandest ships. The river was too shallow to bring them in, so only sixteen or so smaller, but capable vessels are close enough to be viewed. Some of the images are obscured by occasional rain.

"WATCH OUT!"

Everyone flinched as the giant monitor showed a metal orb heading straight for the crowd, then out of the frame.

The narration continued, "At first, the ships were too far away for the fort's cannons to strike them, but some of them approached, believing they had done significant damage. Our cannons soon put them to flight. As night fell, the rain increased. The night sky was occasionally lit by a flaming rocket."

Hindsight pivoted on its mobile platform to show various views, including the seeming chaos of fort defenders. Last of all, the panel was turned to face a flagpole, then tilted upward.

"Finally," David concluded, "the sun rose to reveal a damaged, but standing fort, and soon the ships sailed away in defeat—for our flag was still there."

The final scene brought tears to eyes and lumps to throats. The equipment's hum was less distracting in the open air, but the sound was clearly increasing. Hindsight was shut down after outdoor lights were turned on. Team members helped their audience escape their protective suits. The twenty-minute demonstration had taken its toll on women's hair and make-up. And while everyone had reduced their clothing to the reasonable minimum, no one was dry.

Dr. Knab apologized for not advising them to bring a change of clothes, but most participants shrugged the apology aside as unnecessary. They were too enthralled by what they had witnessed to care about how they looked, felt, or smelled. They rejoined their attendants with a sense of awe.

The idea that Hindsight's ability was supposed to stay classified seemed lost on the legislators. They couldn't wait to describe the presentation to those sequestered. The longer they talked about what they witnessed, the more they sounded like excited children.

Jacob gave the committee's vice-chairperson a secure website link that members could access to download a video of what they had just witnessed. In return, the director was promised quick action by the legislators. The

Hindsight team returned home proud of their impressive demonstration and eager to learn what legislation would be drafted.

As it turns out, when it comes to the federal government, *quick action* is a relative term with relatively little meaning. The joint committee did meet to discuss possible recommendations, but that was as far as it went. No other action was taken during the current legislative session—nor the next. Welcome to Washington.

Chapter 11 - Discovered

Buoyed by successfully tracing the path of Hindsight's clandestine caravan last year, Sheri Curtis was the last investigative reporter to chase down leads. Her tabloid employer was growing impatient, so Sheri would submit an unrelated "scoop" every once in a while—imaginary things that she claimed to have discovered while on the road. Those and her occasional progress on the time machine story held her editor at bay.

Having discovered both the restaurant and hotel the team had visited, Sheri was following her third hunch for the most likely path the convoy would take into Arkansas. She stopped for lunch in a city forty miles from the base.

"You ever hear of strange goings-on around here?" she asked her waitress, who tried not to smirk.

Reasoning that sharing some good gossip might bring in a better tip, the server answered, "Whatcha lookin' for? My momma says the priest is a drunk, among other things."

"Nah," Sheri responded, moving on to her standard approach. "I'm an insurance investigator, following up a hit and run, but I'm pretty much at a dead end. The accident happened ten months ago, and I can't find the convoy that was involved."

"Convoy?" the young lady questioned. "A whole convoy hit someone?"

"No, just one of the trucks. A witness claimed there were two trucks, a van, and two cars traveling together." Sheri was used to getting blank stares when she told the story, but it was the best one she had come up with. "Yeah, I guess no one will get the reward."

"Reward?" An eavesdropping customer inquired.

"Yup!" The reporter reeled in her catch. "Five-thousand dollars to anyone with information that leads to finding the culprit."

"Wow," the waitress exclaimed. "Wish I could help."

The customer turned back to his meal, shaking his head.

"Thing is," Sheri prodded, "they're probably part of a big organization. It just irks me."

"Me too," the server agreed. "But there ain't no big outfits 'round here."

"Even that Army base is less than a quarter full," the customer inserted, without looking back at the reporter.

"Army base?" she asked, her Spidey senses tingling. Desperate for any lead, Sheri got directions to the base.

Once in the nearby town, Sheri confirmed with locals that a group of vehicles like she described did exit the base several months earlier. With that information, she rented a room at the only motel in town and began investigating further.

Not one to be subtle, Ms. Curtis asked pointed questions to those she thought most likely to know anything of value. She found banks and schools unhelpful, citing confidentiality. She didn't even try the local Urgent Care facility. Most patrons she found in grocery stores and gas stations responded cautiously to the stranger's inquiries. Even contractors who had been on location to do plumbing, electrical, and construction work were confused by her interest in the mostly abandoned base.

As far as the community was concerned, the facility housed a small contingent of specialists working on undisclosed military projects. Despite the absence of information, the locals had no reason to believe anything dangerous or highly secretive was going on. Many of them had been on base for birthday parties and other events. The forty or so families in base housing comprised almost ten percent of the schools' enrollment. As a last resort, Sheri went to a hairdresser for a trim and some gossip.

"Yup, sounds like the Army's stuff," one lady waiting her turn commented when Sheri told her story. "I wonder why their trucks aren't camouflaged. I guess so nobody knows they are military."

The date stood out to one of the other ladies because it was her grandson's birthday when they saw the unusual number of vehicles exit the base.

"About the same number of vehicles returned less than a week later," the cosmetologist offered. "Funny thing—hadn't seen those trucks since until last Sunday. Must be an annual outing or something."

"Those trucks left on Sunday?" Sheri asked. "Which way did they go?"

"Only one way to the interstate, dearie," she answered. "Don't know which way they headed from there."

Ms. Curtis convinced her editor to put her up at the local motel for a little while longer. "The trucks were off base for just a few days the last time," she told him. "If they follow the same routine, they should be back any time now."

She gave her cell phone number to the few people she was able to befriend and asked them to call her if the trucks were sighted. She wanted to avoid staking out the base entrance for several days and nights by herself.

Just before seven o'clock on Thursday evening, her phone dinged. The two-word message simply stated, "They're back." Sheri quickly replied with her thanks and hurried to her car. As she arrived at the base, she could see the convoy less than a quarter mile away. Instinctively, the reporter turned into the entrance where security tried to wave her off. Pretending that she did not understand the officer's signal to leave, Sheri stopped her car and rolled down the window.

"I'm sorry, but no guests are allowed on base at this time. You have to leave immediately." The guard was agitated. He could see the Hindsight team approaching and was anxious to send the visitor on her way.

"But I need some help," Sheri responded, ignoring the soldier's instructions. She mumbled as she fumbled through her purse. Her stall tactic was effective, and she was soon boxed in with a row of trucks and cars behind her and a lowered vehicle barrier ahead. The car immediately behind her quickly moved to provide space for the visitor to back out. When Sheri hesitated, the guard placed his hand on his sidearm and flipped open the securing strap with his thumb. A second soldier exited the guard post, brandishing a semi-automatic weapon.

Taking the hint, Sheri raised her hands in surrender, then backed her car away from the entrance and turned around to leave. Then, taking a deep breath, she drove her sedan into the first box truck in line, trying ever so hard to make it look like an accident. She jumped out of the car with her cell phone in hand.

"Oh, I'm so sorry! I just…that man with a rifle rattled me so. I just lost control. Look, I'm a nervous wreck." The reporter extended her right hand to show it shaking, which was more real than contrived since she didn't know what might happen to her next. A soldier tried to escort her to the guardhouse, but she insisted on taking pictures of the accident for insurance purposes.

After a few snaps, the soldier took her by the arm and led her to his post. Other security personnel arrived and took pictures of their own before moving the reporter's damaged car. The line of vehicles blocking the lane finally entered the base and made their way to their respective garages, all except for the damaged truck. It was pulled onto the base property where the driver and passenger awaited police.

Sheri's rash decision didn't give her time to think through the fact that she would have to provide her personal information as part of the police report and insurance investigation. She briefly considered how she might escape the situation since her car should be drivable.

"I need to get my purse out of the car," she said as she stood up from the metal folding chair. When the guard walked her to the vehicle, she realized it was foolish to try to leave. She retrieved an envelope from the glove compartment and her clutch purse from the floorboard in front of the passenger's seat.

By the time she returned to the guard post, a police deputy had arrived on the scene. She remained outside as the officer spoke briefly with the truck driver, then one of the soldiers. He finally approached the offender and asked for her driver's license, car registration, and proof of insurance, which she provided. As the policeman recorded pertinent information from the documents, he asked for Sheri's statement.

"I was lost, so I pulled in here to get directions. Those soldiers threatened me with their guns. So, while I was pulling away, I lost control and ran into that truck." She motioned to the box truck in question.

"The driver says it looked like you hit him on purpose," the officer asserted.

"That's ridiculous! Why would I do that?" was the nervous reporter's retort.

Having finished recording the necessary report information, the deputy continued the questioning. "Where is it you are trying to go?"

"What?" Sheri asked, stalling to think of a believable answer.

"You said you are lost and stopped here to ask for directions," the officer reminded. "Where are you heading?"

"Oh, uh, I'm looking for a good place to eat." Her answer sounded even lamer when she spoke it than it did in her head. Sheri was certain the deputy was aware that she was lying, so she was surprised when he said he had all he needed and that she could go.

"Maybe these small-town cops really are like the stereotypes," she thought. Then she took a chance. "What about their truck? Shouldn't you see if anything inside is damaged?"

Having reverted to her normal quick thinking, the keen investigator argued. "Not that I don't trust them, but they could tell my insurance company that something in the truck was broken during the accident. I just think we should make sure everything is okay before I leave."

The officer motioned for the truck driver and his passenger to come closer. "Ms. Curtis is concerned that you might exaggerate your claim to her insurance company. Would you tell her what you told me, please?"

The driver explained, "We do our own repairs and there is not much damage anyway. We won't be making a claim against you or your insurance company. Accidents happen. Don't worry about it."

"Even have it in writing," the deputy said, pointing to the signature declining to prosecute or seek compensation for damages. The reporter was at a loss. She knew that pressing the issue further wouldn't yield any better results, but she decided to try a different tactic before leaving.

"So, what do you all do here anyway?" she asked, batting her eyelids to draw attention to her dark brown eyes. "I mean, none of the people who drove in were wearing military uniforms. But this is an Army base, right?"

The officer's face indicated that he had a secret he was about to reveal. "Ma'am, I know who you are and why you are here. I was at the station on Tuesday when you came in asking questions about this facility. Your snooping around made us curious. So, we've checked you out and know that you are a reporter of some sort. That's fine. We really don't care, but if you are not off this property in two minutes, I will arrest you for trespassing. Savvy?"

Defeated and a bit embarrassed, the sleuth returned to her car and drove back to her motel room. From there, she called in her report. Taking the biggest chance of her career, Sheri told her boss that she had found the location of a time machine. Her article with some unrelated pictures added by the editor made the publication's front page.

News traveled fast for a rag with a small web presence and even smaller print circulation. Soon the town was inundated with photographers, journalists, investigators, and sci-fi enthusiasts. Residents were not accustomed to being a tourism town, and many of them were put off by rude and pushy paparazzi and professional news gatherers. Eight days of chaos did turn out to be good for business, almost doubling some of the small businesses' annual receipts.

Motel rooms were full. Restaurant owners had to make frequent trips into the big city to get supplies. While nobody engaged in deep price gouging, the cost of most items increased considerably. Naturally, this irritated the locals.

It didn't take long for the dozens of men and women who positioned themselves at the base entrance to realize that they would not get any news scoops that way. So, they canvassed the neighborhoods offering incentives for information. Several newspeople had run-ins with the law when they tried to interrogate teenagers coming out of school. Reporters were especially trolling those who rode the school bus from the base.

Three days after the plague of reporters descended, the base went on lockdown—no one in, no one out. The only exception was the two trucks sent to gather supplies needed to support the families during the quarantine. Unfortunately, the only trucks available were the same ones used to transport Hindsight and related equipment.

Both trucks were followed by several vehicles filled with eager reporters and photographers. When the trucks went different directions, each vehicle of investigators had to choose which one to follow. The group that ended up at a big box store in the next city waited patiently while base employees shopped. Camera shutters rattled and video equipment rolled, documenting every move as groceries and paper products were loaded into the truck.

While this vehicle was parked in plain view on the store's parking lot, the other truck made its twisted way through alleys and side streets toward its final destination. Those following the second truck had reason to believe they were on the trail of a hot lead. Following the truck could not be done covertly, though the snoops tried.

When the truck stopped, three people exited the cab. One of the men had a holstered weapon. The other man lifted the truck's roll-up door while the sole female knocked on the building's back door. The two men repeatedly entered the truck's cargo area to bring out baskets on wheels like those used by hotel laundry attendants. The baskets appeared to be lined with tarps and half full of something heavy. A lift-gate was used to lower the containers to the ground. There was no movement for a while after six containers were taken into the building.

Some brave investigators approached the truck on foot, hiding behind garbage bins and parked cars. They positioned themselves to be able to see that the truck was empty. Soon, two containers were wheeled out of the building and put into the truck via the lift-gate. The baskets seemed much heavier, and ice cubes could be seen piled up in the middle.

As soon as the men being surveilled reentered the building, three trackers (two with cameras) jumped into the truck to have a look. Digging through the ice, they found a variety of wrapped meats: poultry, fish, pork, and beef.

"This must be a meat market we're at," one of the disappointed investigators said.

This revelation caused those inside the truck to drop their guard and begin talking amongst themselves. Suddenly, they heard the rolling wheels of two more carts approaching. They barely made it to the back of the truck when they were met by the three base employees. Both groups were startled, and the armed man unholstered his gun but kept it pointed at the ground. Those still in hiding took pictures and video of the confrontation.

Even that was a dud. There was no shooting, no yelling, no threatening. After the initial shock, the unarmed base employee motioned for the trespassers to exit the truck. Then, the two men put the bins in place and went back into the building for the final two containers. The woman, who was one of the base cooks, stood guard at the truck to discourage any more encroachments. With the suspense ended, all those in hiding revealed themselves and made their way back to their vehicles. Some of them waited to follow the truck back to the base. Most didn't bother.

When no reprieve was apparent by Monday, Dr. Knab called D.C. for advice. "Should I give a statement or hold a press conference so we can try to send these reporters on their way?" he asked. "I was thinking that we might be stoking their curiosity by remaining silent."

"No, just ride it out," came the answer. Not much help, but Washington types lean heavily on denial, deflection, and stonewalling as strategies.

It became clear that there was little value in staking out the base, so the uninvited visitors left. When they did, even beneficiaries of the business boon were relieved. Still, it was a long week for those on base. Several victims of the lock-down mentioned its similarity to the stay-at-home orders of the 2020 coronavirus pandemic.

Even weeks after newspeople and their cameras disappeared, there was some residual effect from their invasion. The local community that had passively received the new base crew with its small economic bump became more suspicious and inquisitive.

Students were frequently questioned and teased by classmates. Spouses were met with glaring stares while shopping. Even members of the police force made sure to look into the vehicles of base residents whenever they were observed off campus. This added uneasiness caused the workers and families to somewhat self-sequester, making relationships among the isolated more important, necessary, and special.

Chapter 12 - Hired

"You're going where?" Katy asked, looking up from her book.

"Greece," David repeated. "You know, in Europe."

"Why?"

"Maybe that wasn't the best way to bring up the subject," her husband confessed. "I just thought it would be dramatic. Isn't it cool?"

She closed her book and laid it on her lap. "But why?"

"Some rich guy is renting Hindsight," he stated. David was happy to talk about work at long last. The invasion of reporters all but confirmed that the base housed the secret past-revealing machine. There were still lots of forbidden topics, but general discussions about the project were allowed among adult family members who lived on base and had signed non-disclosure agreements.

"So, you went from hiding your secret machine to renting it out to strangers overnight?"

"Kinda seems that way, doesn't it?" David agreed. When the conversation quickly turned to Katy's day with their son, David figured the news was far less interesting to his wife than he'd hoped. The subject didn't come up again until they were in bed.

"So, you aren't interested in the details of my trip?" David asked rather sheepishly.

Katy turned to face him and answered, "I figured you would tell me what you could. I've gotten tired of asking questions you can't answer."

"That makes sense. I'm sorry, I thought you were just giving me the cold shoulder."

She sighed. "So, what about this trip to…where is it?"

"Greece."

"Why Greece?"

"We are going to use the equipment to record some of the ancient wonders of the world."

"Why?"

"So, we can see what they really looked like."

"Why?"

"I don't know. The man just wants it. And he's paying big bucks for it. You should be happy. It's providing some job security," David answered.

"I should be happy about you running around the world while I'm stuck here? That was never part of the plan," Katy complained.

David wanted to accuse her of being jealous but bit his tongue. Nothing good could come from prolonging the escalating argument. He simply said, "I'm sorry…plans change."

They both rolled over and went to sleep, but not before Katy's pillow was wet with silent tears.

* * *

The job in Greece wasn't easy to come by. When legislation regarding Hindsight did not materialize, representatives of Wentsome Industries and the Sycra Foundation coordinated their efforts. They lobbied fervently to make the device available to individuals, organizations, and friendly nations willing to pay an exorbitant fee. Since there was little reason to consider the project secret any longer, news of Hindsight's availability was made known to allies. Unfortunately, solicitations to friendly foreign nations were met with skepticism.

It was determined that someone with high-level connections was needed to act as a sales agent. Jacob reached out to some ex-ambassadors to no avail. Brokerage firms, multi-national company executives, and marketing experts were just as uninterested. Finding a qualified salesperson was far more difficult than he thought it should be.

"I've never seen Dr. Knab so grumpy," Carol commented to her colleague.

"I know. He is at his wit's end," Trina agreed.

"About what?" The office manager stepped away from the copy machine so she could hear her confidant without Trina raising her voice.

"He's been trying for weeks to find a salesman," the executive assistant confided. "They finally decide to make Hindsight available, and he can't get anyone to make sales calls."

As the office manager, Carol was aware of almost everything that went on at the base even though she was technically a middle-tier employee. She knew that the gag orders were modified, but she wasn't aware that the director was looking for a salesman. Later, she complained to Carson.

* * *

"Sometimes I don't understand what they want from me," she complained to her boyfriend. "I've been going through all the resumes from when this project began, pulling out the ones with certain words and phrases. I had no idea why until today."

"What's up?" Carson asked.

"There's this big employee search going on. You'd think as much as I do at that place, they would keep me in the loop."

"I thought you said the place was downsizing. What jobs are they trying to fill?"

"Well, I told you what our machine does basically."

"Not exactly what the news describes."

"I know, right?" Carol continued. "Now they need someone to find customers to rent it."

"They're going public?"

"I don't know the details, but Dr. Knab is looking for a salesman. So, I have to go in early tomorrow, now that I know what I'm looking for in those resumes."

"Really? Well, that makes this a little awkward," Carson said, his tone soaked with disappointment. "I wanted to surprise you with a fancy dinner out tonight."

"You did? Wow, we haven't been anyplace special in months."

"I know, but I wanted to ask you something." He bit his lower lip. "But now is not the right time, I guess."

"What? I mean, you're right that I shouldn't stay out late, but you can still ask me." Carol's heart was panting for a marriage proposal, but her head kept shouting, "Don't get your hopes up."

"No, really," Carson insisted. "I want to do this right. Can we go out Friday night?"

"Yes!" Carol almost shouted. After composing herself, she added, "It's a date."

"Good. Well, I better head out."

"So early?"

"You need your rest," was his excuse. Then he thought of a better one. "Besides, if I stay, I might ruin the surprise."

* * *

The next morning, Carson made a beeline to the unrestricted coffee shop and waited patiently for the director or his assistant to appear. When asked, he simply told people that he was waiting for Carol. Finally, Dr. Gordman came in for his ten o'clock coffee.

"Hey, chief," the stalker called out. "Carson Trout," he said, identifying himself.

"Yes, Mr. Trout. We can't help but know who you are," Carl replied. "I see you on base more often than I see some of my staff."

"Please, call me Carson. Can you join me while I wait for Carol?" Trout asked.

Carl rarely received invitations like that, so he motioned for Carson to take the empty chair across the table. They chitchatted for just a few minutes before Carson made his play. "It's too bad your machine isn't available to civilians. I know some people who would pay big bucks to see it in action."

Carl was not too surprised about Trout's awareness of Hindsight's ability despite the visitor never signing a non-disclosure agreement. Some information came as a result of the failed criminal trial and subsequent investigations from journalists. More information was leaked by someone connected to the legislative joint committee. And no doubt, Carol had inadvertently revealed additional details. Dr. Gordman was so unconcerned that he continued the discussion as if Carson was an employee of the project.

"How is it you know people like that?" Carl asked. "I thought you were an inspector, or product reviewer, or something like that."

"I am...in a sense," Trout acknowledged. "But the work I do is for people and companies with deep pockets."

"So, you think you know someone who would pay us for the use of Hindsight?" Gordman queried.

"Absolutely! I would be happy to contact him for you," Carson offered. "Of course, the first thing he will want to know is how much it will cost. He has more money than he knows what to do with, but he will still ask. Do you want me to call him?"

Gordman stroked his beard. "Not yet. It's not my decision, but I will pass the word along. Did you say you were waiting on Carol? I don't think she's coming. Looked like she was buried in paperwork."

"Oh, that's alright." Carson declared. "I'll catch her tonight. Don't bother telling her I came by. It will just make her feel bad for missing me. I better get going." Carson tossed his empty coffee cup into the trash receptacle as he strolled out of the shop. Carl finished his java and headed straight to his boss's office to share some hopeful news.

After learning of Trout's offer, Dr. Knab called Ms. Castle into his office to get more background on her fiancé. While she was easily satisfied with her beau's explanations of his work, she realized that her answers to the director were pretty vague.

"Carson came to see you?" she asked the director.

"No, Carl said he ran into him, and in their conversation, your boyfriend mentioned some client he had who might be interested in Hindsight."

"Funny, he didn't tell me," Carol complained. "Could have saved me a lot of work."

Jacob was anxious to get someone on board who could produce results, so he called Trout to arrange an interview. Because the work area of the compound was still restricted, Dr. Knab arranged to meet Carson in a small, unused office in the same building as the coffee shop. Trout arrived a little early, and Jacob joined him a little late. They exchanged pleasantries before the director got right to the point. "I understand you have connections that might help us."

"Yes sir, I believe I do," Carson affirmed. The two talked at length with Carson detailing some of his contacts and background. Knab explained that there would be a vetting process before Trout could join the team.

"I completely understand," the prospective new hire said. "Let me know what you need."

"Our attorney will be in touch. I do know we will need your Social Security number, driver's license, and fingerprints."

A fairly comprehensive background check raised no concerning flags. His Chinese parents came to America from Hong Kong before Carson was born. He was offered a reasonable salary that would convert to commission-only compensation in three months.

"If I make a sale earlier, will the commission pay start then?" he asked.

"Sure," the director agreed. "That would be great, but I don't want to put too much pressure on you."

Carson chuckled, "I thrive on the challenge to exceed expectations."

The leadership team had discussed pricing, and some general numbers were established, but there was never a potential client to share those details with. Carson encouraged an overhaul of the pricing plan, increasing the numbers significantly. After some pushback from unconvinced decision-makers, Carson requested a test period.

"Give me thirty days. If I can't sell our services at my recommended pricing within the first month, I'll drop it and you can set pricing as you see fit."

"Won't hurt to let him try," Carl suggested.

"All right," Jacob agreed. "One month. Good luck."

Next came his orientation to the facilities and equipment. Trout was a quick study with an incredible memory. In less than two weeks he had digested and could regurgitate everything he needed to know for and about his job.

Six days later, Trout knocked on the director's office door. Through the window, he could see Dr. Knab on the phone, but motioning for him to enter. As the salesman stepped in, Jacob punched "End" on his cell phone and placed it on his desk. Carson held out the contract proposal he needed to be approved. Knab took it without realizing what he was looking at. His eyes widened as he glanced over the document.

"Is this for real?" Knab asked in obvious disbelief. "This guy, Seaval, is good with these numbers?"

Just two days earlier, Carson revealed that a Greek billionaire, Theodor Seaval, was interested in using Hindsight to get true images of the famous seven wonders of the ancient world. The project seemed innocuous enough, so Dr. Knab approved offering a proposal. The numbers Seaval had agreed to were staggering.

The terms of the contract called for six-hundred-thousand dollars per day, including travel days. It also included one thousand dollars per mile that the equipment traveled. The distance was estimated at seventeen-thousand miles, which included two Wonders destinations. Raw digital video recordings would be given to the client immediately upon production. Expecting the project to require three weeks, the total price tag was almost fourteen million dollars.

When Jacob realized that Trout's commission would come to over a quarter of a million dollars, he understood why Carson offered to work for a commission of just three percent. Dr. Knab congratulated his salesman profusely while signing the contract. The team had two months to work out the details of the mission.

* * *

"Does this mean you'll be traveling a lot?" Katy asked. The couple hadn't talked about David's trip to Greece for almost a week. The two short business trips he took earlier weren't a real problem for her, but she was afraid things were about to change. This trip seemed to portend he would be gone much more. Before he could answer her query, she added, "How long will you be gone?"

"About three weeks."

"Three weeks?!"

"It's a very big deal. This one job will put the project on sound financial footing for a year."

"But three weeks? What will you be doing for three weeks?"

"I already told you what I could, but it will be safe and educational."

"And you will be gone for three weeks."

David decided it was unwise to try to convince his wife that she was overreacting. Instead, he got up from the couch and knelt with one knee by her chair. He placed his hand over the one she was resting on the book in her lap and looked her in the eyes.

"I know this is hard. It isn't what we signed up for. I don't know if this is a one-time thing or if it will become a regular part of my job. After this trip, we can talk about me quitting if it's too hard on you." David was sincere in his promise, but he was also being a bit manipulative. He learned long ago that promising to let Katy have her way usually ended up with him getting what he wanted. In his mind, he justified the approach by misapplying First Peter 3:7, "Husbands, dwell with your wives according to knowledge."

As usual, David's commitment reduced Katy's anxiety. She understood that his vocational ambitions meant more sacrifices in the short run, but she constantly struggled with the fear that he would lose sight of proper priorities. Her father was a workaholic who often excused his absence as "doing it all for the family."

"When do you leave?" was Katy's next question.

"In about seven weeks."

"Oh, that long? Good. Your other trips were pretty sudden."

"This one is different. It requires a lot of planning."

"What am I going to do for three weeks?" she asked.

"You could visit your mom for part of that time if you want. She would love to see Reese."

"She will probably read into it that we are having marital problems."

"Maybe, but you can convince her otherwise."

"I doubt it. She's pretty convinced that all men are jerks."

"She's probably right," David said with a grin.

"I know she is," Katy giggled while leaning over to hug David, followed by a kiss, followed by a longer kiss.

* * *

Meanwhile, Carson and Carol were just finishing dinner at the most expensive restaurant in the *big* city. It must have been a night for romance. At least she hoped it was. It was looking that way. Carson pulled out all the stops and treated his girlfriend like a queen. It was so refreshing to feel special again. Until recently, she felt like he was slipping away—losing interest in her. Tonight was different.

Though she kept trying to push it from her mind, there was one thing that concerned her. As they walked along the riverwalk, holding gloved hands, she finally broached the subject. "Why didn't you tell me you were going to apply for that salesman job?"

"What? Oh, that. Why? What's wrong?"

"I don't know. It just seems like you went behind my back." She immediately wished she could take that last statement back. It was too harsh, too blunt. She stood still with her head bowed, knowing she had ruined the mood and probably any chance of him proposing that night. "I'm sorry," she said, shaking her head at her stupidity.

"Don't be," he answered sympathetically. "Look, when you told me about the job, I didn't think anything about it at the time. When I got home, I started to realize that I had connections that might benefit your business. I started to think it might be great to work together, especially if we are husband and wife."

Carol gasped at his use of those last three words. She desperately wanted to stay on that subject. She no longer cared about that nagging feeling of being used. She just wanted him to propose, but he wasn't finished explaining.

"But what if they didn't want me, I wondered. Would you reject me too? I just thought if I applied for the job and didn't get it, no harm done. You wouldn't think less of me if you didn't know I failed."

"I wouldn't have anyway," Carol insisted.

"I guess it's just my pride. I want so much for you to respect me."

"I do."

Carson looked at her with a wry smile. "Are you willing to say those two words again?"

"What two words?" she asked, thinking back. "I do?"

Carson took a knee and pulled a black ring box from his overcoat pocket. As she peered down, her gaze alternated between his face and the box, her smile growing with anticipation. He opened the box to reveal an engagement ring. "Carol, will you ma—"

"Yes!" She exclaimed as she removed the glove from her left hand. "Yes, I will. And yes, I do."

Chapter 13 - Wonders

The Greece project planning committee included Carl, Carson, Darren, David, and Trina. Even though she would not travel to Israel, Trina's involvement was necessary because she would be the one to carry out most of the early plans that the boy's club devised. David frequently filled Jonathan in on details since he would be running the equipment. Darren was keen to identify likely transportation problems and possible solutions.

Attorney Debra Minx was occasionally called in for legal advice. She, in turn, conferred with a respected attorney group they had put on retainer. Debra was diligent in making sure they stayed within the law, both foreign and domestic. Carson was just as helpful in planning as he was successful in selling. And Carl kept the director informed of their progress.

"How are we going to get Hindsight to Greece?" Debra asked, "or anywhere else in the world, for that matter?"

"I guess we will have to charter planes, won't we?" Carson suggested.

"Not just planes. We will need trucks, at least two," Darren added. "I hope we won't have to retrofit them. If so, we will have to buy them"

"And leave them behind when finished?" David asked.

"Probably," Carson answered. "We will also need to hire a private security firm to protect everything and everybody."

Trina asked, "Where will we stay?"

"Hotels, of course," Darren grinned. "Nice ones."

"Sounds like this is going to be very expensive," David warned.

"No problem," Dr. Gordman assured, keeping a running tally in his head of approximate costs. As was his usual M.O., Carl had already researched the topics at hand, including pricing. "I estimate the total cost, not counting employee salaries, to run between three and four million dollars."

During the planning stage, the billionaire client offered to provide an expert on the ancient Middle East to brief the team on what to look for and expect. Dr. Carla Combs's orientation, via a Zoom call, was quite helpful. While she shared more information than was probably needed, the historian was easy to listen to and understand.

"As you know, Mr. Seaval is particularly interested in the Seven Wonders of the Ancient World as listed in the first and second century B.C. What he wants is an accurate depiction of as many of them as possible for a special wing of a museum he is commissioning. I've been told that your equipment can get those images. As I go through the list, I will suggest which monuments might be the easiest to include in your project.

"The Great Pyramid of Giza is the oldest wonder, built by the Egyptians in the third century B.C. Since it is still standing, there is little reason to include it now. Because its original appearance was significantly different, Mr. Seaval may request it at a future date.

"The Hanging Gardens of Babylon would be his first choice if it wasn't impractical. It is unclear if they ever existed. If they did, we don't know where. They were supposed to have been built by Nebuchadnezzar II along the Euphrates River around 600 B.C. Another theory is that they were built three hundred miles north of Babylon a century earlier. In any case, attempting to find them would likely be an expensive and time-consuming wild-goose chase.

"The statue of Zeus is high on Mr. Seaval's list, but we can only narrow its construction in Olympia to within ten years."

"That's no problem," Jonathan assured the expert. "Once set up, we can screen a century in seconds."

Carl interjected, "The main thing we need is an accurate location."

"We have that," Carla guaranteed. "The statue of Zeus is a good option since it existed in Greece. We will have the added benefit of seeing the temple it was housed in before it was moved to Constantinople.

"Next up, built by Greeks, the Temple of Artemis at Ephesus was, of course, in Turkey—as was the Mausoleum at Halicarnassus. Traveling and working there would likely present additional challenges. The Lighthouse of Alexandria in Egypt is desirable, especially if we could see it both in daylight and lit up at night."

"When I googled the Seven Wonders, I found some early lists included the walls of Babylon instead of the lighthouse," Darren mentioned.

"That's true, but we are...that is, Mr. Seaval is more interested in the lighthouse. The Colossus of Rhodes is another obvious choice since it too existed in Greece. I am particularly interested in knowing if the enormous statue's legs straddled the harbor as in some artist depictions or if the legs were joined to support the statue's size."

The expert provided her phone number and email address, promising to remain available for questions while the team discussed a proposed plan of action. Carla lived and worked in Greece, so everyone expected she would participate in the project.

"It seems pretty obvious that the most logical candidates for this first civilian project are the two monuments that were built in Greece," Carl stated at their next meeting. "Being the patron's home nation, permissions to work should be relatively easy to come by, hopefully."

"The contract does call for Mr. Seaval to make all legal arrangements once an itinerary is determined," Debra reminded the group.

Legal documents and permission to travel to and from desired destinations were a bit harder to obtain than expected. Carson worked with Trina and Debra to get the necessary approvals. The only easy task was making hotel reservations.

Trout's connections made the planning as efficient and effective as possible. Every time the team hit a dead end, the miracle worker came through. Well before the deadline, every step of the plan, with contingencies, was in place. The project's total cost was almost a million dollars more than Carl's estimate. Carl blamed the difference on the team's choice of high-end hotels, unexpected expenses, and bribes paid to facilitate necessary approvals. Dr. Knab was grateful he let Trout go for the big bucks.

The two destinations were quite far from each other. Olympia was near the far west coast of the Peloponnese peninsula while Rhodes was the island farthest to the east. The team decided to visit Olympia first.

* * *

"Are you all set to visit your mom?" David asked while packing his suitcase.

"I think so. I'm glad you suggested I fly," Katy answered as she took the empty hangers her husband handed her.

"That's too far to drive by yourself, especially with a toddler."

"Yeah, but I feel pretty limited in what I can take. At least with the car, I could pack everything I want."

"That's true, but you're only going to be there for ten days, right? You should be able to buy anything you need with the budget we planned on."

"I know. I just hate to waste the money."

David stopped packing. "It's not a waste. It's yours to use." Then a thought occurred to him for the first time. "I wonder how Reese will react to my being gone so long."

"Hey," Katy interrupted David's musing. "How do you plan to handle the social end of this trip?"

"What do you mean?"

"Well, you never accept your friends' invitation to join them for drinks here. Won't you be a little more trapped in that environment? I understand alcohol is a staple in Europe."

"Hadn't thought about it," David answered honestly.

"Well, you should. If you don't purpose in your heart ahead of time, you might get careless in the moment, and later, regret it."

"Look at you—preaching the Word."

"David, I'm serious. You know I don't care if you decide to have wine with your meal or something if that's what is expected, but would you go to a dance club if everyone else does?"

"Sweetheart, I wasn't mocking you. I'm actually impressed that you've thought all this through. I really do appreciate you bringing it up. I've been thinking about the logistics of the job so much that I never considered the "social aspect," as you call it. Thank you."

"You know I trust you. It's those Greeks I'm worried about," she said with a smirk.

* * *

As the day of departure approached, the Hindsight crew's emotions vacillated between excitement and nervousness. The ensemble included three team leaders and almost half of their staff. Including the private security detail Knab hired, over thirty people participated in this make-or-break, inaugural endeavor.

Convoy travel to the East Coast was uneventful. Most of the employees went directly to a hotel while Darren and his crew took the two box trucks to be loaded onto a cargo plane. Darren decided to take Hindsight vehicles instead of trying to procure transportation in Greece. Four security guards followed them in a van. Three of them stayed on the plane to keep watch while the fourth drove Darren's team to the hotel. Guards worked four-hour shifts. All but two of the guards traveled on the cargo plane, while everyone else flew coach on a major airline. The cargo went directly to the Kalamata while the passenger plane landed in Athens.

"Look at the water," one person commented. "It reminds me of the Caribbean."

"Those little islands are breathtaking," one of the few female team members opined.

The Athens airport was smaller than expected, but it housed an interesting museum that everyone visited during their layover. Even with a connecting flight, the team arrived a few hours before the cargo plane. At Kalamata, the crew was rejuvenated by a trip to a local restaurant. Since sleeping on the plane is never restful, the idea of a good night's recuperation in a hotel was appreciated by all. Unfortunately for some, the thrill of being in Greece overrode the need for rest. Several employees ran into each other wandering the streets well after midnight.

The next morning began very early, much to the dismay of those who enjoyed only a little sleep. Hoping that adrenalin would make up for the fatigue, everyone pressed on in rented vans and the two Hindsight trucks. Dr. Combs joined the Americans as they were loading into vehicles. They arrived in Olympia about breakfast time. While much of the crew helped Darren and Jonathan unload and unpack, a few surveyed the site to determine where Hindsight should be positioned.

"Mr. Seaval has arranged for the site to be closed to tourists for three days by donating a handsome sum to the appropriate parties," Carla informed the team. Like many of the excessively rich, he lived by the tenet that there is no limit to what money can buy. Of course, he insisted that his donations be deducted from the cost of his project.

Since the ruins indicated the likely location of the ancient statue, a plan of action became rather obvious. Equipment was carried into the Temple ruins and set up on its mobile platform so that it could be repositioned as often as necessary. Hindsight was ready for action by lunchtime. After devouring a tasty Greek meal on-site, everyone prepared themselves for Hindsight's revelation.

"The temple was built before the statue, in the early to mid-fifth century B.C.," the expert advised. "If you can set the time to start at 500 B.C., we should be good."

"No problem," Jonathan answered, and typed the desired time into his computer. "Let's turn this baby on."

"Wait!" one concerned employee shouted. "Aren't we supposed to be wearing protective suits like Mr. Daniels and his helpers have?"

"That's not necessary," Dr. Knab announced. "We've monitored radiation exposure during all of our tests and demonstrations. The data confirms that only those who work closely with the equipment or position themselves between the emitters and the screen have any risk of negative consequences due to radiation."

"So, we just need to stay away from the equipment?" another asked.

"Right, but anyone concerned is welcome to don the uncomfortable outfit," David offered. "We brought a dozen, so there are eight still available."

Three people requested a protective suit. Once they were dressed, the equipment was turned on. Jonathan changed the timeframe by ten years every few seconds until the temple appeared.

"There it is," he announced.

"Amazing," Dr. Combs declared. "I saw videos of this machine in action, but I couldn't believe it worked. It really does."

"It does indeed," Jonathan said a bit smugly. He backed the time up to the beginning of construction and created a time-lapse video with a frame every day for twenty years. The resulting recording was four minutes long.

"Look at those pillars," Trina said excitedly. "So, that's how they built this stuff way back then."

"And the attention to detail," Carla marveled.

"Let's move Hindsight inside the temple ruins," Jacob suggested. Darren and his crew tried to move the entire contraption, but the ground was too uneven. They ended up disassembling several of the parts to move them more easily. The ground inside the temple ruins was a bit more level. After reassembling the equipment and refilling the generators, Hindsight was ready for phase two.

Jonathan fast-forwarded until the king of Greek gods burst onto the scene. Hindsight was moved even closer so that the statue filled the screen. Then he backed up the time to record its construction. Another time-lapse video was rendered of the chryselephantine statue's creation with one frame per hour.

"Looks like they are building it with wood," a spectator commented.

"Just wait," Carla encouraged.

"Ah, there's the ivory," one of Jonathan's technicians announced.

"Why is it pink?"

"That's a tint from the panel. It can be cleared up in post-production."

"The skin is fashioned by carved panels of ivory with his garment and instruments covered in gold." Carla found herself explaining the process as they watched it unfold. "It looks like they used some precious stones to accent the scepter in his left hand and statue of victory in his right."

Upon approaching closer still, Daniels recorded the finished statue in real-time. Darren's crew moved the equipment several times to get as many views of the impressive god as possible.

"How tall is it?"

"Over forty feet, and Zeus is sitting."

"Incredible."

The team was so enraptured by the view that they hated to turn off the equipment. But it was growing painfully loud, and Dr. Knab did not want to cause any damage. Hindsight was back in secured storage and team members at the hotel by supper time. No one could believe it only took one day to accomplish the monumental feat. This unexpected speed at which the job was done was celebrated in Olympic fashion.

"You coming?" someone asked David as they left for a party destination.

"No, thanks. Jonathan and I still have some work to do."

"Don't bother them," someone else shouted. "Having fun is against their religion." The two could hear others laughing until the front doors closed. Those who worked directly with David or Jonathan never treated them disrespectfully to their faces. After all, David was a team leader. But crew members from other departments were not so averse to poking fun, especially after indulging in a few adult beverages.

After looking over the videos with Jonathan, David excused himself and headed to his room. He wanted to stay up till midnight so he could call his wife. With the eight-hour time difference, he didn't want to disturb her before eight in the morning, her time.

Jonathan was pretty exhausted, having run the equipment all day, but he wasn't quite ready for bed. So, he ordered a soda from the bar and went outside to marvel at the stars. The night was warm, and the sky was clear. Music from down the street was not loud enough to be disturbing.

"You are American?" one of the two women passing by paused to ask.

"Yes," Jonathan answered.

"You are alone?"

"I guess. Tonight anyway,"

"You want girlfriends?"

"No thanks. I'm engaged."

"Her not here. We are."

Finally, the naive man realized who he was talking to. He later learned that prostitution is legal in Greece, although most purveyors were unlicensed.

"Okay, um, thanks. I mean, no thanks. Uh…bye." Jonathan hurried into the hotel, left his empty glass at the bar, and ran up the stairs to his floor. He fumbled nervously with his key as if he were being chased by gun-toting mobsters. Once in his room, he locked and bolted the door, then leaned against it.

He looked at his watch and determined that David was probably still awake. "It's only eleven," Jonathan thought. "I know he is planning to stay up to call Katy later. "The distraught man unlocked his door and cautiously looked into the empty hallway. He scurried to his friend's room four doors down and knocked.

"Who is it?" came a voice from inside.

"Jonathan."

A click signaled the door was opening. Progress was stopped by a chain that was still engaged. David looked through the three-inch gap. "What's up?"

"I just need some company."

"It's late."

"Please?'

Hall welcomed his colleague into his room and the two sat down, Jonathan on the only chair and David on his bed. Jonathan used the remote to turn on the TV. The image startled him.

"Whoa!" He exclaimed as David lunged for the remote and turned off the program.

"What was that?" Jonathan demanded.

"I was flipping channels when you knocked."

"Look, I know you are my superior and my elder, but you are also my friend."

"I know. I was just flipping channels, waiting to call Katy. It's not porn... but it is risqué. You can turn it back on and see for yourself. The girls are sexy, but they are clothed."

"Barely," Jonathan didn't know what else to say. It wasn't that the dancing scene was all that appalling in itself. It was the guilt written all over David's face that convinced Jonathan the man wasn't being honest. He came to David because of his encounter with prostitutes. Should he even tell his friend they exist and are available? David, on the other hand, was more embarrassed than ashamed. What he was watching on the television was no worse than regular broadcast programming in the States. Still, he wouldn't have been watching it unless he was alone.

"Katy warned me about being careless," David confessed. "Now that I'm over the shock of you confronting me, I can say I'm glad you came."

"Really."

"I guess it's true. The best thing that can happen to a Christian who is starting to make bad decisions is to get caught early."

"Before the decisions get worse."

"Exactly."

David thought for a moment then asked Jonathan for a favor. "This sounds weird, I'm sure, but would you hang around for my phone call? I want you to witness me telling Katy that I messed up."

"Is that necessary? I trust you to tell her without me listening in to your private conversation."

"It is necessary for me. I don't trust myself to tell her without some accountability."

David did tell Katy and offered a heartfelt apology. She expressed disappointment in her husband but accepted his apology, and thanked him for telling her about the indiscretion.

Once off the phone, Katy talked to God. "Thank you, Father, that David is so sensitive. Few men, including Christians, feel guilty about what he just confessed to me. Please protect him from further temptation. Amen."

* * *

Everyone on the team treated the next two days as vacation. Even the security detail took advantage of their free time, reducing the number of guards on duty to two at a time. Carson enjoyed some hero status even though he wasn't very involved in the project activities.

David and Jonathan spent most of their waking hours together or within eyesight of each other. Neither wanted to be tempted so both became a bit paranoid. Some team members thought their aversion to the good life was ridiculous. A few respected their consistency, especially being away from loved ones. Finally, it was time to head to the next destination, Rhodes.

Chapter 14 - Triumph

Besides serving as an expert on ancient Greece, Dr. Combs became a liaison for Theodor Seaval. Upon receiving a digital copy of the Hindsight recordings, she sent them to the project's patron by messenger. A bit disappointed in the reddish hue, the magnate didn't wait for the Hindsight team to do their post-production work. He had the videos professionally enhanced that day to produce more true-to-life color.

Once that was completed, he was thrilled and impressed by the results and encouraged the virtual archeologist to marshal on. So, after their R&R, the team prepared to head to the next stop on their itinerary. They packed up with a sense of accomplishment and confidence, loaded the vehicles, and headed for the airport.

"Ty enay aut? No!" one of the drivers exclaimed.

En route, a flashing blue light caught the attention of all the drivers. The mostly-white police vehicle positioned itself between the two box trucks, making clear that they were to pull over. No doubt, the officer was surprised when the entire convoy obliged. Those with a clear line of sight could see him speaking into the microphone of his vehicle.

"What is it?" Darren asked the driver he was riding shotgun with.

"Don't know. Ah, police say stop."

"Did everyone pull over?"

"I think so."

The officer did not emerge from his car until backup arrived. Even then, he kept looking behind him nervously as he approached the truck in front. Dr. Knab wisely arranged for nationals to drive all the vehicles with Hindsight employees riding alongside. After a brief conversation in Greek between the policeman and driver, the latter opened the truck door and spoke to Darren.

"He says for you to show papers."

Darren produced them from the glovebox. As the officer looked over paperwork, both David and Jacob stepped out of their respective vans to lend aid if needed. They were quickly ordered to return to their vehicles. Though the command was in a language foreign to them, the message was clearly understood from the backup officer's body language, voice inflection, and hand signals.

The first lawman returned to his car, its single 360-degree strobe light flashing incessantly. Again, he spent several minutes communicating with his station. Finally, he returned to the truck and handed the paperwork back to the driver. Since everything was in order, he waved the team on. From their side mirrors, drivers and passengers observed the two police officers staring at the convoy, hands-on-hips, as they drove away.

Despite the trip interruption, the team made it to the Athens airport several hours before the passenger plane was scheduled to take off. This was plenty of time to get the trucks back onto the chartered cargo plane and passengers to the proper gate of the terminal. Once in place, most everyone experienced both relief and a little fatigue.

"We have two stops before getting to Rhodes?" Darren asked, looking at his boarding passes.

"Yes, but the layovers are pretty short," Trina answered.

"Not even enough time to get coffee," David teased.

This time, the cargo plane arrived several hours before the team. Airport personnel complained that it was sitting on the tarmac too long. So, the plane was taken to a hangar to await Hindsight employees. Trucks were not unloaded until they and extra guards arrived.

"Okay, folks!" Jacob addressed the group in the hotel conference room where they met after putting belongings in their rooms. "We originally planned for three days in Olympia and two weeks here. The Colossus project will be more complicated, so don't be discouraged if things don't go as smoothly and quickly here."

Carla spoke next. "One reason the project here in Rhodes is more challenging is that the statue's exact placement was unknown. The first order of business for this week of work is to find a high enough elevation so that Hindsight will have a clear view of the third century B.C. harbor location and its surroundings."

Jonathan spoke up, "Once that site is determined and the equipment deposited, our operator-in-waiting, Beth Auger, will use Hindsight to determine Colossus's location."

Jonathan's protege was anxious to get her turn at the wheel. She was first to finish breakfast and load into the transport. With her eyes closed, she imagined operating the equipment via a computer keyboard. Much like a pianist practicing on imaginary ivories, Beth held her hands in front of her, fingers tapping away in the air.

"You'll be fine." Jonathan startled her with his encouragement. She was so engrossed in her pantomime that she didn't notice anyone joining her in the van. Soon everyone was on board, and the caravan made its way to the first destination.

A late summer breeze refreshed the team atop the hill as Beth set the time for 250 B.C. and panned the harbor landscape. Every eye was on the metallic screen or adjacent larger monitor. The roar of several generators running to provide power seemed to diminish as attention was concentrated on the image.

"There! Is that it?" a voice from the back of the crowd called out. "Zoom in. Oh, I forgot. You can't."

"That's just the harbor, I think."

"Wow, it looks a lot different."

"Well, that was a long time ago."

Beth was not nearly as fast and proficient as Jonathan at operating Hindsight, but she needed the real-world experience because Jonathan needed a backup technician. After twenty minutes, spectators were growing weary of waiting.

"What am I doing wrong?" Beth asked Jonathan. He, of course, had been watching her movements closely, evaluating her performance.

"Nothing, Beth," he answered. "It just takes time. You're doing fine." A moment later, he added, "Why don't you try clearing the preset and doubling the pass rate?" She was the only one who understood what he meant. It took another ten minutes of trial and error before the group finally got a glimpse of the giant statue.

"Wow, we almost missed it," David commented. Less than half of the bronze structure was visible on the left side of the screen.

Carson agreed. "If it wasn't for the large monitor, we might not have noticed it at all."

Beth did not even have to step out of the pilot seat for Darren's team to reposition the platform so the statue was in the screen's center. The landscape more than two millennia ago was somewhat different from modern times.

"We should take pictures and determine landmarks so we can figure out where to position Hindsight for a closer look," Darren suggested. "By the time Hindsight can be disassembled, loaded, and moved, it will be too late for another shooting. Instead, scout out the best areas to operate."

"Good idea," Jacob agreed. "Except for those needed to get our equipment moved, let's divide up between our Greek hosts and find a good location. Take pictures, and we will compare notes at the hotel."

Teams of four separated and surveyed areas of a map they were assigned to. Using landmarks from digital pictures captured on cell phones, each team recorded the coordinates of their best options. They didn't see each other again until supper.

"We've had a pretty long, hot day in the sun," David said while feasting on dessert. "Let's meet after breakfast to make a plan."

Carson voiced his approval, "I'm all for that." Nobody objected.

It took until lunchtime to narrow the options to five choices. Key personnel visited the sights and narrowed the field to two. The next task was to ensure safe passage and permission from the appropriate people. Considerable dispute with local authorities necessitated another call to Mr. Seaval. Once he satisfied objections with his wallet, Hindsight was placed where it could record the statue's construction process. When Hindsight was activated at the closer range, anticipation was replaced by a collective groan.

"What's that?" one of the crew called out.

"I think we are looking at the statue from the backside," Beth offered. "We couldn't tell what direction it was facing from our first vantage point."

"Why is it facing that way?" Jonathan wondered out loud.

"Here, let's look at what we recorded from the hill," Dr. Knab suggested. As they did, the mistake became obvious.

"I noticed the harbor had changed over time, but I didn't realize how much," David admitted. "The way the statue is facing makes sense considering how the harbor was laid out back then."

Darren's team moaned when they realized that the equipment would have to be moved again without any progress being made. Disappointed that they would have to wait until the next day to continue, the team packed up and returned to their hotel. Security crews guarded the trucks in four-hour shifts, four guards per shift. Everyone else went to their rooms early, exhausted from Greece's summer sun.

The next morning, Hindsight was taken to a new location, this time with less resistance from the locals. From this third position, the statue's front was visible, though still at an angle.

"Interesting," Dr. Combs commented. "I'm surprised the structure only vaguely resembles any of the artist renderings we have."

The legs were only slightly spread apart, with a himation or mantle held in the sun god's right hand and draped over the left shoulder. The bronze garment reached the ground behind the feet of Helios, effectively providing a sturdy base for the hundred-foot-tall construction.

The statue did sport the expected curly hair with apparent rays protruding from its head. The left hand shielded its eyes, but nothing covered its loins. The Colossus filled only two-thirds of the screen height, but moving Hindsight yet again to get a closer view would have been a waste of the day. So, they determined to record from their current location and scout a closer venue later.

Jonathan helped Beth set the program parameters to produce a time-lapse recording like was done in Olympia. Her confidence growing with each hour, the protege relished the opportunity to practice her skills. Beth took most of the day to complete the project. Afterward, the team returned to their hotel with more enthusiasm than the day before. Despite minor complications, the project was moving more smoothly and quickly than the schedule anticipated.

Jacob approached Carson with some bad news. "You know, this project will not take nearly as long as we estimated."

"I know. Isn't that great?"

"In one way, yes."

"Is something wrong?"

"We are going to have to adjust pricing significantly. That will affect your commission."

"Is that all?" Carson chuckled. "Don't worry about that, boss. I'm not greedy. Besides, I've got more jobs coming down the pike."

"Thanks for understanding."

"Sure thing. Giving some of his money back will be good *P.R.* too."

On the third full day, Hindsight was carried in pieces to the flat rooftop of a downtown factory. This location was as close to the statue's site as they could get. The arrangement cost Seaval two-hundred-thousand euros to evacuate the building for the day.

"Today's goal is to show as much detail of the structure as possible," Jacob explained before Hindsight was turned on.

"Wow, we are close," Beth commented when she realized she could fit only half of the statue in the frame.

"Let's begin at the base and pan up," Jonathan instructed his assistant. With Hindsight recording the closest view yet of the sun god, the workmanship seemed sub-par to the observers. Many of the comments were made by unidentified team members.

"Looks like the statue has an iron frame."

"Yes, and large sheets of bronze are attached."

"Why are they filling it with stones?"

"Probably to give extra weight to the base," Darren suggested.

"The rivets on the bronze sheets are pretty obvious."

"The metallic details aren't very impressive even this far away."

"There is no comparison between the Zeus and Helios statues. This one looks like a junior-high student designed it."

Carla grew weary of the insults. "You should remember that Zeus was built to be worshipped in a temple. Colossus is more like your Statue of Liberty. He welcomes ships to the harbor. Helios is a minor god, whereas Zeus is the king."

"This statue is way bigger too," Darren commented.

"And intended to stand outside, not protected in a building," someone added.

"Colossus is impressive in its own right," Jonathan said. "After all, it made it on the Seven Wonders list."

"True that," Darren responded.

While the leaders wished they could get footage from additional angles, there didn't seem to be any more rooftops worth renting. Instead, two days were spent recording the statue's construction up close, using the time-lapse approach. A third day was spent at the previous position, recording the construction with the entire structure in view. That evening, Dr. Combs regaled the troops with stories of ancient lore, including the earthquake that toppled Colossus.

"You mean it only stood for sixty years?" Carlson asked.

"Less," Carla corrected.

"And it still made the list."

"Since we know when it happened, why don't we record the statues toppling?" Debra suggested. Some of the party preferred to call it quits since they had already accomplished more than expected, but the growing chorus of advocates spurred Dr. Knab to acquiesce to the suggestion—only after a day off.

Except for the guards who had to work two four-hour shifts every twenty-four hours, everyone spent the entire free day as they wished. Most went to the beach. Some went shopping. A few just stayed around the hotel, sipping beverages and taking a nap or two. Everyone understood that nightlife activities should be limited because of an early start the next day.

It was raining as the team was awakened to get ready, but the clouds rolled away before breakfast was finished. Their last trek took the Hindsight team back to their most recent vantage point, where most of the harbor could be seen along with the entire colossus. It was the ideal location to view the statue's position, the earthquake, and its effect on the statue, including where it fell. Daniels resumed his role as the technician, so it didn't take long to find the right timeframe. Instead of a time-lapse recording, the earthquake was recorded in real-time.

"Oh, no!" Trina exclaimed. Until it appeared on screen, no one considered the human element of the tragic event. The people in view were too tiny to see faces, but panic was obvious from their running around helplessly. Visually, the earthquake was not impressive, but the resulting damage was.

"It never occurred to me that we would be watching people die," a team member said somberly.

"Yeah, that was…not good," another agreed.

"I thought the earth-shaking would be more dramatic," the historian commented, trying to change the conversation.

"Right," Darren agreed, "it was hardly noticeable except for the destruction it caused."

Trying to take everyone's mind off the loss of ancient life they had just witnessed, Jacob said, "The collapse of Colossus was truly monumental." His pun was met with several groans and shaking heads.

People returned to the hotel pretty somber, but as the evening progressed, spirits revived. Flights had been rescheduled, so they had two more free days before heading home. After a late night of festivities, few ventured very far for the rest of the visit. Even though it was three days early, there was a general feeling that it was time to go home, especially among those with family at the base.

And home they went. Seaval was excited to receive the video footage from Rhodes. Dr. Combs was grateful for the surreal experience. Dr. Knab was relieved all had gone well. Beth's proficiency with Hindsight equipment improved greatly. And everyone had a story or two to tell (if allowed). By any measurement, the trip was a great success.

* * *

David arrived home just two days after his wife and son returned from her mom's. "I missed you," he offered.

"Me too," she answered. "That was just too long."

"Barely over two weeks," he thought to himself. "I even came home early."

"Daddy home," Reese was ecstatic to see his long-lost father again and wrapped himself around David's left leg. Daddy sat on the couch instead of his favorite chair. He pulled his son up to sit on his lap as Katy sat next to him. The child looked at his mother and said, "Mommy, me hungry."

"Wow!" David exclaimed. "He's speaking in sentences—kinda. Have I been gone that long?"

"Seems like it," Katy was more interested in sharing her perspective than alleviating his guilt. "I hope…we hope you will be home for a while. I wish you wouldn't go on any more long trips."

David didn't respond, but he knew there would likely be frequent trips. People at work viewed him as third in command. He hoped that he would soon own that title officially. Such a promotion would require even more dedication to the project.

* * *

Even with some unexpected expenses and a partial refund, the project profited about five million dollars. Jacob's main concern was that his salesman would retire after his windfall. Carson, however, showed no signs of slowing down. Within a month of returning, he had brought up three possible projects. Two of them were approved; one of them signed.

While the team was planning the next project, Carson brought in five more requests. Even though most of the proposals were limited to eight- or nine-day jobs, Hindsight was looking very lucrative as a booming business. Executives at Wentsome Industries and the Sycra Foundation were happy to split three percent of all income as compensation for their investments. There were even some raised eyebrows in Washington when ledger sheets showed a positive balance for Hindsight.

More and more job requests were coming from foreign governments. Those from countries that were deemed hostile to the United States' interests were disregarded. Requests from allies and friendly nations were considered closely. The director wanted to make sure that approved projects were not politically motivated or even especially beneficial to one political persuasion. To play it safe, he was more eager to approve projects for individuals or businesses instead.

With over two thousand billionaires in the world, there seemed to be no shortage of possible clients. Hindsight presented the possibility of owning priceless videos and images of history. In the United States alone, there were many candidates: the first Thanksgiving, the Boston Tea Party, the signing of the Constitution, Abraham Lincoln's assassination, and any number of famous battles fought in the early days of the nation.

Many clients simply wanted accurate images of historical figures. One request, a video of Leonardo da Vinci painting the Mona Lisa, was abandoned after several days because the assumed location of the artist's studio in Florence, Italy, turned out to be incorrect. By contrast, Italy's desire for a recording of Mt. Vesuvius's eruption and the resulting devastation was easy to fulfill.

Theodor Seaval was a little frustrated that he had to get in line to have more ancient wonders recorded. He insisted that being the first customer qualified him for special status. After a bit of arm-twisting, Dr. Knab acquiesced. Seaval's next project was slated for just after a Jewish philanthropist's order to see Solomon's Temple.

* * *

Every time David informed his wife of another trip, she grew more bitter.

"You told me you would stop traveling after your Greece trip if I wanted you to," Katy complained. "You've gone on six trips since then and each time I've asked you not to go."

"Five," he unwisely corrected. "And I didn't exactly say you could make the decision. I said we would talk about it."

"Have we?"

"Have we what?

"Talked about it."

"If you call arguing every time a trip is planned, talking." Next, David tried the never-successful approach of turning the tables. "I'm doing this for us, for the family."

"That's what my dad always said—right up to when Mom divorced him."

David looked into Katy's angry eyes and wondered if that was a threat. He wanted to continue arguing but thought better of it. He couldn't understand why she was so adamantly opposed to his trips—his job. Where was that supportive wife he married five years ago? Was it really all his fault? Couldn't be.

David decided to do a spiritual check-up on himself. "I'm reading my Bible and praying regularly—not with as much enthusiasm, but I'm doing it. I'm not watching porn or doing anything else immoral. We're faithful to church and give our tithe. I haven't missed many special events with Katy and Reese."

Then the thought struck him, "How do I know what I haven't missed—or what I have? All those phone calls with Katy are a blur. I couldn't tell half of what she said ten minutes after we'd hung up. Oh Lord, it is my fault, isn't it? Has work become my top priority? Am I sacrificing my family for my job?"

Chapter 15 - Israel

"Recording Solomon's Temple will be our most challenging project to date." Dr. Knab began his meeting with a realistic observation. "Because of the geopolitical and religious animosity between Jews and Muslims, it will be difficult to obtain necessary approvals. Even that will be easy compared to the pushback we are likely to get from the locals."

"The site of Israel's first temple was fairly well established," Dr. Gordman joined in, eager to play some role in the enterprise. "While the Temple Mount is technically controlled by Israel, the Jordanian royal family maintains control over the Dome of the Rock, which sits on that very spot."

Jacob continued, "The Dome of the Rock is one of Islam's most sacred shrines. It was built at the end of the seventh century, long after the second Jewish temple was destroyed. Solomon's Temple was lost many centuries before that."

"During the Six-Day War, Israel captured the land from Jordan," Carl again interjected. "But in order to preserve peace, the Jerusalem Islamic Waqf was allowed administrative control of the Temple Mount."

"How do you know so much about it, Dr. Gordman?" someone asked.

"Google."

"Our client doesn't have as much pull there or as deep pockets as Mr. Seaval did in Greece. So, we will have to do much of the leg work ourselves to get this done," the director concluded.

Dr. Knab met with Debra and David. "Over-the-phone negotiations were non-starters. We need to meet the decision makers on site. I want you two to join me."

David squirmed a bit before responding, "Director, I've been on every trip so far. I need to bow out of this one if that's all right."

Jacob wasn't accustomed to rejection, so it took him a moment to come up with plan B.

"I'm fine with going," Minx said while Knab was thinking. "I'd love to see Israel."

"I would too, believe me," David argued. "It's just that Katy is struggling with me being gone so much, and so often."

"I understand," Jacob answered. "I'll see if Carson can go with us. He seems to have a rapport with our clients. Maybe he can use his charm on the Palestinians."

* * *

"You'll be proud of me," David announced when he arrived home. Reese hurried to his father, who noticed that he no longer had a comical waddling walk. He was distracted, thinking about how quickly his son was growing up.

"Why will I be proud of you?" His wife asked.

David returned to his announcement. "I turned down a trip to Israel."

"You can do that, can you?" Katy answered, sarcasm dripping from her lips.

"Really?" he said, lifting his son.

"I'm sorry. I'm glad you turned down a trip. Should I be suspicious of the reason?"

"No, I just told the director I've been gone too much."

"Thank you." Nothing more was said. David was a bit disappointed he didn't get more credit for being a good husband. Then again, he realized it was likely to take more than one concession to start mending the emotional fence.

* * *

Negotiations to allow Hindsight on location were tense. The Arabs had no interest in promoting Israeli pride. Finally, one wise politician asked the Waqf leader if he would be interested in seeing what the Dome of the Rock looked like when it was built.

"What do you mean?" the Grand Mufti asked. The cleric in charge had been arguing against the Hindsight project without really knowing what it was. All he understood was that high-tech equipment would be used to promote Israeli nationalism.

Hindsight's capabilities were briefly explained. Following that, Carson suggested that, in exchange for allowing Hindsight to record Solomon's Temple, the patron paying for the project would also pay to have images of the seventh-century Dome of the Rock provided to the Waqf.

Video clips of recent Hindsight projects were shown to demonstrate that the operation was legitimate. Once the Sunni Muslim cleric was assured that he and/or his representatives could observe the process, a contract was written up and signed. The Jordanian's insistence that the Dome of the Rock be recorded first fell flat. Everyone in attendance knew that the Temple project would somehow be sabotaged if left for last. Finally, the Arabs and Jews had an agreement, and the trip was scheduled for six weeks later.

David was happy to take a break from traveling but had no intention of missing this opportunity to visit Israel, even if it was to work. Katy understood his excitement at visiting the land where Jesus walked, so she was almost supportive of the trip—*almost* being the operative word.

* * *

Security was extremely tight in Israel. It is not unusual to see military personnel patrolling airports and train stations in Europe, but Israel's precautions were a notch or two higher, and considerably more intimidating. It created dueling emotions, being nervous about all the visible weapons and feeling safe because of exceptional security.

Since the first couple of jobs went without any serious issues, Dr. Knab started sending his associate, Carl, on some projects. Unfortunately, both men had scheduling conflicts. So, this was the first assignment headed up by Hall. Both he and Daniels were thrilled to visit the land of Christ, but David's excitement was tempered by his failure to deal with problems at home.

By this time, Katy understood that work projects come first. The mostly tranquil marriage was beginning to suffer from neglect on his part and bitterness on hers. That their relationship was strained was apparent to those closest to them.

"I know that it's mostly my fault," David confided to Jonathan. "But if she would be a little more understanding and patient, she'll see that it will all be worth it."

"How is that?" His friend challenged.

"I won't have to work this hard forever," Hall asserted.

"You don't have to work this hard now," Jonathan argued. He grew even bolder, and suggested, "You need to reexamine your priorities."

Jonathan's words fell on deaf ears. David had convinced himself that *just a little* more would bring some satisfaction. Surely this next trip would make a difference to his spirit too. It was a life-long dream to visit the Holy Land. And to be the one in charge of the project was icing on the cake. Secretly, he hoped they might record something from the time of Christ while there.

Despite his excitement, David projected a professional persona. He had prepared well for the trip and was aware of likely challenges and possible conflicts. Gavi Braum, the philanthropist funding the enterprise, was close at hand with his entourage. His gaggle of assistants, lawyers, historians, bodyguards, and government liaisons almost matched the Hindsight team's number. The auburn-colored Pekingese he cradled in his arms was a curious distraction.

Everyone spoke perfect English when dealing with the Americans, but they usually spoke Hebrew amongst themselves. The occasional chuckle or outright laugh was a bit disconcerting to the visitors, but David just encouraged everyone to ignore the apparent humor at the team's expense and carry on with their responsibilities.

After settling into the hotel, David, Jonathan and Darren took a survey trip with some of Braum's people to determine the best place for a preliminary view. Although they anticipated where Solomon's Temple had been located, a good vantage point was not easy to determine.

"Remember how we almost missed finding the Colossus because he wasn't where we expected?" he reminded his team. "Let's start further back than necessary to make sure we know where to head."

"But we know where the site is exactly," Braum complained.

"I'm sure you are right. It's just a precaution. It won't cost you any more." David's assurance that he wasn't running up the tab put the almost billionaire's mind at ease.

* * *

Early Wednesday morning, Hindsight was set up at the most convenient location to get a wide-angle view of the Temple Mount and surrounding areas. Two teams of private security monitored the perimeter as Jonathan worked his magic. Beginning with the Dome of the Rock in the center of the screen, he "tuned in" to the correct time period.

Nothing. There was no temple—no significant structure at all. Jonathan checked his settings. They seemed correct. "Could the calibration be off?" he wondered. He moved the timing forward, thirty years at a time for a couple of centuries. Still, there was no temple. He had just asked Darren to move the platform so he could pan a wider area when one of the historians offered a suggestion.

"Please, can you set your time machine for AD 200?" the scholar asked.

"It's not a time mach—" Jonathan caught himself, then took a breath. "Sure, AD 200 coming up."

Suddenly a temple appeared, but it was nothing like anyone expected. The historian explained, "That is Jupiter's temple, built by Hadrian in AD 135. The Christian emperor Constantine tore it down almost 200 years later."

"Well, we know the timing is still calibrated correctly," David stated, even as the same thought passed through Jonathan's mind. "Let's go back to the time of Solomon's Temple and get a panoramic view. Maybe the temple was located elsewhere."

Darren's recent improvements to the mobile platform made panning easier. With the Dome visible outside the far right side of the screen, Hindsight was re-engaged and the platform slowly turned to the right. Just as the Dome was beginning to protrude past the far left side of the screen, there was a collective gasp. The Americans glanced around to see their counterparts facing down, apparently praying. A few were even on their knees, face to the ground. Even the Christians in the group were surprised by the reverence displayed by the Israelis.

The Americans turned their attention back to the screen and waited for the unexpected reaction to Solomon's Temple to run its course. Curiosity overpowered awe in short order, and the Jews were soon staring intently at the image of Solomon's Temple. One of the assistants was soon on the phone, telling Braum that the temple was in view. It was quickly determined that the structure was just southwest of the Dome. One helpful historian seemed the least surprised by the discovery. She explained why.

"Scripture indicates that Solomon's Temple should be built at the sight of a threshing floor that King David purchased. He offered sacrifices there to stave off an angel of God who was sent to punish him. While tradition has placed the two Jewish temples at the top of Temple Mount, there has been a growing consensus that such might not be the case."

She continued, "When the conquering Arabs asked where the Jewish temples had stood, they were directed to the Temple Mount. Caliph Abd al-Malik then built the Dome of the Rock on that site. Whether the Jews who were asked lied or were just ill-informed is unknown. In any case, now we know that our temple site was never desecrated by that hideous shrine."

Several Hebrew men spat with an exaggerated head bob.

"Please," the assistant addressed David. "Mr. Braum would like to meet you at the hotel to discuss the next step."

"Of course," David agreed, then gave the order to take any necessary notes of the correct location before packing up. "We'll get a fresh start tomorrow. We need to figure out exactly where we should be to get the best view of our objective."

The crew was used to five-hour workdays. Only occasionally was it necessary to operate Hindsight for more than a couple of hours at a time. The team was as adept at packing, loading, and transporting the equipment as a roaming circus troupe is with theirs. They were back at the hotel in less than two hours.

Meanwhile, David was taken straight away to meet with Gavi. Mr. Braum was seated at a table in the empty dining area of the hotel when David arrived. Stroking his dog, Gavi sported an enormous smile. He stood excitedly and extended his right hand, still cradling the pet in his left. A handshake was not enough. He handed the Pekingese to an assistant and wrapped his arms around David.

"Thank you, thank you so much." Gavi released his bear hug, took hold of David's shoulders, and leaned back so the men could see eye to eye. "I feared that this venture would end up being a disappointing waste of money, but you, my friend, are a godsend."

Hall was not sure how to react. He certainly didn't see himself as any kind of hero, but he did not want to stifle Braum's enthusiasm. He smiled and said the only thing that came to his mind, "Just doing my job, sir." He closed his eyes and slowly shook his head, embarrassed that his response sounded like a corny line from an action movie.

"No, no, you are a great man!" Gavi would not allow modesty. "Your name will go down in Israeli history. Do you have the video?"

"Yes sir. I knew you would want to see it right away." David opened his computer and inserted a thumb drive. They watched the video together. David expected that the raw footage would be a bit disappointing to the multi-millionaire, but Gavi resembled a child staring at a mountain of presents under the tree on Christmas morning. When the short video ended, Hall admitted, "We still have lots of work to do before we fulfill our part of the contract."

Gavi insisted upon celebratory beverages before discussing business. By the time he was finished making merry, the rest of the team arrived. This allowed other key players to participate in the discussion. One of Braum's people pulled out a map and indicated where the temple was sighted.

Those of Gavi's team who accompanied Hindsight's survey crew the day before arrived an hour after the rest. They had already discovered and secured the spot where Hindsight should be placed for the best view of the ancient temple. Everyone was impressed, and Darren was grateful. The crude video was viewed over and over throughout the evening. After a very late, multi-course dinner, happily exhausted colleagues went to bed.

* * *

Thursday morning was met with anticipation and hangovers. Gavi arrived early and prodded the Americans to finish breakfast quickly. For the first time, his pet was not in tow. Everyone noticed, but no one mentioned it until they headed to their vehicles. Then, three different Americans asked about the canine's whereabouts.

"This is Adie's day at the spa. Besides, she does not do well in the sun for prolonged periods," Braum explained.

The group assigned to bring Hindsight left forty minutes before the rest. Everyone else climbed into luxury vans except Gavi, who left in the limousine that brought him to the hotel. Despite having showered David with accolades the night before, Braum did not invite the American to ride with him.

The two groups arrived within minutes of each other, and Hindsight was assembled. Jonathan allowed his assistant to run the equipment this morning. He had been alternating with Beth to give her more hours on the machine. This time, he had an ulterior motive. He wanted to enjoy the show with less distraction. And what a show it was!

The screen view captured the entire front of the temple and just a glance of its south side. The historian had determined a perfect spot, just inside the outer walls of the complex. Beth asked Darren to spin the platform 360 degrees to capture everything in the front courtyard. Then, the platform was moved another twenty feet closer to the temple to get the best images possible. Because of natural and man-made obstructions, that was the closest they could get. Since the entire temple fit on the screen, intricate details of the building remained unclear.

In general, the structure shared similarities with typical artist renderings, but the temple was different enough that few people would identify it as Solomon's Temple if it were in a police line-up. It did have enormous, ornate pillars in front, next to the doors. And it seemed very tall. Compared to modern edifices, the temple was not as impressive as the Americans expected. The Israelis, however, marveled at its majesty.

A huge sacrificial altar stood just northeast of the temple, with smoke wafting up. To the south sat an enormous vessel on the backs of sculptures resembling oxen. A rather large porch graced the front of the temple. After the initial enthusiasm wore off, some expressed disappointment that the image could not be magnified.

Perhaps the most moving part of the scene was watching priests perform their religious activities. The temple soon became secondary as observers witnessed sacrifices being offered and ceremonial washing taking place. The courtyard was not particularly pristine. Trails of blood were evident. Ashes from the altar were gathered and taken away.

After a few moments of recording the centuries-old image, a seated Braum motioned to one of his assistants who leaned down to hear him whisper instructions. The attendant nodded and quickly stepped away to make a phone call. Gavi then asked out loud, "Are there any other vantage points we can access to see more angles of the temple?"

"Sadly, no sir," one from his security detail lamented. "Nothing close anyway. Nor can we get near enough to view the temple's interior."

"We've looked at every possibility," another voice echoed. "We can't get around these buildings to get a closer look."

Gavi watched with anticipation as his assistant returned from making his phone call. The attendant was nodding his head excitedly, and he hurried to report success. Gavi smiled broadly as the news was whispered to him. A plan was in the works. He stood to walk to David, who met him halfway.

"What do you think of using a helicopter to get an aerial view?" Braum asked cautiously. "I have one available that is large enough to fit your machines."

David hesitated. His first thought was about safety, then practicality. "And the platform?"

Gavi nodded, then waited impatiently for a response. David held up an index finger to indicate his need for a moment, then motioned to Jonathan and Darren to join the conversation. After some discussion, the team agreed to take Hindsight to the airport and see if Gavi's suggestion was a viable option.

The helicopter was the largest one most of the team had ever seen. The platform fit easily in the cargo bay. Once secured to the platform so it would not move while in flight, Hindsight was positioned the only way it would fit, facing the back. Due to security issues, the aircraft was put into a hangar and two of Braum's men joined the American guards.

Chapter 16 - Airborne

Because Sabbath begins at sundown on Fridays, everyone was up before dawn so they could be finished early in the day. Jonathan decided to take over for his assistant, both for her safety and to ensure the best job possible. Beth was happy to relinquish her role and stay on the ground. Those who were not on the flight made their way to the temple site to observe.

Gavi stayed on the ground with his pooch back in tow. An attendant held a closed umbrella which she deployed once the sun's heat became uncomfortable to her boss or his pet. Soon the hum of a helicopter could be heard. Even wearing sunglasses, everyone shielded their eyes as they looked into the bright, cloudless sky. They watched as the craft circled the target area several times, each time a little slower. Braum was in contact with the helicopter via some type of walkie-talkie.

Suddenly, several police vehicles could be seen in the vicinity with lights flashing. One arrived where the ground crew was witnessing the action. The siren sounded two brief blasts, then two officers emerged to interrogate those present. Gavi didn't even stand. A lawyer approached the police and handed them a paper. After reading it, they got back into their vehicle, and one spoke into the microphone. Within two minutes, all the car lights ceased flashing, and the police cars began leaving. The Americans were quite impressed with Braum's connections, as well as his proactive approach to problem-solving.

Inside the copter, Jonathan was manning Hindsight while David watched the screen and gave instructions to the pilot. Darren stood in the back with one helper in case they needed to adjust the platform (what little they could). The co-pilot watched out the front window for power lines or anything else that might be a hazard. Two security personnel and two of Braum's men were also on board. One of the guards asked if he should open the bay door so the team could see outside.

"That's not necessary, thanks," Jonathan answered and explained, "Since the helicopter did not exist three thousand years ago, it won't show up on the screen or block our view."

The first couple of passes were practice runs to see how close they could get and allow Darren to adjust the equipment at the correct angle for the best view. The final three passes provided near-perfect images of the entire structure. Those in the cargo bay could not see how dangerously close to the current buildings the pilot was flying.

Seeing the temple details was deemed worth the risk. Close up, the holy building was even more impressive. Its artisanship was magnificent. Too bad existing structures precluded getting a look inside.

About ten-thirty, they radioed to the ground team that they had finished and were heading back to the airport. Those on the ground went back to the hotel to await the flight crew's return. Even before seeing the recording, Gavi was clearly conflicted. He was happy about what had been accomplished but frustrated that they could not get inside images of the ancient temple.

"Find out what it would cost to purchase the buildings at the temple site," he told the attorney standing nearest him. "I want to tear them down so we can take the machine *into* Solomon's Temple. I want to see the interior." In a moment of self-reflection, he added, "Except the Holy of Holies, of course. It would be sacrilegious to go in there."

Knowing that Braum always expected immediate action to his demands, the lawyer grabbed her briefcase and left with a cell phone to her ear. It was over an hour before the flight crew arrived back at the hotel. Gavi was happy with the video they had captured and eager to tell them of his plan for a future project. After a late lunch, everyone settled down for the Sabbath rest.

* * *

Hindsight was packed into the cargo plane late Saturday night to be ready for an early morning take-off. The team's commercial flight was scheduled to leave for America late on Sunday afternoon. After saying their goodbyes, the Hindsight crew waited to board their flight.

As with most airports, announcements from the public address system were frequent. Suddenly, the tone was different, less scripted—more urgent. "All flights are temporarily suspended. We will update you with more details as soon as possible. We apologize for the inconvenience." The message was repeated in several languages every few minutes.

All eyes were on television monitors as news of a cargo plane's crash just outside of Jerusalem was reported. As details emerged, it became apparent that the plane had been targeted by a surface-to-air missile shortly after takeoff. David's cell phone rang, identifying Dr. Knab as the caller.

"I just got the news," said the voice from the United States. "That was our plane. Hindsight is gone."

Although the missile strike occurred several miles from Tel Aviv, the airport was shut down for the rest of the day. When the team finally did arrive home, they were still in a daze. Most of the Hindsight staff and their families were gathered to greet the travel team. Katy ran to David and threw her arms around his shoulders.

"I'm so glad you're okay," she whispered into his ear. It was the warmest embrace they had shared in weeks. After a quick kiss, David gathered his luggage and carried it all with his left arm so he could hold his son's hand while they walk to the car. He was surprised to find keeping up with the child was such a challenge.

Once home, the shell-shocked man shared his heart and mind more fully than he ever had before. Katy listened intently.

"I've been a fool. All this time and effort for a project that is gone in an instant. Do you know what I feel most guilty about? My first thought was how terrible losing Hindsight was for me; how unfair. I didn't even think about the ones who lost their lives. I'm not even sure how many people were on that plane.

"Then I thought about us and the toll this job has taken on you. I did think I was working so hard for the family. I was just fooling myself. I'm so sorry."

"Me too. When we first heard about the bombing, we thought everyone was gone. We didn't realize it was just the cargo plane." She paused. "You know what I mean. All I could think about was how bitter I was and how I treated you the last several months."

"But you were right about my priorities," David said. "Even Jonathan said I was working too hard. Now, I may not even have a job."

Both regretted the emotional chasm that had grown between them. After putting Reese to bed, Katy sat across from David at the dining room table.

"It is so…surreal…unreal," he commented, "like a dream, or really, a nightmare." He took a sip of his cooling coffee, then set the mug aside. She reached across the table and took his hand reassuringly.

"What are you going to do?" she asked.

"I don't know," David responded. "Depends on Dr. Knab, I guess. We could make one more Hindsight, but if something happens to it, the project is finished. I'm sure we will meet to talk about it soon." His aimless gaze indicated his thoughts were suddenly distant. Finally, with his eyes welling up, he said, "People died, Katy. What's worse is that I was in charge. People died."

Just then, his cell phone dinged. The message from Dr. Knab was sent to all employees. It stated that everyone should take the rest of the week off and meet in the gymnasium at ten o'clock the following Monday morning. Just two minutes later, a more targeted text message informed David of a leadership meeting on Friday at nine.

"Well, I guess we'll find out soon," the weary man said under his breath.

The trip leader had not been able to sleep well since the incident. His first night home was no different. He laid in bed with an arm around Katy, who was curled up comfortably next to him. He stared up at a ceiling he could not see.

"Stuff is so temporary," he thought to himself. "How could I get so caught up in things that don't last?" He glanced over at his wife who fidgeted just a bit before settling back down with a smile he could barely see. He closed his eyes and fell asleep himself.

No terrorist group took credit for the cargo plane's downing. A consensus formed that the attack was retaliation against Braum for failing to provide video of the original Dome of the Rock as promised. Since Solomon's Temple was never at the shrine's sight, the Hindsight team didn't need the negotiated access.

Despite all his money and connections, Gavi was unable to broker a deal to retrieve any of the broken meteoric metal that was recovered at the crash site. Investigators insisted that nothing could leave their possession until after a full investigation of the event. Such an investigation could take years. To one unknown person, this was unacceptable.

* * *

One night, a clandestine crew of four made their way safely into the hangar where recovered items from the crash were being sorted through, categorized, and stored. Instead of using flashlights that might be noticed, they wore night-vision goggles as they searched. Debris was laid out in a very orderly fashion with labels indicating what was in each designated area.

They found parts of the x-ray and gamma-ray machines, but no sign of the Hindsight screen. A barking dog froze the men in place for just a moment. Then they quickly hid as a door was opened by a security guard accompanied by his canine partner. The dog continued to bark while the guard panned the hangar with his flashlight.

"See, nothing here," the unexpected visitor said to his four-legged partner, speaking in Hebrew. "I know you want to check the whole place out, but I can't let you loose. If you mess something up, that will be the end of both our careers." He panned the area again and pulled the leash to remove the reluctant dog from the hangar, then shut and locked the door.

Once the threat of being exposed subsided, one of the spies noticed an unmarked metal chest with a tamper-resistant lock. It had a hole on the top about the size of a typical mail slot. Two of the men turned the chest over as quietly as they could. The contents rattled inside as they made their way towards the small opening. A third man joined in the effort to gently shake the chest, hoping some of the contents were small enough to fall through the slot.

The fourth person held a bag under the hole to catch whatever came out. They were careful to avoid anything metal clanging on the concrete floor. One piece finally emerged, and the bag holder quickly reached inside to pull it out. It looked like part of the screen. The men continued shaking the chest until they heard the dog barking in the distance again. Quickly, they replaced the chest and took their leave with several small pieces of mangled Hindsight screen in a bag.

* * *

News of the attack and loss of Hindsight reinvigorated interest by the national media as well as publications dedicated to conspiracy theories. Headlines like *Time Machine Lost* and *Government Secret Project Doomed* were common for a short news cycle. That cycle lasted long enough for some accurate information to be disseminated as well. It was revealed that the material necessary for Hindsight's success came from unique meteorites. Somehow, a picture of such meteorites made it to a TV exposé of the project.

The revelation of Hindsight's "secret sauce" predictably led to a search for more of those space rocks. Only one of the original meteorite collectors was still alive. Eager for his fifteen minutes of fame, he made himself known. A government lawyer warned him that breaking his decades-old confidentiality agreement was a federal crime.

"What are you going to do, put me in jail?" The ninety-one-year-old man asked sarcastically.

He explained in interviews, "We considered the search we conducted in the mid-1900s to be pretty exhaustive, but then, we didn't know how valuable these space stones would become."

Two of his grandchildren arranged for him to meet with anyone willing to pay for information about where the original meteorites were discovered and how to tell if they found the real deal. Of course, the grandchildren managed both the old man and this new income until he died. Afterward, they tried to pawn themselves off as experts, a failed effort. It was, still, a very lucrative eight months for the pair.

A new gold rush was on. Instead of pans and pickaxes, these modern "forty-niners" used metal detectors. Some prospectors were able to make use of higher-tech tools. Naturally, the search began in the deserts of New Mexico, where the first meteorites were discovered, but it wasn't long before treasure hunters were searching on almost every continent.

Meanwhile, Hindsight leaders, along with government liaisons and corporate sponsors, discussed the next step. There was only enough meteoric metal to construct one more panel of sufficient size to complete a replacement contraption. Naturally, Wentsome and Sycra wanted to press ahead. They didn't want their cash cow to dry up. Shortly after the powwow with lobbyists, Carson caught Dr. Knab in a hallway.

"I just received a strange call," Trout said. "Someone claims to have pieces of the Hindsight panel from the crash site."

"What?" Knab asked in unbelief. Then he wondered out loud, "Why did they call you?"

Carson answered, "Well, he probably got my number from one of my contacts. Your number isn't exactly public knowledge."

"True," Jacob conceded. "So, how much do they have? Are they trying to sell it?"

"Not much, I don't think," Trout answered. "He's looking to make a deal, though."

A secret meeting was arranged to see and evaluate the alleged Hindsight screen shards. Dr. Gordman was tasked with validating their authenticity. A clandestine meeting was arranged, but not in a dark alleyway. Carl would not have survived a mission impossible scenario. Despite meeting in broad daylight in a crowded venue, the expert's nerves frayed in the middle of his examination. His twitching eyes concerned the seller's representative, who kept glancing at bodyguards.

"What's wrong with him?" the agent asked, clearly agitated.

"He's fine," Jacob assured. "He's just a little nervous."

"Well, he better get over it quick, or I'm out of here."

"All five of these look to be genuine," Carl finally confirmed. "But they are not much to work with."

"Can you get more?" Knab asked the stranger.

"I don't know anything about it," he answered. "I'm just here to show them to you and tell you the seller wants three million dollars."

Carl shook his head. "We don't even know if this metal can be recycled. We've never tried to remelt it."

The seller would not allow Knab to take a sample to see if it could be reused, but they finally agreed on a price of eight-hundred thousand dollars, which was paid in cash. The fragments amounted to a small fraction of the full screen, but enough to melt and remold into a tiny plate. The appropriate department was temporarily restaffed to recycle the shards. Remelted scrap created a screen that was just nine square inches in size, barely three by three. With this remelting, the resulting screen was not at all translucent. Instead, it looked like rusted metal. When bombarded with gamma rays, no image appeared. X-rays had the same non-effect. Looking at the material microscopically, scientists discovered that the molecular structure of the metal mutated with a second melting.

* * *

Once it was clear that the substance could not be recycled, the decision about melting down the remaining meteorites became more difficult. An expanded leadership team met to discuss the dilemma.

"I appreciate that this is the best use of the meteorites, as far as we know, but shouldn't we keep some of it in reserve?" Dr. Gordman cautioned. Like many others, he was concerned about losing the remaining metal to another attack. "It just seems prudent to keep half of what's left in reserve."

"I understand your concern, but half of the metal will not provide a very useful tool," David argued, having decided to lobby for creating the best screen possible with the remaining metal. "A half-sized screen will make Hindsight less effective while creating more work for our crews. We will just have to take more precautions for its protection."

"Easier said than done," Darren stated. "I'm not opposed to making a full-sized screen, but protecting against every possible threat just isn't realistic."

Carson joined it. "What use will the stuff be locked up in a safe?"

"Who knows what other possibilities the metal might offer? We stopped experimenting once its time-viewing capability was known," Carl stated.

"I've read the reports—most of them," Trout argued. "This stuff has been tested to the extreme. I say we go for it."

The director was normally the voice of reason, seeking accommodating compromises. However, there didn't seem to be a compromise possible. Jacob finally put in his two cents. "I understand and agree with your concerns, Carl, but I think David and Carson are right. Our first screen was very small. It offered no practical value except to show us we needed a bigger one." He then turned his attention to David. "We…the world cannot afford to lose another Hindsight. How do we use it and protect it at the same time?"

David was prepared for that logical question. "First of all, we can't go globetrotting to fulfill the fancies of billionaires. Hindsight should be restricted to essential services. What I mean is, Hindsight should be used for serious endeavors only."

"Those billionaire pet projects are what pay the bills," Carson argued. "Doing projects for the government is expensive. How will we be funded if we don't take lucrative jobs?"

"Maybe Congress could be convinced to include funding for Hindsight in the next budget?" Debra suggested to rolling eyes. "It could happen."

"Not likely. Congress won't even pass legislation recognizing, let alone regulating, Hindsight." Jacob reminded. "We need the funding that independent sources provide, but we also need better protection while on location."

"As well as traveling to and from," added Darren.

The decision was made to use the remaining metal to build another Hindsight. Carl was visibly agitated about not saving any meteorites. He relapsed to some tics that he was thought to have conquered. It was not uncommon to see him scratch his belly while rocking to and fro from then on.

As the meeting participants rose to leave the conference room, Jacob tapped David on the elbow and motioned with his head to follow him. Soon they were in the director's office.

Chapter 17 - Gamble

"Have a seat," Knab offered politely, as he took his place behind the desk. "I think it is time to make something official."

"What's that, sir?"

The director looked David in the eyes. "When you joined us, I expected your tenure to end when Hindsight was completed; however, you've continued to prove yourself to be invaluable to the project."

"Thank you, sir."

"So," Knab continued, "I want to promote you to Assistant Director of Hindsight."

David was hoping for some recognition of his contributions to the project, but this promotion was completely unexpected, especially with the loss of Hindsight on his watch. Then a question came to mind.

"What about Dr. Gordman?"

"Oh, Carl is still Assistant Director in charge of research and development," Jacob answered. "You will be in charge of operations."

"By chance, have you run this by him?" David asked. "I know he doesn't like change, and he is already upset that we are melting down all of the remaining metal."

"Carl is on board. We were considering someone else for the position, as well."

"Carson Trout?" The name slipped out before David could shut his mouth. Once said, he completed the thought. "Was Trout the other candidate?"

"Yes, but he didn't know it, so don't say anything," the director ordered. "But Dr. Gordman chose you—and I agree. There's just one thing."

"What's that?" David asked hesitantly.

"We all know you are a religious man," Jacob began while David took a slow deep breath. "There's nothing wrong with that—you're entitled to believe whatever you...believe."

"But?" Hall said, anxious for his boss to get to the point.

Knab continued. "Some people feel that you're a little too vocal about God."

"How so?"

"Well, when you pray before eating lunch, for example,"

"I bow my head and pray silently. How is that being too *vocal*?"

"You're right," Jacob admitted. "Bad example, but someone did see you corner an employee that's not even in your department and push her to pray with you."

David thought for a moment. "You mean Bethany? Rhonda Spalding told Bethany she asked me to pray for her mother when she was sick some time ago. Bethany came to me and asked if I would pray about something for her. I try to do that whenever I'm asked. I didn't coerce anyone."

The director was beginning to see that the complaints he'd heard were pointless. And he could tell that David was getting tense about his confrontation. Still, he wanted to make a point, so he continued.

"Faith is a private matter."

David let his frustration take over. "Do you know that we have two Muslims who stop working to pray?"

"Yes, I've heard."

"Have you confronted them about how they are making their *private* faith a public spectacle?"

Knowing his was a losing battle, Knab concluded his exhortation. "The point is, with this new title, you'll need to be extra careful about wearing your religion on your sleeve. You won't be able to lead people who think you consider yourself better than them."

Taking the opportunity, Hall explained, "Being a Christian has nothing to do with being better than anyone. In fact, you can't become a follower of Christ unless you realize you are condemned as a sinner. Believers in Jesus are not better, we are just forgiven." He knew that was all he would be able to say without being interrupted. "I'm sorry if I seem contrary. Do you want to reconsider my promotion?"

Jacob chuckled. "Of course not. Seeing how well you handle yourself under pressure convinces me even more that you are the man for the job."

Hall couldn't wait to get home and tell Katy the news. Their relationship had improved greatly since he returned from Israel. Other aspects of his life had improved as well. He was back to fruitful Bible reading and happy church attendance. He and Katy were even teaching a children's Sunday school class at the hundred-member church.

Katy shared David's excitement about the news, not because of the increase in pay or prestige. In these few short weeks, she became confident that he could handle the promotion without jeopardizing their relationship. At least, she hoped so.

* * *

When word got out that another Hindsight was being fabricated, Trout got to work rescheduling canceled projects and taking new applications. In anticipation of higher security costs, pricing was adjusted up by fifteen percent for new projects. That didn't seem to matter to the kind of people willing to spend millions of dollars on pet projects.

Once the decision was made to build another Hindsight device, a brand new atmosphere permeated the base. The excitement was reminiscent of the project's early days, except this time everyone knew what the outcome should be. This untempered optimism was much like that of someone watching the replay of a football game, knowing his team won. The only thing that could make it better would be for more meteorites to be found.

Unfortunately, that seemed less likely with every passing week. The treasure hunt seemed to enrich only those who sold tools and information to the scavengers. Clever charlatans found ways to make money from those eager to join the meteorite hunt. Software programs promised to help determine likely deposit sites. Special metal detectors were supposedly configured to react to only the unusual space metal. Special goggles were designed to recognize the unique stones. Stories were invented to lend credibility to these high-priced tools. The gullible were guaranteed improved chances of success.

Enterprising entrepreneurs suspected that anyone willing to waste their time searching the deserts for special rocks would also be willing to spend their fortunes to aid in that enterprise. They were right about this bunch of treasure seekers. While many hit the hot sands unaided, those who could afford extra "advantages" purchased them with little question.

Those who capitalized on the hopeful hunters by selling them useless tools were unscrupulous. Worse yet were the charlatans who perpetrated more extensive frauds on unsuspecting targets. Con men (and women) came out in droves. Desperate seekers were easy targets for their clever schemes. Hundreds of people lost their life savings by purchasing stakes in a variety of "guaranteed" opportunities.

In the grand scheme of things, the few thousand people who joined the search was a small number, but it was enough to create plenty of fodder for tabloid publishers. For several weeks, every clue with promise even made local, if not national, news.

After ten months of "mining," no new meteorites that matched the first eight were discovered. Hindsight people were as disappointed as anyone. Leadership would have paid top dollar to restock their shelves with the rare meteorites. By the time scavengers gave up, the second Hindsight was already completed.

* * *

The first step in building another Hindsight screen was to heat meteorites enough to separate the metal from silicate minerals. Both assistant directors were on hand for the event. The remaining space stones were laid on a table from the smallest to the largest. Before the process proceeded, David picked up the smallest one and carried it over to Dr. Gordman.

"I've been thinking," he said, holding the rock waist-high toward his associate. "Maybe you're right about keeping back some of this material. This small one won't provide a significant amount of metal. Why don't you keep it someplace safe in case it's needed in the future?"

Dr. Gordman stopped scratching his stomach and slowly took the meteorite from David's hand. No one ever saw Carl cry, but he came close that day. He put the stone in his lab coat pocket, not a particularly secure place, but David said nothing, knowing that the good doctor would guard it with his life.

Even with past experience to guide technicians, the greatest of care was taken to properly remove metal from the meteorites. Once removed, it was melted and poured into a mold that was designed to create the same size screen as the last one. The screen ended up being eight percent thinner than the last one. The difference was not discernible to the naked eye.

With little concern about the likely success of a second Hindsight screen, some engineers were able to focus attention on potential upgrades. One of those improvements was a filter for the cameras. Earlier videos of history had a reddish tint that had to be adjusted in post-production. Future renderings would be recorded by cameras outfitted with filters to eliminate the tint.

* * *

Some brainstorming sessions took a surreal turn. Even level-headed scientists can fall victim to overly imaginative ideas and embarrass themselves with unrealistic suggestions, or flat-out dumb questions. One such conversation centered on the purchase and retrofitting of a cargo plane.

"Instead of chartering cargo planes in the future, we are going to purchase one with defense capabilities from the military. There are several possibilities ready to be decommissioned that we can choose from," Darren announced to his crew.

"Do any of them have stealth capabilities?" a twenty-four-year-old new hire asked.

"Um…stealth technology is only used on warplanes. Besides, it only reduces the plane's radar visibility," a colleague explained.

A more mature crew member followed up, "What about cloaking? Doesn't that make planes invisible to the naked eye?"

Darren's first assistant couldn't resist. "Maybe Wonder Woman's invisible jet is available for sale."

"I don't think it's big enough," the down-to-earth colleague answered, deciding to play along. "We should just develop our own cloaking technology so we are the only ones who have it—except for comic books."

Darren ended the bizarre discussion; "We'll get right on that tomorrow. For now, let's deal with reality." He distributed pictures and descriptions of planes within the project's price range. "We need to decide which aircraft to recommend to Dr. Knab and the rest of the leadership team."

During the discussion, someone brought up the idea of purchasing a helicopter. "It seems like a chopper designed to transport Hindsight would open up a lot of venues that we can't get access to on land." As consensus grew for adding a helicopter to the shopping list, the choice of a cargo plane was limited to the three that could carry a helicopter and two armored vehicles.

The two armored trucks would each be outfitted to hold plenty of staff inside. New platforms were designed that allowed equipment to pitch significantly, yaw completely, and roll slightly. Earlier platforms had to be moved manually. These new platforms in both the helicopter and trucks were mechanical. Control of these functions could be routed to the Hindsight operator or an alternate crew member.

Another issue was contracting the best private security possible. Jacob was content with their current company, Safeguard, but he didn't expect them to stay on board after losing six agents in the plane's downing. Carson encouraged the director to talk with Safeguard before looking elsewhere for security services. Sure enough, the company was willing to continue providing services with three stipulations: an increase in the number of agents, permission to carry higher caliber weapons, and a twenty percent price increase.

Carson scheduled a meeting with Dr. Knab to make another suggestion. "Now that the base is known to be home to Hindsight, what do you think about beefing up security here?"

"What do you mean?" Jacob asked.

"In my previous work, I researched and tested many security products. I can recommend great equipment to monitor and protect sensitive areas." the salesman replied. His boss recognized the wisdom of this suggestion and asked Carson to prepare a report with his recommendations.

It wasn't long before Carson was making his proposal to the executive staff, explaining the purpose and value of each high-tech device he was recommending. The cost of the total package seemed reasonable, so the enhanced security tools were purchased, and Darren oversaw their installation, with Trout tagging along.

The new security equipment revealed a hitherto unknown weakness in the military police assigned to the base. They were fully capable of guarding the entrance and patrolling the grounds, but they did not fare well when it came to learning how to use the new surveillance equipment. Hall met with Carson and Darren to discuss the issue.

"Darren," David began, "you were involved in setting up our new security. Did you find it difficult to understand?"

"Not really," Oats answered. "Of course, I haven't been through the full training regimen."

"No insult intended, but perhaps we aren't getting the sharpest knives in the Military Police drawer," Carson interjected. "Most of our MPs seem pretty young."

"I think they are fine," Darren protested. "I don't understand why they can't get a handle on this stuff."

David shook his head. "Me either. I've talked to several of the soldiers who have been through the training. They say that the instructions are complicated and even seem contradictory. Some complain that the steps are counterintuitive."

"Maybe some of the Hindsight staff should go through the training," Darren suggested. "It wouldn't hurt to have some backup available. Plus, we might be able to see why the military folks are having such a problem."

"I'm not sure it's a good idea for non-security people to know how the equipment works," Trout argued. "Wouldn't that partially defeat the purpose of security? What if one of our own is a spy?"

David was surprised by Carson's suggestion that security was aimed at Hindsight personnel. He just assumed it was to protect against outsiders. This new perspective left him at a loss. "What do you think we should do then?"

"Why don't we contract our private security company to operate and monitor the new security features?" Trout responded. "We could even replace the military personnel with them."

"I don't see any reason for that," came Darren's retort. "I think our security crew does just fine."

Sensing tension building between his colleagues, Hall decided to cut the meeting short. "Let me share what we've discussed so far with Drs. Knab and Gordman. I think they need to decide how far outside the box we should think. I'll let you know what they say."

Darren Oats was normally the consummate team player, but something about Carson Trout rubbed him the wrong way. While rules against discussing business outside of Hindsight facilities had never technically been loosened, no one ever suffered repercussions for doing so. There was very little left to be kept secret, so Darren often spoke of work at home.

* * *

"Are you sure you're not just jealous of him?" Destiny asked her husband after he complained to her about Trout. "I understand why you would be."

"I ain't jealous of no one," Darren responded. "'specially not him."

"Well, I heard he is making a lot of money from this project you've put so much work into," the understanding wife offered. "It's only right to be frustrated about that."

"I don't care," the operations chief insisted. "I'm telling you there is something wrong. That man has too much influence, and his suggestions just keep giving him more power. I don't trust him."

Darren wasn't the only one to question Trout's motives. Carl was starting to feel boxed out in his role as assistant director. He didn't mind Hall being an assistant as well, but Carson seemed to have Knab's ear at least as much as his two lieutenants did.

At first, Jacob didn't like the idea of turning all security over to a private company—partly because of the added expense. But when his request for more seasoned military police fell on deaf ears, he decided on a balanced approach. Since the new security equipment seemed beyond the MP's abilities, Jacob hired additional Safeguard personnel to man that equipment —if they were able. The military presence was reduced to those needed to patrol the grounds and man the entrance.

The Safeguard tech staff flew through the training with flying colors. With security upgrades operational, the base was more secure than ever. There were cameras and/or sensors in obvious places and a few unusual locations. Hindsight employees felt spied upon for the first few weeks after the improvements, but soon, the new cameras were less conspicuous, and everything seemed back to normal.

Following copious notes from the first endeavor, the team was able to duplicate the process of creating the metal plate flawlessly. They were especially happy that the difference in screen thickness did not affect its function. There had been concern that the thinner plate would make a difference in the time spanned by various frequencies.

"I was afraid that we would have to go through the same tedious process as before to calibrate the settings for this Hindsight," Daniels confessed. "But our few tests indicate that X-rays and gamma rays have the exact same effect on this one as the last."

"That's good," Carl agreed. "Are you concerned at all about the thickness of the screen being reduced?"

"A little," Jonathan admitted. "It seems that this one would be a little easier to damage, but I think the reinforced frame Darren built will protect it while in use."

"And the new traveling case is very sturdy," Darren added.

One frustration that key team members shared was the occasional meeting that wasted both time and mental energy. One of those meetings centered on upgrades that the CIA pressed for. Convinced that the agency could make use of Hindsight without congressional action, the Vice President's chief of staff arranged for a sit-down.

Thirty-something Cody Smith was a no-nonsense CIA agent who was no more excited to bring his request than the Hindsight team was to hear it. "The

Central Intelligence Agency would like you to pursue an upgrade that will significantly enhance your machine's usefulness."

"What kind of upgrade are you looking for?" Hall asked.

"We would like you to work with our team to add the ability to tag a person or object for the purpose of identifying its origin," Smith explained. Noticing confusion on everyone's face, he continued, "Let's say a bomb goes off in…uh…London. And we take your…thing…"

"Hindsight," Jonathan offered.

"Okay, Hindsight then," the agent went on. "We scan the area and discover that the bomb was delivered in a suitcase. I understand that this could help identify the delivery person, but what about the person who sent the bomb? What about the person who built the bomb? How can we identify them?"

After a brief awkward silence, David spoke up. "I'm not sure what you are getting at? What are you wanting us to do?"

"We want the ability to tag that suitcase, electronically or virtually or whatever you would call it. Tag it so that we could follow it throughout its history." Everyone understood the words Smith was saying. They just couldn't believe he was saying them.

"You understand that Hindsight can only reveal the past of what has occurred directly in front of its screen," David stated, almost as a question. "The only way to follow something or someone's past movement is to physically move Hindsight along the same path."

"I understand," Smith interrupted. "But what if we could tag that suitcase and register its dimensions, color, and any distinguishing marks into a database? So, we don't have to physically follow it. When it appears further in the past, our computer recognizes it."

"How would it 'appear'?" Dr. Gordman asked.

"Via our extensive surveillance abilities," the agent answered.

"I don't know what you need us for," Carl insisted. "In a scenario like you described, we could get the best images of the item, from as many angles as possible. Your people could do whatever they need to do to tag it. Then run it through your system to see if it pops up."

"Oh," Smith said thoughtfully.

Jonathan glanced at the time on his cell phone. "Oh crap! I'm supposed to meet Trina in ten minutes." He looked at David. "We are cake tasting for the wedding."

"Go ahead," Hall chuckled, knowing that cake tasting was not on his friend's bucket list. But being a good fiancé, Jonathan was trying to be as supportive as possible as Trina made plans for their wedding.

"Crap," Carl repeated. He had never heard David nor Jonathan use foul language. In a rare exception to his normally deadpan personality, Dr. Gordman joked, "Is that a Christian cuss word?"

The soon-to-be groom hurried off, and David concluded the meeting within a few minutes. No promises were made, but the agent left with some food for thought and a better understanding of Hindsight's limitations. More than a few meetings ended this way, leaving Hindsight staff wishing the project were still secret.

While in development, the new equipment was called Hindsight 2.0. However, once it became operational, it was just referred to by its predecessor's name. Carson continued to work his magic, and high-paying projects started pouring in. That was an especially good thing since most of the project's surplus funds had been spent on new transport vehicles and other improvements.

Chapter 18 - Revived

With a new Hindsight ready for action, the travel team gathered to be briefed on their next project. Everyone was excited about the new and improved equipment. Carson successfully rescheduled all but one canceled project. In addition, several foreign governments expressed interest in seeing if Hindsight could help with difficult-to-solve crimes. Those that requested reduced rates were put on the back burner.

"Looks like you are going to be busy," Katy commented as David looked through paperwork at the table. Secrecy was no longer necessary, so non-classified missions could be discussed off-site. "Will you be gone a lot?"

"I'm trying not to be. I've begged off the easier projects," David answered. "There are so many applications getting approved that scheduling is becoming a problem."

"How many of the trips will you have to go on?"

David hesitated. He knew his answer would not be well received. "Right now, half of them, but I'm working on it."

"Isn't there anyone else who you can rotate with?" Katy's disappointment was turning to frustration. "Part of a good director's job is delegation."

"Don't tell me how to do my job!" David responded in a slightly raised voice. "I'm sorry," he said more softly. "I've just got a lot on my mind."

"Okay, just do your best," Katy knew not to press any harder. She went to check on Reese, who was playing in his bedroom. In the end, David missed only six of fifteen trips.

* * *

Most of the first projects were like the early ones—billionaires looking to own videos and images of marvels from ages past. One Civil War buff paid for a full-length video of two major battles. An Italian businessman wanted to see the Roman Colosseum in all its glory, including action in the arena. A proud Greek requested the famous battle of 300 Spartans. That was an expensive disappointment compared to the Hollywood versions.

Next on the list were some of the famous conspiracy theories. The JFK assassination was chief among them. The team went to Dallas to capture images from multiple vantage points, including the sixth-floor room and window from where the fatal shots were supposedly fired.

Some conspiracies gained momentum because *red tape* halted the investigation. The questionable suicide of Jeffrey Epstein was a prime example. Despite everyone expressing a desire to reveal the truth, the team kept getting the runaround. It was never discovered who blocked the project.

Other mysteries were far too expensive to investigate. Did Shakespeare write the works bearing his name? Was King Arthur a historical figure? What about Robin Hood? Who was Jack the Ripper? Was Atlantis a real island? If so, where is it now?

Then there were the Sasquatch and Nessie investigations. Based upon purported sightings, approximate times and places were scanned for Bigfoot. Most of the stakeouts turned up nothing at all. The three times where a creature did appear, Hindsight was able to get close enough to show that the figure was a human wearing a costume. On one occasion, the fraudster and his camera-toting accomplice were recorded together with the monster's mask removed.

The Loch Ness project turned out a bit differently. Starting onshore, using dates and times provided by eye-witnesses, Hindsight observed something strange in the water. Using that data, the team took to the air in their custom helicopter. While this vantage point brought them considerably closer, they were still limited by the height at which they had to hover. It was unsafe for the helicopter to get any closer to the water that the creature bobbed in and out of. This made being in the right position to get clear images difficult.

There was something alive coursing through the water, but even multiple passes could not provide definitive evidence of what the creature was. Once back at their Irish Bed and Breakfast, the team watched and rewatched the footage. While it could still be an elaborate hoax, these new witnesses were more than reluctant to assert or even suggest so.

Soon, the subject of returning for another try at a discounted rate was being discussed. Noting limitations of both the land and air approaches to getting useful images, the idea of a watercraft from which to operate Hindsight was bandied about. Two vessels were suggested. The obvious one was a motorized boat. The second option was an underwater vessel, a type of submarine with a very limited depth potential. Something that could obtain underwater images would show what the object looked like under the surface. An underwater view would probably reveal what Nessie was.

Any return visits could not be scheduled for at least twenty months, so discussions about the Loch Ness monster dissipated. Conversations about water-based Hindsight platforms, on the other hand, continued.

* * *

"Well, we should have expected that unidentified flying objects would eventually be on our list of projects," Director Knab told his team. "To make matters more complicated, no one person with an interest in UFOs has the means to sponsor such an expensive project. So, a group of over thirty moderately wealthy enthusiasts have joined together."

Carson jumped in. "They've sorted through pictures, film clips, eyewitness testimonies, and news releases to find the most likely candidates for positive identification, or, in this case, un-identification. Since several of the members are especially suspicious or curious about Area 51 in Nevada, it too is part of the project, along with Roswell, New Mexico."

Priorities were established, and a plan was pretty well developed before the co-op met with Hindsight representatives. In an effort to save money, the land-based discovery method normally used to get a proper bearing was eliminated. Hindsight was operated from a helicopter for the entirety of the UFO project.

The information provided by co-op reps was surprisingly accurate. It wasn't long before Hindsight zeroed in on a shining object hovering in the air. Keeping the time period constant, the helicopter drew closer to the orb. Suddenly, it disappeared.

"Where'd it go?" David asked, a bit perturbed. "Did you have a glitch in the time setting?"

Jonathan ignored the question as he pivoted Hindsight 180 degrees. "There it is. The object's small size made it appear to be further in the distance than it was. So, when the copter reached and passed it, the disc seemed to disappear."

Being an unbeliever where UFOs are concerned, Jonathan expected the object to be bogus and reacted quickly. The helicopter hovered close enough to the object to determine that it was between five and six feet long from end to end. It was definitely man-made.

Several UFOs turned out to be everything from metallic-looking frisbees to kites to outright frauds. Some appearances turned out to be natural phenomena. The helicopter circled what looked like slits in the sky, only to find them to be optical illusions. There were some sightings, though, that Hindsight could not identify. Some were too high in the sky for the helicopter to get close to.

Area 51 was examined as extensively as the military permitted. After discovering what became famous debris, Hindsight was set to operate in reverse, automated by Jonathan's newly enhanced program. The camera followed the surreal image of metallic fabric floating up, into the sky. A somewhat circular shape eventually formed out of reconstituted material.

It was no weather balloon. Of course, that early explanation had been debunked long ago. The copter circled the object, which looked to be about thirty feet long and twelve feet high. Intrigue guided the team to follow the airborne object toward its place of liftoff. That dream was shattered as a fighter jet suddenly appeared, followed by a military helicopter. The latter's pilot signaled for the Hindsight crew to change course.

Jonathan quickly adjusted Hindsight's timing feature to fast-reverse to capture the object's path as it disappeared into the distance. To avoid another close contact with military-grade weapons, the copter headed to the airport and ended the day a bit early. No one from the military ever contacted Hindsight about the encounter.

As it turned out, what was recorded could well have verified the most recent official statement concerning the Area 51 crash site and destroyed craft. Upon review, the object did not appear to be extra-terrestrial. It was, indeed, part of a secret project. Its purpose was never explained, and its value was never quantified.

While some would call the discovery a "nothing burger," others felt it vindicated their efforts to expose unnecessary government secrecy. A video of Hindsight's viewing was released to national and cable news networks. This prompted the military to provide a spokesman to do some interviews.

"The 1950s was a different time, with different thinking. While there are certainly military secrets still kept from the general public today, during the Cold War, misinformation was an essential component of staying ahead of our enemies. Some things our predecessors chose to do might embarrass us today, but they made the best decisions they could with the information they had, for the times they lived in."

Not exactly the mea culpa conspiracy theorists wanted, but it satisfied the general public, which made for a short news cycle. For the most part, co-op members that paid for the UFO Hindsight investigation were disappointed in the results. However, there was enough ambiguity in some of the sightings that true believers and those who make a living promoting conspiracies had fodder to chew on and share.

As lucrative vanity projects began to dwindle, serious thought was given to friendly foreign governments who requested Hindsight help. Since the division was making money hand over fist, the decision was made to serve Interpol for two weeks at a thirty-percent discount. Federal representatives of both the executive and legislative branches lobbied for the goodwill gesture, citing the positive PR and additional cooperation it should bring.

* * *

The elite British investigative agency had three important cases that were approaching dead ends. Leaders hoped to reinvigorate the investigations with fresh information harvested by Hindsight. Interpol sent a couple of agents to the US base a week earlier to discuss the cases.

"The first and most urgent need is terrorist-related," the Brit stated. "A second case involves human trafficking. And the third case is considerably more sensitive. It involves a member of the royal family who is suspected of several crimes. It is not nearly as urgent, but certain powers that be want it resolved."

Hindsight was helpful in the first two efforts much the same way it aided the FBI in its inaugural mission. The equipment was set up in suspected areas of criminal activity. The time was set for earlier than necessary and fast-forwarded until suspicious motion was detected. Once illegal activity was identified, Hindsight was moved closer to get a better look at the culprits. Besides aiding in the intended cases, Hindsight inadvertently revealed several other crimes taking place. Several months after returning to the States, the Hindsight team received emailed newspaper clippings from London authorities, highlighting criminal prosecutions that resulted from Hindsight's revelations. The Americans' involvement was never revealed to the general public or courts.

Despite successfully identifying questionable behavior, the team never heard a peep about the Royal whose past they surveilled. The non-disclosure agreement all participants signed restricted them from even talking about the cases amongst themselves. Any action taken against the aristocrat remained private.

This was one of the rare times when the travel team could not report project results to the stay-at-home team. Homecomings normally included a celebratory gathering that included everyone on base. This time, after being away for seventeen days, the travelers had to remain mum. While those tethered to the base were disappointed to be left out of the loop, they were happy to see their comrades again.

After a short hiatus, all the employees were gathered for the next project's announcement. A simple gymnasium was the only building on base large enough to accommodate all the employees and their families. Since the old bleachers were uncomfortable, folding chairs were set up in the middle of the basketball court.

Originally built as a multi-purpose facility, the gym boasted a stage at one end. The sound equipment was old but functional. Its intermittent hums and squeals prompted attendees to wonder why new equipment wasn't installed. After all, the project was flush with cash.

Most people arrived early, while those with a reputation for tardiness did not disappoint. Dr. Knab watched the room fill. Though eager to make his announcement, he patiently waited for late arrivals. Finally, seventeen minutes after the scheduled start time, Jacob approached the lectern. The first few words of his address were only faintly heard without amplification. He paused until the sound technician signaled that it was safe to proceed.

"Let's try this again," Director Knab said, leaning toward the microphone. Satisfied that it was working properly, he relaxed. "Hindsight employees are more than a team. We are a family. Every one of you is an intricate part of this endeavor. Unfortunately, only a few of you have witnessed Hindsight in action. Some of you have never even seen our baby. That is about to change.

"After our next project, we have the biggest one of our careers. It begins in four months and is scheduled to take fifteen weeks to complete. We intend to record the geological history of our planet. Since it is impossible at this time to take Hindsight to the International Space Station, we are chartering the newest airship large enough to carry our equipment and several passengers.

"This space-aged, blimp-like craft is capable of flying almost one-hundred-thousand feet above sea level. At that height, we will be able to view an entire continent at one time. The airship can stay airborne for six hours, which gives us plenty of time to view and record history.

"Here's the exciting part. We will arrange for every employee to participate in this mission if you would like. We will pay for your travel and lodging for five days at one of our destinations. On one of those days, you will get to ride in the airship and witness Hindsight in action. You can treat your four other days as bonus vacation."

Excitement with a fair measure of disbelief permeated the gymnasium. The crowd's murmuring grew louder and louder as they spoke amongst themselves, first in whispers, then in raised voices. Soon, there was cheering and even some tears of joy. This was just the spark many of the staff needed to revive their passion for the project. That Jacob was still at the podium might have gone unnoticed had he not persisted in vying for the audience's attention.

"Flying with Hindsight is only available to employees," the director continued, "but the trip is for everyone who lives on the base. Whatever family members live with you can accompany you to your chosen destination and enjoy every part of the trip, except the airship flight.

"Pick up a flyer at the doors on your way out to see what destinations you can choose from. Miss Benson—that is, soon-to-be Mrs. Daniels and her staff will be in the office all day tomorrow. Stop by and sign up for your first and second choices so we can begin making arrangements."

Knab's concluding "Thank you" was drowned out by the loudest cheering ever heard in that gymnasium. This morale booster would cost over three million dollars, but judging from the initial response, it would be money well spent.

Katy didn't stay after the announcement. David didn't think too much of it, figuring she wanted to get Reese home for his occasional afternoon nap. Jonathan caught David in his office just before quitting time.

"Wow, that's some undertaking," Jonathan marveled.

"The geological study? Yes, it is. Sorry I didn't give you a heads up."

"No worries, but the director is going to expect Hindsight to look back millions of years."

David took his point. "Oh, that's right. Hindsight doesn't work that far back."

"Well, maybe it works, but there is nothing to see. We've never received permission to test that far back in time."

"I'm sorry. I did try a couple of times to make that happen."

"I understand," Jonathan answered. "I'm just wondering if we should warn Dr. Knab about my earlier non-findings or just surprise everyone."

David chuckled. "Part of me wants it to be a surprise, but if Hindsight proves that the earth is young like the Bible describes, our scientists will end up looking like fools, including Jacob. That would not be very kind."

"My thinking exactly. I don't want to come off as smug when the truth is revealed—if that is the truth. We still don't know for sure."

"I'll talk to the doctors as soon as I can," David committed.

* * *

When he arrived home just an hour later, David found his wife sitting at the kitchen table, crying. "What's wrong? Are you okay?" David asked, concerned.

"How long will you be gone this time?" Katy complained. "I hardly hear from you anymore when you're away."

Over the recent trips, David's nightly calls home had become inconsistent, and briefer. It seemed to Katy, that instead of wanting to talk to her, he was just doing his duty. She wondered if she was wrong to think that David would not revert to making the job his top priority, but that wasn't the main thing on her mind at this time.

"Who is Hindsight's lawyer?" Katy asked. It took three years for her to discover the only Hindsight attorney was the attractive redhead.

"What?" David was genuinely confused. "Who?"

"The lawyer you took that trip with?" she pressed.

His mind raced to remember what trip she might be talking about. She stared angrily at him until he answered.

"You mean Debra Minx?" He asked innocently. "She goes on most trips. Which one are you talking about?"

"Which one? The one you went on alone with her. You said it was just you and the project's lawyer."

"Oh," he finally realized what she was talking about. "That trip was ages ago to meet a judge."

"Why did you lie to me?" Katy asked, keeping her voice down only to avoid disturbing Reese, who was watching TV.

"I didn't lie," David answered firmly. "I knew you would overreact if I told you. Nothing happened. I made sure our hotel rooms were on different floors to avoid any suspicion."

"How am I supposed to trust you?" She asked defeatedly. "You keep secrets from me. You're gone all the time. And even when you're here, you're not here. Reese doesn't have a father. I don't have a husband."

"I even avoided eating meals with that woman," he continued, defending himself. Even though Katy exaggerated, David took her point. It was so hard to balance work and relationships. David felt like he was on a pendulum, swinging between a focus on family and work obligations. In reality, his choices were more like a balancing scale. He continued to give more weight to work than to family. He was back to his old ways and didn't even realize it. David stepped behind his sobbing wife and gently placed his hands on her shoulders.

"I'm so sorry, hun," he offered, sincerely. "I don't want to neglect you—really. And there has never been another woman—never."

She looked up at him to see his reaction when she announced, "I'm pregnant."

Chapter 19 - Poisoned

The travel team gathered for a briefing on one short mission still to be taken before the grand worldwide project. Beth Auger, the assistant Hindsight operator, hurried into the conference room. Already seated were Drs. Knab and Gordman, Trina, Darren, David, Carson, and Debra.

"Is something wrong?" David asked Beth, who wasn't supposed to attend the meeting. "Have you seen Jonathan?"

"I just got off the phone with him," she answered in an ominous tone. "He's too sick to come in. He sounded really bad."

"He canceled our dinner date last night," Trina added. Her face revealed guilt for being frustrated at the cancelation. "He must be really ill. He's never canceled on me before. I'll go check on him after the meeting."

"Beth," Dr. Knab cautioned, "make sure you take good notes, just in case you end up flying solo this trip."

"Yes, sir," she answered. Beth was more than ready to take the reins, so she had mixed feelings about her superior's condition. The meeting went pretty much as normal except for Beth's request for clarification on some issues. She was taking copious notes to be sure she was fully prepared.

Trina took her leave as soon as the meeting was adjourned and headed straight for the barracks where Jonathan lived. She once asked him why he didn't opt for one of the base houses since his employee status more than qualified him. He just shrugged and said, "This is enough for me." He commandeered two rooms and put a door between them to afford more space and create a more apartment-like domicile.

She passed through the main barracks doors and knocked on the one that led to Jonathan's living area. Impatient, she knocked again, more loudly. No answer. Trina stepped to the next door, which opened to his bedroom, and knocked again. No answer. "Jonathan!" she shouted as she pounded on the door. She thought she heard a groan. She tried to turn the doorknob. It was locked.

Trina hurried back to the first door, only to find it locked as well. By then, a couple of off-duty MPs had stuck their heads out from their rooms to see what the ruckus was about. "Something wrong, Miss?" one of them asked, wiping the sleep from his eyes.

"Yes, I think Jonathan needs help, and I can't get in." Trina pleaded. Her panicked expression convinced the men to hurried, half-dressed, to her aid. After knocking loudly himself, one of them lunged at the door with his shoulder. A cracking sound indicated he needed only a little more force the second time, which he appropriately applied.

The door flew open as a chunk of the door jam sailed halfway across the room. Trina ran in and opened Jonathan's bedroom door. The second MP joined the first just inside the damaged door, which he examined while awaiting Trina's return. They could hear a man moaning, followed by a high-pitched, "Help!"

The men joined Trina in Jonathan's bedroom to find him writhing in pain. Sweat had soaked through his T-shirt and boxer shorts so that his bed was noticeably wet. One of the men ran back to his room to get his cell phone and call an ambulance. The other man watched as Trina tried to communicate unsuccessfully with her fiancé.

After the 911 call, guards at the base entrance were notified of the impending ambulance arrival. EMTs were on the scene in less than ten minutes. Trina could offer no pertinent information regarding Jonathan's condition, so he was transported with little paperwork. She didn't even know if her soon-to-be husband had any allergies.

Trina was permitted to ride in the ambulance. She phoned David and Dr. Knab while in transport. The closest care center was a community hospital that could satisfy most needs, but Jonathan's symptoms were not readily diagnosed in the ER. When the director arrived, he rushed into the treatment room, introducing himself as Dr. Knab.

Using his title inappropriately was enough to get the confused receptionist to buzz him through the security door. Once with Jonathan, he pressed the attending physician to test for radiation poisoning.

"Radiation poisoning?" the doctor objected. "Why would we test for that?"

"This man is in contact with X-rays and gamma rays on a regular basis," Jacob explained. Then he asked, "Aren't his symptoms consistent with radiation poisoning?" He knew what radiation poisoning symptoms were because all staff was trained to recognize them.

"We're just a community hospital. If he has radiation poisoning, we will have to send him to the city," the attending physician stated.

"Fly him," Knab demanded. "Now!"

It took twenty minutes for the helicopter to arrive. By then, morphine had calmed Jonathan to sleep. David drove Trina to the city hospital. Jacob followed, Darren with him. They all waited impatiently as Jonathan's condition was assessed. About an hour into the wait, Destiny Oats, Katy Hall, and Carol Castle arrived to comfort and console Trina.

"I didn't even know if he has allergies," she lamented, sobbing. "Almost every question the EMT asked, I had to say, 'I don't know.' What kind of fiancée can't answer those questions?"

The three female friends assured Trina that she was a great fiancée and would make a wonderful wife. The two married women offered their own embarrassing experiences as evidence that Trina was better suited for marriage than they were when they said, "I do."

Discussions among the men were less related to the event at hand. It is hard to understand how fishing, sci-fi movies, and athlete's foot make it into hospital waiting room conversations, but with these men, they did. Every once in a while, someone would belt out a hardy laugh that was met with stern stares from the women.

The three-hour wait seemed more like ten when a doctor finally joined the anxious crowd. At first, the physician was unsure about sharing Jonathan's medical information with anyone, including Trina. The ever-prepared Dr. Gordman had sent a folder with Jacob. In it was a notarized document with Jonathan's signature that allowed for medical disclosures to Hindsight representatives. Upon seeing it, the physician asked Dr. Knab and Trina to join him in a consultation room.

When several others seemed surprised that such a document existed, they asked to look through the folder he left with David. One by one, he handed each team member the paperwork they had signed upon being hired. "I forgot we signed these," Darren confessed. "Good thing we did." David collected the papers and returned them to their folder.

The consultation room was just large enough for a small table and three chairs. The doctor entered first and stood next to his seat behind the table. He motioned for Jacob and Trina to be seated. He began speaking as he sat. "Whoever suggested that Mr. Daniels is the victim of radiation poisoning was correct. I have never seen the degree of exposure he has suffered."

Trina was speechless, so Jacob asked the obvious question. "So, what is the treatment?" Since both had been fully briefed in early orientation sessions, they knew that mild cases could be dealt with successfully. They were not expecting the answer they received.

"I'm afraid there is no treatment. Mr. Daniel's organs are rapidly deteriorating. All we can do is medicate him for his comfort. I don't think he will survive until the weekend."

Trina burst into tears. Jacob awkwardly placed his arm around her as she leaned her head into his chest. Her upper body heaved as she sobbed uncontrollably. The doctor was familiar with this response, so he just waited a moment before continuing.

"We will keep him as comfortable as possible. By sometime tomorrow though, I suspect that he will have to be sedated to deal with the pain. Any family members who want to see him need to be here by morning. I can't guarantee that he will be lucid enough to communicate, but we will do our best to find that balance for a few hours at least."

The stunned look on Trina and Jacob's faces as they rejoined the rest informed everyone of Jonathan's prognosis. As Knab shared the news, the ladies surrounded Trina. Their hugs and tears were appreciated but provided little comfort and no relief. After a while, they encouraged Trina to go home and rest before returning in the morning.

"I won't be able to sleep," Trina explained. "Besides, it's over an hour drive each way. I need to be here if he wakes up and can communicate."

Carol's offer to stay with her friend was accepted, and the others made their way back to the base. Destiny took Trina's house key so she could bring fresh clothes in the morning.

Sleeping in the hospital waiting room was almost impossible due to uncomfortable seats and unrelenting grief. Trina's mind was racing. She felt that it was her responsibility to contact Jonathan's parents, but she was glad David promised to do so when he returned to his office. After all, she did not have their contact information with her. She had not even met them. Jonathan had made it a point to meet her parents months before, but she kept putting off her "meet the in-laws experience." Now, their only encounter would be at his funeral. A fresh stream of tears began to flow.

* * *

The next morning, before heading back to the hospital, Dr. Knab called a meeting with the entire staff. "I'm sure most of you are aware that our great friend and model employee Jonathan Daniels is in intensive care with no hope of recovery. We will soon be joined by OSHA investigators. You will fully cooperate with them. During the investigation, all projects will be put on hold, including the Hindsight mission planned for next week."

Before anyone could ask a question, the director was out the door. His wife Kathleen was waiting for him in their car. Dr. Gordman was left to clean up any messes—that was not his forte. Before dawn, Destiny went to Trina's home and collected some clothes and other personal items. She arrived at the hospital before Trina or Carol was awake. She knew how important and evasive rest would be, so she sat nearby and waited quietly until one of them stirred.

Carol yawned, stretched, and wiped her eyes. She looked around for her glasses, which she forgot she had placed in her purse. That little bit of movement was enough to disturb Trina from her restless sleep. She groaned as she sat up. Too tired to stretch, Trina just cupped her head in her hands, elbows anchored to her knees.

She looked up as Destiny stood to bring her the requested belongings. "Oh, thank you," Trina sighed. She got up and slowly carried the bag into the restroom to freshen up and change.

"Sweetie, you look like you didn't get an ounce of rest," Destiny said as she placed her hand on Carol's shoulder. "When you are up to it, you can take my car home. We will pick it up later."

Carol wanted to argue, but she also felt as if she had done her duty. Perhaps it was someone else's turn to sit with her friend. She waited until Trina returned before taking her leave. "Thank you so much, Carol. I didn't realize how badly I needed someone to stay with me last night." They hugged, and Carol left with Destiny's car key.

Shortly thereafter, a nurse approached. "Miss Benson?"

"Yes," Trina answered.

"You can see your fiancé now," the nurse announced. As they walked toward the intensive care unit, Trina was warned not to expect much interaction from Jonathan. "Mr. Daniels is in a lot of pain. We have reduced his medication to help him stay awake for a little bit, but he may still slip in and out of consciousness. You will only be able to stay with him for a few minutes."

His was the third of ten glass doors in the semi-circle that made up the ICU. The nurse opened the door and pulled a curtain back enough for Trina to enter. Jonathan was awake but not very alert. His head moved about like a bobblehead doll in slow motion. His eyes darted around the room as his mind tried to make sense of his surroundings. Then his gaze fell on Trina.

Jonathan smiled.

He tried to speak, but his voice was hoarse, and the sounds were gibberish. She approached his bed, and he tried to reach out to her. His hand barely raised two inches before it fell. His head tilted forward, and his eyes closed. Trina looked nervously at the equipment monitoring his vitals. She sighed in relief when she realized that he had just fallen asleep.

Knowing she had precious little time, Trina touched Jonathan's hand and softly called his name. His eyelids fluttered, then opened wide. He grimaced in pain, then smiled at Trina again. She leaned over and kissed his stubbled cheek. He closed his eyes as she whispered in his ear.

"I love you...so much."

She could only hope that he heard her before losing consciousness. Jonathan didn't wake again before a nurse informed her that she would have to leave. As she stepped out the door, Trina looked back to see the dose of her fiancé's pain medication being raised. This time, the tears did not flow. They just barely trickled down her cheeks.

Trina grabbed a couple of tissues from the nurse's station as she left ICU. When she returned to the waiting room, Jacob and Kathleen were there to greet her. She couldn't make eye contact without crying, so she just shook her head as she looked toward the floor. Kathleen and Destiny sat on either side of her, alternating between holding her hand, rubbing her arm, and stroking her hair.

About noon, Jonathan's parents arrived from out of state. Before connecting with the Hindsight folks, they were ushered in to see their dying son. When they finally arrived at the ICU waiting room, Mr. Daniels had to help his wife make her way to a chair. She wasn't crying, but grief was evident as she nearly collapsed twice before getting to a chair.

Jacob took Kathleen by the hand and went to introduce themselves to Jonathan's hurting parents. They were particularly broken over news that their son would likely never regain consciousness.

"He won't even know that we were here," his mom sobbed. The elder Daniels held his wife close as they cried together. Trina kept her distance as they grieved. After several minutes, her would-be father-in-law made eye contact with her. He greeted her with a smile that mirrored his son's. As she got up to walk toward them, he nudged his wife and motioned for her to look up.

"Trina?" Mrs. Daniels asked, glancing up for just a second.

"Yes, ma'am," Trina answered as she sat down and took her hand in both of her own. "I...I don't know what to say. I'm so sorry."

"I know, dear, I know," the distraught woman answered comfortingly. "We were so looking forward to meeting you."

"Me too," Trina lied, but she wished it were the truth.

"Jonathan talked about you all the time," Mr. Daniels said softly.

"When he would call, anyway," Jonathan's mom quietly interjected. Her eyes finally fixed on Trina's. "He really did love you."

Kathleen motioned to Jacob that they should leave the three alone. Quietly, they joined Destiny, who was watching from across the room. Soon, they left the waiting room entirely. "Let's find some breakfast and bring it back to them," Jacob suggested.

The middle-aged couple and Trina were alone in the waiting room when a doctor entered somberly and informed them that Jonathan had peacefully and quietly passed away. The physician stood silently for a minute while the three wept loudly.

Jacob and the two ladies returned with breakfast to find the trio huddled in sorrow. They could tell what news had been delivered, and Kathleen whispered, "He's gone." They never made their presence known. They just left, leaving the three to grieve alone.

Together, but alone.

Chapter 20 - Investigation

Carson knocked on the director's office door as he opened it. Jacob looked up from his laptop in surprise. One of the few courtesies he expected from visitors was to wait at his closed door until invited in. Everyone understood and respected that, so the salesman's behavior was unexpected and unappreciated.

"Can I help you?" Knab asked bluntly.

"I'm sorry, Dr. Knab, but there is a rumor going around that we aren't going to India next week," Carson blurted out, slightly out of breath from rushing through the building to confront his boss.

"I'm afraid that's so," Jacob confirmed, lowering his hands from the keyboard to fold them in his lap.

"We have to go," Carson insisted. "This is a really important client." Knab folded his arms and leaned back in his chair. Carson continued, "Look, I understand that Jonathan's death is a shock, but the best thing for everyone is to keep moving forward. He would want that, right?"

"You think?" Jacob queried. "Why is it that everyone assumes that the recently departed would want us to just move on?"

"I don't mean any disrespect." Trout adjusted his demeanor to reflect some empathy. "I guess I'm thinking too much about our client and not enough about the team. Sorry. How about I try to reschedule for next month?"

"I don't think so, Carson." Knab explained, "No telling when we will be operational again. It's out of my hands. OSHA has to conduct an investigation and clear us before we can make any plans."

Carson huffed, shook his head, and left, leaving the office door ajar. Jacob marveled at how quickly his temperament could change. He went back to working on the comments he would make at Jonathan's memorial service. Carol peeked in, curious as to why the door was open. Knab sensed her stare and looked up.

"Do you need anything?" she asked sheepishly.

"Just some privacy," he responded. "Shut the door, please."

Carson made his way to the break room that the private security detail frequented. He chit-chatted with the few in the room until the security chief entered and sat down. "Well, I'd better get a move on," Carson commented, dumping the remainder of his coffee in a sink. He leaned behind the chief to toss his empty cup into the trash receptacle, whispering, "We need to talk tonight."

Trout left the room, but not before making eye contact with the chief, who acknowledged the message with a slight nod and raised eyebrows. Carson never moved onto the base even though his job title warranted a private dwelling. He spent his twenty-minute commute home formulating a plan.

* * *

Meanwhile, a team from the Occupational Safety and Health Administration arrived to investigate Jonathan's radiation poisoning, evaluate the effectiveness of and adherence to established safety protocols, and mandate any changes that might be needed. The team of five met with the director and his two assistants to explain their mission and answer questions before beginning their work. The men committed to full cooperation. Security guards were called to escort the visitors. Dr. Knab gave them explicit instructions.

"I'm assigning these OSHA members to you. Allow access to every place and every person they request. No sites are to be considered off-limits."

The OSHA leader announced assignments, "Andre and Vivian, visit the lab where most of the radiation was discharged. Johnson, you measure radiation levels throughout the base. Peitry and Harris, interview everyone who has been in contact with the equipment or the deceased technician within a week of his poisoning."

"Jonathan," David stated, unhappy with the leader's impersonal identification. His correction was ignored.

* * *

At the barracks, Trina helped Mr. and Mrs. Daniels go through Jonathan's belongings. His parents were surprised at the lack of clutter. "Too bad he never keep his room this clean when he was a teenager," Mrs. Daniels remarked. When she entered his bedroom, she noticed a picture of her and her husband on the wall with a Bible passage engraved on a plaque below it. She sat on the bed and read the message out loud.

"The father of the righteous shall greatly rejoice; he who fathers a wise son will be glad in him. Let your father and mother be glad; let her who bore you rejoice. My son, give me your heart, and let your eyes observe my ways, Proverbs 23:24-26."

With tears in his eyes, Jonathan's dad walked over and sat down with his wife, putting his arm around her. Trina traced the recessed words with her index finger. "I've never heard anyone speak as glowingly about his parents as Jonathan did. I couldn't count how many times he referenced one of you when making a decision…or just in conversation," she remarked.

Mr. Daniels reminded his wife about an upcoming phone appointment with the funeral home. They decided to have Jonathan's body shipped home to be buried in the family plot. There would be a memorial service at the small church he, Trina, and the Halls attended in town, but the funeral would be back home in Iowa.

After arrangements were made, Jonathan's parents invited Trina to ride home with them. She declined, preferring to drive herself. She was afraid that the joint journey would become uncomfortable. She thanked the several ladies who offered to accompany her and help drive the long distance.

"I just feel like being alone. I promise to travel wisely and safely. There is enough time before the funeral that I won't have to push myself."

"Sweetie, I'm afraid you will feel like an outsider at the funeral. Are you sure you don't want one of us to come with?" Kathleen implored.

"I know the memorial service will be more meaningful for me, but I'll be okay up there."

"When is the memorial service here?" Destiny asked.

"It won't be until after the funeral, so I have time to get back and participate in it as well."

Everything project-related on base was at a standstill while OSHA did its thing. Employees spent a lot of time in break rooms and the cafeteria speculating about the outcome.

"They are going to shut us down. I just know it."

"They won't shut us down, but they will put so many restrictions on us that we will wish they had."

"It's been three days. This shouldn't take so long. I wonder what they've discovered."

Finally, the OSHA team appeared to be packing up. They scheduled a meeting with Dr. Knab and his leadership team for nine o'clock the next morning. Just before eight, two black sedans arrived at the front gate. The drivers identified themselves as FBI Special Agents. In all, four agents joined the OSHA team leader in his meeting with the Hindsight leaders and lawyer. The OSHA representative began the meeting with a report of their findings.

"Fortunately, we discovered no issues with escaped radiation anywhere on the base. The labs you primarily expose to radiation are well protected. After you adopt some minor recommendations and one major mandate, we can clear you for continued service."

A collective sigh of relief among the Hindsight troop was short-lived when the speaker explained the reason for the FBI's presence.

"Our investigation has turned up one very serious concern. The protective gear that Mr. Daniels wore was faulty. We tested all the other garments and helmets. They were deemed safe. We thought because Mr. Daniels experienced unusually frequent and extended exposure to radiation, his equipment degenerated more quickly. Our tests indicated that the garment's worn condition may have been enough to poison your employee.

Besides that, the gear was definitely tampered with. That's why we called the FBI."

An agent held up Jonathan's protective outfit and pointed out a large panel in the torso of the suit. Another agent explained, "Someone cut out a section of protective material and replaced it with similar-looking material that provided no protection at all. The sabotage was aimed to seriously injure, if not kill, the wearer of this suit."

The team sat dumbfounded. "Who would do such..." David's words trailed off.

"So, you're saying someone killed Mr. Daniels?" Carl asked. The accusation was clear, but it seemed preposterous.

"This entire base is now a federal crime scene," an agent stated. "You may go about your normal activities during our investigation, but everyone must remain available for interrogations."

"Interviews," another agent corrected.

"Understood," the baffled director responded. "How much do we tell the rest of our employees?"

"Nothing!" the lead agent insisted. "If asked, we are carrying on a routine investigation to ensure everyone's safety."

"Should we assume you need to interview those in this room?" Hindsight's attorney asked. Debra Minx's education and experience had not prepared her to aid clients in a murder investigation, but she understood that she might have to fill that role, at least in the interim.

"Yes, we will begin immediately with Mr. Hall. Dr. Knab, you are free to meet with the OSHA rep to finish reviewing their report," Agent Maxwell explained. "Special Agent Brier will sit in on that meeting to ensure you don't speak to anyone else until after we've interviewed you."

The three went to the director's office to complete OSHA's reporting. Two agents took David and the lawyer to a vacant room down the hall for his interview, and the last agent stayed with Dr. Gordman while he awaited his turn to answer questions.

Questions asked of leadership were neither intimidating nor accusative. Still, Carl was noticeably uncomfortable. He had no problem discussing the science behind what the team did, but when asked about his impression of various people, his emotional disability kicked in. He would say one thing, then correct himself because he thought his comment was too negative. When asked follow-up questions, his answers were vague.

David was also helpful in explaining technical issues of the equipment, and he demonstrated a better grasp of the strengths and weaknesses of those who worked in his department. Once Dr. Knab was finished with OSHA, he was able to fill in most of the blanks, giving the agents a solid foundation upon which to question others.

Even before the initial interviews were completed, several vehicles filled with a dozen more FBI agents arrived on base. The investigators were briefed and given instructions, which they began to carry out aggressively. It was barely lunchtime when an agent showed up at the make-shift control center with evidence.

"We found this material from the victim's suit in a plastic garbage liner at the bottom of a dumpster," he announced. Along with it were scraps of the material used to replace it. There was no obvious evidence that might identify who had discarded the items. So, the bag was sent to a lab for closer examination.

No one believed that the FBI was conducting a *routine* investigation. The number of agents and the pace of their activities made it obvious that something serious was afoot. The military personnel seemed to take the activity in stride, but much of the private security staff were noticeably nervous. Just before five o'clock, the Safeguard chief approached Dr. Gordman to explain there had been an accident in the Hindsight lab.

"One of my men noticed that the large monitor on Hindsight—the TV, not the special panel—was tilted oddly. While he was checking it out, someone opened the door and startled him. The screen crashed to the floor. I'm very sorry. We have already ordered a replacement. It should arrive tomorrow. Our company will foot the bill since it was our fault."

In a rare expression of empathy, Carl responded, "Don't worry about it. We can't use Hindsight right now anyway. Thanks for letting me know. I will tell maintenance to expect the replacement tomorrow. Everyone seems to be on edge with all this FBI stuff. I'm surprised that there haven't been more incidents."

As part of the investigation, several FBI teams were sent to the homes of people who had more than casual contact with Jonathan, including his fiancée, Trina. She had already left for his funeral, so authorities had to wait for a warrant before examining her residence.

Once in, agents conducted a thorough, quick sweep. They observed nothing to support their suspicions until they reached her bedroom.

"Look here, in the carpet." One agent called the other over. "These threads must have missed the wastebasket here." Barely noticeable were some sewing threads that were a visible match to the material used to sabotage Jonathan's suit. They were bagged and sent to the lab.

In the meantime, efforts to contact Trina continued. Oddly, she didn't answer her cell phone. It seemed to be turned off completely, giving no hint as to her whereabouts.

"She's on the run," an agent asserted.

"She's on her way to a funeral," Knab argued angrily. He knew his executive assistant was not involved in Jonathan's death. He wanted to berate the agent but bit his tongue instead.

"Where and when is this funeral?" the lead investigator asked.

"Carol can get you that information," Jacob answered and left in a huff.

* * *

David arrived home to find the Oats children playing with his son and Destiny talking with his wife. Katy got up and hugged him.

"What is going on? Why is this happening?" she pleaded for understanding. "First, Jonathan dies. Then, we hear he was murdered? And they think Trina did it?"

David glared at Destiny. All that information wasn't public knowledge yet. Darren must have told her, and she told Katy. Quick to deflect suspicion, Destiny explained her presence.

"Katy was suffering from morning sickness, all day. She finally called me at about two and asked if we could entertain Reese while she rested. Darren called me while I was here, and I guess she heard his side of the conversation."

David looked back at his wife. "Look, I don't know what's going on, but God does. And He is in control."

"I know. It just doesn't feel like it. Everything in our lives seems to be falling apart. Even your job, if Hindsight is shut down."

Again, David looked sternly at Destiny, who avoided eye contact. "We are going to get to the bottom of this. I'm sure there is an explanation that doesn't involve Trina killing anyone."

Katy released her hold on David to rub her tummy. She was beginning to show, and the stretching was itchy.

"We better run," Destiny said, gathering up her children. "If you're home, Darren must be too. I wonder why he hasn't called to ask where supper is."

Chapter 21 - Infiltration

While fairly sure they were on the right track in pursuing Trina as Jonathan's murderer, the FBI continued their efforts to uncover evidence both related and unrelated to her. They were nearly finished with their interviews and searches when word arrived that Trina was located.

She had indeed gone to Jonathan's hometown to attend his funeral. Authorities found her easily by tracking the use of her credit card. She seemed genuinely confused by the FBI agents' arrival at her motel and their urgent, even rude, insistence upon speaking with her just hours before her fiancé's funeral.

"Miss Benson, could you tell us the nature of your relationship with Jonathan Daniels?" the interrogator asked.

"He was my fiancé," Trina answered. "What is this about?"

"How was your relationship?"

"What?" Trina became indignant. "I don't know what your problem is, but I need to go bury the only man I've ever loved. The only ma…" Her voice cracked. She paused and took a deep breath, but she couldn't restrain the grief, and now anger, building inside. Suddenly, Trina fell onto the concrete sidewalk outside her motel door. The second agent caught her in time to avoid a full impact, but she still scraped her knees. She then slumped to the ground.

Trina didn't faint, but she seemed to be incapacitated by a nervous breakdown. The agents helped her inside, leaving the motel door open to avoid any appearance of impropriety. One agent filled a glass with water that she sipped while the other explained their visit and asked about the evidence they had found in her home.

"Wait—what? Are you saying Jonathan was murdered?" she asked, struggling to free her mind from its fog.

"It's looking that way. Can you explain these bits of thread we found in your bedroom?"

"You were in my bedroom?" She asked, still trying to absorb the shock of this news and the FBI's belief she was involved. " I don't know anything about threads. I don't even know how to sew."

When asked again, Trina stated with more clarity, "I have no idea where the threads you're talking about came from—especially ones that match Jonathan's protective suit." Then she added, "When that gear is not being worn, it is kept locked up by our security company."

"Why do you have your phone turned off?" the agent asked, still skeptical.

"My phone? Did you find my phone?" Trina asked.

"Not yet, but I'm sure we will unless you've discarded it," came the answer. "Where is it?"

"I thought you said you found it," Trina responded. "This is all very confusing. I know I laid my phone on the passenger seat while packing my car for this trip. But when I started to leave, I couldn't find it anywhere. I ran by Katy's to say goodbye. When I told her about losing my phone, she lent me hers for the trip."

"Katy?" the agent interrupted.

"Katy Hall. Her husband works…worked with Jonathan," she explained. Then she reached for her purse and pulled a smartphone from it. "She insisted I take it for the GPS and in case of an emergency."

As Trina's answers were relayed to the special agent in charge at the base, he began to suspect they had been sent on a wild goose chase. Never one to cut corners, he instructed his team to find Mrs. Hall and check out Trina's story. Then you told the agents with the suspect, "Take Ms. Benson to her fiancé's funeral. If she turns out to be innocent, I don't want to have kept her from that service."

* * *

After his interview, David wandered to the lab where Hindsight was stored. The revelation that his friend had likely been murdered weighed heavily on his mind. "I'm the one who told him I needed him here. If it wasn't for me, he would still be alive." David wanted desperately to be of some help in solving the crime, so he went where he and Jonathan spent so much time together—just to think.

The new hundred-inch monitor had been installed, the damaged one removed, and the area thoroughly cleaned. David sat in his usual chair and stared at the empty seat from whence Hindsight was controlled. He could imagine Jonathan sitting in his familiar setting. His gaze moved to other parts of the equipment, ending at the miracle screen itself. Even through tear-filled eyes, David noticed something peculiar.

"What the—" he stood quickly and hurried to the usually translucent panel. The color was virtually the same, but when he placed his hand behind the plate, it did not show through like normal. He touched, then tapped the front. He pulled out his cell phone to call the director.

"You need to come to the Hindsight room right away. Bring the FBI."

Soon Knab, Gordman, and several FBI agents joined David to examine the imposter screen. They pulled it out of its frame to reveal it to be aluminum, painted on both sides to look like the irreplaceable Hindsight part. Agent Maxwell called for the base to be locked down, and a search ensued for the genuine article.

All of the military personnel were called to duty. They and the paid security employees were sent to monitor the perimeter while looking for evidence that anyone had exited the base by scaling the fourteen-foot walls. Security video was reviewed only to discover that video from the room in question was missing. Adjacent hallway footage was gone as well. The FBI called for reinforcements while the ones already there worked hurriedly.

The ringing of Knab's cell phone startled him. He almost ignored it due to the chaos around him. The screen revealed that the caller was Darren Oats, so he answered. "Darren, where are you?" Jacob asked before Oats had a chance to announce himself.

"I'm behind the general store in town," he answered in a soft voice. "Something struck me funny about the security guys replacing the broken monitor next to Hindsight."

"I thought maintenance took care of that," the director interrupted.

"They should have." Darren continued. "I was with maintenance when they arrived to install it, but the security guys said that their captain told them to do it since it was their fault it was broken. When they hinted that we should leave, I became suspicious. You need to send the FBI over here. Behind the general store off Main Street."

"Yeah, I got that," Knab responded. He had already changed his phone to *speaker* so that the FBI agent with him could hear the conversation. The message was relayed to Maxwell, who sent two cars to the location. In the meantime, Oats continued his report.

"After my men and I left the lab, I watched for the security guys who chased us out. I figured they put the broken monitor in the box that the new one came in, but the two guys carrying it treated the box pretty carefully like it held more than a broken TV. I watched them put the box in the back of an SUV and head for the front gate. Since it was security guards who were doin' it, I didn't know who to tell. So, I followed them myself. They've been sitting back here for a couple of minutes now. Looks like they are waiting for someone."

Suddenly, there was a thud, then the phone went silent.

* * *

Jonathan's hometown in Iowa was a small, close-knit community. Many of the citizens were farmers or factory workers, so only the funeral home staff and presiding pastor wore suits. Everyone else, except the Jonathan's parents, Trina, and FBI agents dressed rather casually. Trina's arrival with the men sparked lots of whispers among attendees. The agents took seats in the back of the church while Trina made her way through the memorabilia that represented Jonathan's life.

The guest book at the front gave Trina pause. She glanced over the list of names above the blank space intended for her information. The book only asked for name and address. She couldn't help but think that she would end up as forgotten as her signature would soon be. There were lots of childhood pictures, Sunday school perfect attendance pins, sport trophies, and Boy Scout badges. A laptop on a separate table played a loop of pictures and short videos of Jonathan's high school and college years. There was virtually nothing from his time at Sycra or Hindsight except for a newspaper clipping about his death.

Jonathan's funeral service was short and sweet. Even though her fiancé hadn't lived there since he left for college, many folks regaled Trina with tales of the boy she never got to marry. Some stories made her laugh and some made her cry. All of them made her miss him all the more.

By the end of the graveside service, the FBI had confirmed Trina's story and determined she was no longer a suspect in Jonathan's death. The agents with her offered to escort her back to the base, but she declined. She decided to stay another day before heading back.

* * *

Meanwhile, Darren's condition was of great concern. Knab kept hoping to reconnect with his employee. "Hello? Darren, are you there?" Jacob asked. After several minutes, there was still no answer. Finally, the connection ended completely. Knab looked at the agent nervously. While two FBI teams headed for the rendezvous, another pair questioned guards at the front gate.

"Sure, Bruce came by here with another security guy I don't know. He said he had a broken monitor that couldn't be thrown in the trash. He was headed to take it someplace that recycles." The sergeant at the gate confirmed. "That was about twenty minutes ago. Just before the lock-down order." That's when reality set in. "Oh no! Are they who you're looking for?"

"Maybe," the agent responded. "We are just following leads."

"Oh, he was smooth," the soldier declared. "He even asked if I needed to look inside the box."

"Did you?"

The sergeant's closed eyes and bowed head provided the answer.

* * *

The two FBI teams sent to the general store were informed of Darren's sudden "radio silence." They approached the location from different directions. The first one arrived just in time to see the SUV speed off. They pursued, calling for assistance.

The ensuing car chase was hardly worthy of a Hollywood movie. The small town did not provide many obstacles or opportunities for fancy driving. Traffic was almost non-existent. When unaided escape seemed unlikely, a passenger in the SUV aimed a gun at the pursuing FBI sedan. Bullets hit the windshield, causing the sedan's driver to veer off course and crash into cars parked at the general store. The other FBI vehicle soon appeared and approached to check on their partners. The team in the damaged vehicle motioned for them to continue the chase.

It wasn't long before two police cars and three more FBI vehicles were on the search, but the suspects had disappeared. Special Agent Jones called for helicopter surveillance but was informed it would be almost an hour before it arrived. For the time being, he put out a BOLO. All the local police took to the highways, and the FBI patrolled the downtown area looking for possible hiding places.

While patrolling, agents found Darren Oats's car. It was empty except for his cell phone on the floorboard. He was discovered unconscious, inside a nearby dumpster. A blow to the head had incapacitated him, but he regained consciousness on the way to the hospital.

* * *

"There sure are a lot of black cars racing around today," Destiny told Katy over the phone. "Do you know anything about that?"

"Not a clue," Katy answered.

"I tried to call Darren several times, but I just kept getting his voicemail. I'm so tired of him ignoring me. Oops, I've got another call. I'll call you right back."

Katy wanted to call David to see if he could satisfy their curiosity, but she didn't want to tie up the line, knowing Destiny should call back soon. Sure enough, within minutes, her phone rang. It was Destiny.

"Oh my, Darren's in the hospital!" the frazzled woman announced.

"What happened?"

"I don't know, but I've got to go."

"I'll meet you there."

* * *

It didn't take long to find the few places a getaway car could be hidden in town, and to begin searching them. It was the third garage door checked that stirred the hornets' nest. While agents heard nothing inside before lifting the rollup door, once it was in motion, an engine roared and shots rang out. Not waiting long enough to clear the rising door, a car lurched forward, the bottom of the door striking the windshield and scraping the top of the vehicle.

Two agents were winged during the encounter, and the rest pursued their target. The thieves were worse off than earlier since more law enforcement was now involved. Weapons were held out both back windows, and a flurry of bullets flew haphazardly toward pursuers. Soon the guns were back inside

161

the car for reloading. Before they could reemerge, the suspects' vehicle was rammed on the driver's side by another FBI car.

The scene of multiple law enforcement personnel surrounding the disabled SUV (with weapons aimed) looked like a scene out of a television police drama. The local sheriff's deputy who had joined in the car chase remained at his patrol car, some distance away, while federal agents approached the disabled vehicle.

"FBI! Show me your hands."

Windows lowered slowly, and a pair of hands emerged from all four. Agents opened the doors before instructing the occupants to exit.

"On the ground, face first."

Two of the men were Safeguard employees. A third was a stranger who spoke angrily in Chinese to the fourth Asian—Carson Trout, Hindsight's successful salesman. Several weapons were found in the vehicle.

"There is a box in the back," one of the agents observed.

"Looks like a broken TV," an examining agent stated. "Wait. There's something wrapped up in here too." The essential Hindsight part was retrieved from the surrounding pieces of the broken monitor. The thieves were taken into FBI custody, and the rest of the non-military security personnel were confined until they could be vetted.

Carson wouldn't talk, but one of his partners agreed to help as part of a plea deal. Trout was a Chinese spy sent to determine if the rumored Hindsight project was legitimate. Once its existence and value were confirmed, he was tasked with stealing it for the Chinese communist government.

His "cover" was thoroughly developed so that any security check would likely turn up nothing of concern. While most of his clients had nothing to do with the scheme, they were groomed by the communists to ensure Carson would be successful in his salesman function. All the while, the spy was looking for a way to steal the meteoric metal, if not the entire Hindsight ensemble.

After gaining the director's trust, Carson was able to position other spies on base through the security company he recommended to Dr. Knab. While many of Safeguard's employees were innocent bystanders, almost one third were part of the Chinese plan. The company was a well-established and cleverly concealed front for spies.

The theft was intended to take place on the India trip. All the arrangements had been made, but Jonathan's untimely death caused the trip to be canceled. With Trout's superiors growing impatient, the spy decided to improvise.

Further investigation revealed that Jonathan's gear had been tampered with after he was afflicted by radiation poisoning. His suit had failed due to frequent radiation exposure, but Carson determined that he needed a distraction to aid him in absconding with his intended treasure. So, he framed Trina for Jonathan's supposed murder. He disabled and hid her phone while she packed, so no one could contact her while she traveled. He knew this would make her appear to be on the run.

* * *

Destiny and Katy, along with their children, sat impatiently in the emergency waiting room. They were relieved to receive word early on that Darren's injury was not life-threatening, and his condition was stable. While they waited for more information, Katy prayed with the Oats family. "Father, it sounds like Darren was not seriously injured. We thank you for that. I ask that you give him a full recovery and Destiny and the kids peace of mind. If you would use this incident to reveal yourself to them, I'm sure you would get the glory for working in their lives. I ask this in Jesus' name, amen."

Other family and friends were anxious to greet Darren after a medical examination determined he should make a full recovery. Conspicuously absent from the well-wishers at the hospital was Carol Castle. After driving to the medical facility, she just sat in her car for several minutes. After a deep breath and a rare prayer, she opened the car door. She barely had both feet on the ground when FBI officers accosted her.

"Ms. Castle? I'm Special Agent Maxwell with the FBI. We need to ask you some questions."

Carol sighed and nodded. Then she sank back down into the driver's seat, keeping her feet on the pavement. She folded her hands in her lap and patiently answered every question she could about Carson Trout and her relationship with him. While she did, anger built inside her, anger at herself for being duped, anger at the FBI for asking repetitive questions, but mostly anger at the man who used her to accomplish his evil mission.

It was apparent that unfriendly nations had more interest in Hindsight than anyone realized. It was time, once again, to beef up security. With Safeguard out of the picture, the base was secured by an unusually large contingent of the United States military.

As time went on, more pieces fell into place. For example, training on new security equipment and procedures was intentionally designed to confuse and frustrate previous military police. This opened the door for Safeguard staffing. The equipment itself was easily manipulated so that spies could move about relatively freely without leaving a record of their whereabouts.

All the new security equipment was dismantled, examined, and destroyed to make sure that no enemy state could somehow benefit from it. Basic cameras and motion sensors were installed. The base was considered secure in a matter of weeks, with the expectation that new high-tech gadgets would be researched and purchased over time.

Chapter 22 - Scapegoat

Trina arrived back at the base well after the excitement abated. Jonathan's memorial service was postponed yet again to allow everyone time to catch their breath after the theft attempt. Darren was out of the hospital after a one-night stay for observation. The FBI wrapped up its investigation and headed to Washington to report on the findings and to build legal cases against the Chinese spies and their coconspirators.

Everyone hoped that things could get back to normal, or at least, a new normal. Surely, the worst was over.

* * *

Darren Oats spent a few days resting at home. His wife doted over him for two reasons. First, that's just the way she was, always looking for a way to help. And second, because her husband had been right about Carson Trout. She knew he would lord it over her if she didn't eat a little humble pie.

"I told you he was no good, didn't I?" Darren would say, shaking his head with the chin prominently protruding. "I can read people like a book, uh-huh."

"You were right, sweetie," Destiny would usually respond. Finally, when the pie plate was empty, she added, "And it's a good thing you have such a hard skull. So, when he snuck up on you and kung-fu'd your head, it didn't do no damage."

That's when Darren knew he had milked it for all he could at home. It was time to go back to work. There, he thought he might find sympathetic ears and more gracious tongues. Still, he was surprised at just how complimentary everyone was. He relished the role of being a hero, even if just for a couple of weeks.

The stolen Hindsight panel was not returned immediately. It had to be processed by law enforcement. When it did arrive back at the base, it did so with much celebration. Unfortunately, unwrapping it revealed that one of the corners was damaged. The missing section was a triangle that measured less than two inches long on each of the two shortest sides. The panel's frame was large enough to hide the missing corner. So, once it was in place, the damage was unnoticeable.

"It says here that the item was recovered in this damaged condition," Darren said after reading the packing slip from the FBI.

"Yes, someone called me about that," Dr. Knab stated. "The missing piece was never found. Further examination showed that the piece had not been broken off accidentally. It was carefully cut out. Since the frame hides the corners, there was no way of determining when the metal was vandalized."

"We assume it was during the theft, but we don't honestly know," Carl added.

Fortunately, the screen had not been damaged otherwise. The thieves were very careful to protect it. It even escaped the crash unscathed. Hindsight would soon be operational again. Senior staff met to discuss the next steps they should take. The director informed his team that the India trip was canceled.

"We've been informed that Trout, or whatever his name is, planned to steal Hindsight while in India. Since we don't have any way of knowing who his accomplices there might be, I've decided to avoid the trip altogether."

"That's logical," Carl agreed.

"What about the big project?" David asked.

"We still want to do that," Knab answered. "But we will have to put it off for a little while. We need to beef up our security personnel and protocols before taking our baby on the road again."

David leaned forward in his chair, "Are there any other changes we should know about at this time?"

Jacob leaned back in his. "There are. After briefing Washington on our situation, I received some ultimatums that require difficult decisions. I'm letting Carol go."

"Really?" David exclaimed. He didn't ask why because the reason was obvious. It was still a disappointment. He felt bad for Carol, who had already suffered the indignation of being used as a stooge. Now she would lose her job, to boot.

Carl thought it through, out loud. "Carol was our original contact with Mr. Trout, but she's not suspected of being a spy too, is she?"

"No, she's been cleared," Jacob answered.

"You are the one who hired him. He passed your background check." Carl continued. "He weaseled his way into your good graces. You are the one he talked into hiring the Safeguard company, and the security equip—."

"Okay, got it," Knab responded gruffly.

David was surprised at how critical Dr. Gordman was of their boss, and how blatantly he attacked him. He wasn't surprised that the meeting came to an abrupt end.

"Well, that's all for now, David," he said. "Carl, I need you to stay a minute."

Hall left, expecting that Carl was about to get an earful. Since there wasn't anything pressing at work, David went home to play with his son before taking his wife on a date. He arrived to find that Reese wasn't home from preschool yet. That gave him some quiet time to think—and pray.

When Katy arrived with their son, David heard all about school while Mom got ready. Trina frequently asked to babysit ever since she returned from the funeral. The Halls were hesitant to take her up on her offer until she assured them that the distraction was welcomed.

It was always easier to focus on family when the project was at a standstill, but David was determined to keep a proper balance, even if Hindsight got back into high gear. He planned for the couple to start dating again. She was still experiencing odd cravings, so some of her meal choices were entertaining in and of themselves.

* * *

Back in Knab's office, Carl remained in his chair as Jacob stepped out from behind his desk to sit in the recently emptied seat. Gordman wasn't good at deciphering emotional cues, but Jacob's obvious uneasiness was easy for Carl to recognize. Knab folded his hands as he planted his elbows near his knees. He faced down for a moment but looked his friend in the eye before saying a word.

"Carl, I have to let you go too," Jacob revealed. "I'm sorry."

"What? No! What for?" Carl demanded.

"Heads need to roll. It's all political, but I've got to prove that I'm taking the recent problems seriously," the director explained. "We've had a plane shot down, an employee die of radiation poisoning, a spy almost steal the rarest item on the planet, and unexplained vandalism to the screen."

Carl looked confused about the last item.

"The missing corner," Knab clarified.

"What does any of that have to do with me?" Gordman complained, standing. "Hall was in charge in Israel. I wasn't even there. My people regularly test the protective suits. We gave Daniels a new one that he hadn't started wearing yet. I had nothing to do with hiring the spy. In fact, I didn't even like him. And the corner missing from the plate isn't even noticeable when it is in its frame—which is always."

Jacob remained seated to deescalate the situation. He rarely saw Carl worked up so much. He tried to reassure him, "I'm not blaming you. I know it's not your fault. Washington wants a fall guy so they can save face. We've done all the research and development necessary. I need Michaels to run operations. That's why it has to be you. Understand?"

"No!" Gordman looked at his ex-best friend in unbelief. Gradually, something became clear. "You have to fire me to save your own job, don't you?"

Jacob bowed his head. "Yeah," he said softly. Then he stood to meet Carl's gaze. "Yes, if I don't make some changes, I'll be replaced."

"By me?" Carl asked. For a moment, he considered what it might be like to run the entire operation.

"Is that what you want, Carl?" Jacob asked. Finally, Gordman relaxed a bit. It didn't take long for him to realize he wouldn't last a month as the director, and he would hate it the whole time.

"No, no I don't," Carl answered calmly. "I'll go pack my things."

"Don't hurry, my friend. It's not like security is escorting you out today."

"No perp walk?" Gordman asked with a smile.

Jacob couldn't believe his odd friend even knew what that meant, let alone make a joke, however misapplied, about it. "No, buddy. No perp walk." He put his arm around the man responsible for much of his success. Carl wasn't one for physical contact, but he offered a tentative hug in return. The famed scientist slowly made his way to one of the labs. He didn't want to be by himself at home. Somehow, being in the lab, he didn't feel alone—even when he was.

Since Dr. Gordman came to accept his fate quite gallantly, Dr. Knab decided to throw him a going-away party, of sorts. The plan was to make Carl's departure seem like his idea. It should be easy to convince others that the scientist longed for his next challenge. Knab's wife, Kathleen, along with Destiny Oats, put together a reception that included simple decorations and light refreshments.

The sad goodbye took place in the gym just two days later. Someone suggested opening the mic up to anyone who had a story to tell about Dr. Gordman. David could visualize that going badly—and fast. So, that idea was nixed in exchange for one safe testimonial. Dr. Knab took the stage and the mic.

"No one means more to this project than Dr. Carl Gordman—no one. Nobody has done more for this project. No one is more indispensable. And yet, he is leaving us. We mere mortals can't imagine what he would leave us for. We naturally think that Hindsight must surely be the pinnacle of his illustrious career. But when the history books are written, I imagine this will be just one of many ground-breaking, earth-shattering discoveries and breakthroughs that he will be known for. We will miss you, my friend. More than you could ever know."

Carl put on a brave face as well-wishers said their goodbyes. Nobody could imagine Hindsight without him. Most of them said so. Once the refreshments were consumed, the crowd dwindled. Despite being the focus of the evening, Carl was soon sitting alone, as usual. Stragglers left when it became apparent they might be asked to help clean up.

"What is Dr. Gordman going to do?" Katy asked. "I never have heard."

"You know, I haven't heard either," Destiny said.

"It's probably something top secret," Kathleen proposed. "Otherwise, someone would have said."

Even Knab's wife wasn't privy to the reason behind Carl's leaving. Jacob was too ashamed of his selfish decision to admit it, even to her. Chit-chat transitioned to other subjects as the men and women (mostly women) finished cleaning up.

Jacob approached Carl. "You did good. You gonna come by and get your stuff tomorrow?"

"Yes, if that is alright," the emotionally drained guest of honor replied. "I've already got most everything together for inspection." He understood that anything he planned to take out of the building would be searched thoroughly.

By ten o'clock, everyone had left the building.

* * *

"The only constant is change," David mumbled as he slipped into bed.

"Will you miss him?" Katy asked.

"Sure, but the truth is, there's nothing more for him to do here." David answered. "It's no wonder he wants to leave. He's probably been bored for months. Still, it will be weird without him. Seems like everything's been turned on its head."

"Will you have to do more as the only assistant director?" she wondered out loud.

"Nope. I've already warned Dr. Knab that my plate is full," he replied. "He agreed."

* * *

The next morning, two MPs met Dr. Gordman at the front door. He pulled his loaded car into his regular parking spot instead of closer to the building as security suggested. Since his home was furnished by Hindsight, he didn't have much except clothes and books to pack. There wasn't too much in his office or labs that belonged to him either. So, it didn't take long for security to rummage through the few boxes.

After passing them through a metal detector, the MPs helped carry the boxes to his car. Jacob was there to see him off, so Carl stopped to speak with him.

"Do you know what you will do next?" Jacob asked, concerned for his friend's well-being.

"Not yet," Carl replied.

"You're going to be all right," Jacob said reassuringly. But Carl took it as a question.

"I guess so." As the scientist started toward his car, he realized he was still wearing a company lab coat. He turned around and started to remove it. "This is yours," he called to Knab.

"Keep it," Jacob offered.

Carl threw it back onto his shoulders and ran his hand along his name embroidered on the breast. He walked slowly to the parking lot, meeting the helpful MPs on their way back. Gordman got into his car and took one last look at the old military structure. Then he looked at Jacob, who waved. Carl feigned a slight smile and drove away.

Chapter 23 - Dilemma

"After recent heartbreaking news and disturbing events, I'm sure you are ready for things to get back to normal." Dr. Knab was addressing all the project employees in the gym. "This has been the most difficult two weeks of my life. I know some of you feel the same way.

"There will be, no doubt, more changes in the days ahead, but nothing as drastic as what we've just been through. Before we press on, however, I want to encourage you to return here this afternoon for Jonathan Daniels's memorial service. It is way overdue.

"Many of you have asked about our plans to record the geographical history of our planet's continents. That is, in fact, our next project. Dates for each trip are now available. There have been some adjustments. Stop by and see my new assistant, Marjorie Leary, today or tomorrow and sign up, if you haven't already. If you have, make sure you can work with any date changes we've made and confirm your plans. See you this afternoon."

Hall hurried to catch the director as he left the gym. "You got a minute?" Jacob looked at his watch. "It's important," David insisted. The men made their way to Knab's office, waving off would-be interruptions on the way. Hall followed Knab in and closed the door. Jacob went to his safe place, the chair behind his desk.

"There's something I think you need to be aware of before our next job," David began. Jacob waited. "Jonathan told me that he once ran Hindsight back fifty-thousand years and more."

"Without authorization?" Knab's eyebrows raised in surprise, then lowered in displeasure.

"Yes, well, uh…I wanted you to be prepared for a possible problem with our geological project," David continued. "When he tried looking back that far in time, nothing showed up."

"Nothing? What do you mean, nothing?" Jacob's face now expressed confusion. "Did you see it?"

"No, he just told me about it." David wiped some involuntary saliva from his mouth. "It's possible that when we try to record what the planet looked like a million years ago, there will be no image."

"Do the X-ray frequencies not work that far back?" Knab asked.

"I don't know. That's possible. We never tried to calibrate for more than a few thousand years past," David reminded his boss. "Not officially, anyway. As far as I know, he just tried once, and got interrupted before he could determine the furthest back in time that would display an image."

"Are you saying we should scuttle the project?" Jacob asked.

"Not at all," his assistant answered. "I just want you to be aware. I thought it unfair not to warn you."

"It's got to be a glitch, right?"

"That....or..." David struggled to suggest his preferred option. "Or the earth is not as old as the general scientific community believes." Before Jacob could respond, Hall finished his thought. "Some of...some people believe that the Bible account of Creation presents an accurate timeline. If so, the earth is just a few thousand years old."

Jacob laughed before realizing David was serious. The assistant director continued.

"I'm just suggesting we run tests to make sure Hindsight performs as you want it to. I'm not sure why we never have before. I suggested it to Dr. Gordman, but he never approved it."

Jacob crossed his arms. "Are you really one of those people who think the earth is young and flat?"

"Not flat," he answered, "Just young."

"Look, David, I've been happy with how you've kept religion from affecting your work here." Knab complimented. "Let's not mess that up now."

"I'm not," he insisted. "I'm just letting you know what Jonathan told me." David excused himself, wishing he hadn't said anything about the young earth theory.

Two hours later, Hall received a text from his boss. It read, "Something came up. Can't be at the memorial. You cover it."

* * *

What came up was an impromptu meeting with Beth Auger, the newly promoted Hindsight operator. She was instructed to meet the director in the lab where Hindsight was stored and tested.

"I would like you to show me how to operate Hindsight," Jacob requested.

"Of course, Dr. Knab," she answered. "But I'm training two others to do it."

"That's fine, but I'm tired of being asked questions that I don't know the answer to. So, I'm trying to familiarize myself with practical information to save myself some embarrassment."

They quickly donned protective suits, and Beth gave the director a crash course. Jonathan had made operating Hindsight pretty easy; setting a date and pushing a couple of buttons was all it took. Beth explained that operating the platform to control pitch, roll, and yaw was more difficult.

Knab cut short the training session after learning the basics. "Let's save the hard stuff for later."

Beth looked at the time while checking her phone for messages. "Oh, no! We are late for Jonathan's memorial service."

Jacob grabbed her arm gently. "I'd appreciate it if we kept this tutoring session to ourselves. I don't want smart-aleck employees razzing me."

When they arrived at the gym, Jacob paused so that Beth entered a couple of minutes ahead of him. Once inside, the director followed the flow of friends as they made their way around the memorabilia placed on several tables. When he sat next to his wife, David approached.

"You made it after all, good."

"I didn't want to miss it entirely, but I can't stay," Knab stated. Kathleen frowned at him. "I have some important calls to make," he explained.

"They can't wait for half an hour?" she asked, clearly perturbed. He just got up, shrugged his shoulders, and left.

Several people shared their favorite memories of Jonathan. Trina sat in the front, frequently dabbing tears from her eyes. She chose not to speak, but she enjoyed hearing how much respect her fiancé had garnered from his co-workers. It humbled her a bit to think that such a wonderful man wanted to spend the rest of his life with her.

It was common knowledge that Trina was not staying much longer at Hindsight. She couldn't bring herself to keep working at a place that stirred up so many emotional memories. And Trina couldn't ignore that Hindsight was the cause of Jonathan's death. It would be nearly impossible to work under those conditions.

* * *

"That was a nice service for Jonathan," Katy commented while brushing her hair. "Too bad there wasn't more made of his faith."

David nodded as he tossed the blanket back to get into bed. "It was appropriate for the venue, I guess. I know he had a positive impact on several people, but I suppose they didn't want to speak about spiritual things and risk being labeled."

"What do you mean? I didn't think you two got much grief for being Christians."

"Not too much," David answered. "That doesn't mean people don't think we are nuts. Most scientists at work think that belief in God is superstitious. The rest of the staff don't want to look foolish to their superiors, so they tow the 'science trumps religion' line."

Katy joined her husband in bed. "You know what would be cool?" She asked, eager to share her thought. "What if you took Hindsight back to Israel and recorded some events detailed in the Bible?"

"Jonathan and I talked about that more than once," David said with a sigh. "We even tried to figure out a way to approach Dr. Knab with doing just that."

"What did he say?"

"Knab? We never asked. I chickened out."

"If you could, what would you want to see?" Katy asked.

"I don't know. It would have to be something we knew the exact location and timing of."

"What about the crucifixion?"

David thought for a moment. "I don't think I would want to observe that. It seems kind of sacrilegious, not to mention heart wrenching. What about you?"

"Oh, just about anything from the Bible would be neat to see," Katy answered. "David and Goliath, Elisha with the prophets of Baal, and the battle of Jericho come to mind. I think, if I could only witness one event, I would like to see the birth of Jesus."

"That might ruin all the church Christmas programs we've seen," David joked. "But I agree that it should be near the top of the list. I think my number one choice would be the resurrection."

"That would be awesome," Katy agreed. "Do you think there will ever be a chance we see that?"

"Who knows. If Hindsight proves that the Bible account of creation is correct, there will be a clamor to check out other biblical events that even hardened scientists won't be able to resist."

David kissed his wife, rolled over to turn off his bedside lamp, and closed his eyes. "I should have at least asked Jacob to let us record something extra when we were in Israel," he mumbled. "I owed Jonathan that much."

* * *

"Are you sure you don't want me to stay, Dr. Knab?" Beth Auger asked the director. This was Jacob's second exposure to the equipment. The new lead technician found it strange that the director wanted to learn how to run Hindsight; even stranger that he wanted to be alone.

"Yes, I'll be fine," Jacob answered without giving a reason for wanting privacy.

"We haven't gone over how to change angles," she warned.

"I don't need to adjust the pitch or anything. I'm just going to run it in its current position," he promised. "Now, this is set to change by five-hundred-years every thirty seconds, right?"

Beth checked the instrument to be sure. "Yes, you are good to go. I'll be back in twenty minutes."

"That will be fine." Knab answered, and waited until Beth left before beginning the sequence she had programmed into the Hindsight computer. He had no idea David Hall was just outside the lab.

"What do you mean, I can't go inside?" David asked the security guard at the lab entrance. "Is someone operating the equipment?"

"I'm sorry, sir. I'm under strict orders not to disclose that information."

Just then, Beth stepped out. When she saw Hall, she instinctively used her body to block any view inside the lab as the door closed behind her.

"What's going on, Beth?" David asked.

"What do you mean?"

"This guard won't let me in. Were you in there alone?" Beth hesitated to answer. "Oh, I'm sorry. I forgot, with your promotion, you have full access to the lab."

Beth was relieved she didn't have to answer about being in the lab alone. "Yes, sir. Is there anything else?"

"Have you seen Dr. Knab?" he asked. "Marjorie wasn't sure where he was, but remembered he called you this morning."

"He did come to see me," Beth answered, then added, "About a personal matter." She wanted desperately to avoid lying to her boss, but was afraid his superior's demand for secrecy might require it. "Are you sure he is even in the building?"

"Marjorie checked the log and said he hadn't left. Of course, by now, he might have."

David turned to leave, then thought of another question. He turned back and looked Beth in the eyes. "Why wouldn't security allow me into the lab?" He looked at the guilty guard, who just stared straight ahead.

Beth didn't want to throw the guard under the bus, so she tried to downplay the situation. "He must have misunderstood my instructions. I simply didn't want to be distracted by any visitors. He didn't realize that you can go into the lab any time you wish. I was probably too adamant. That's my fault."

David nodded, satisfied with the answer, and again turned to leave. He didn't see Beth mouth a silent "I'm sorry" to the guard, who smiled and shrugged his shoulders. As David started down the hallway, Beth followed. Hall stopped, causing Beth to bump into him.

"Oh, I'm sorry," she said, a bit flustered.

"My fault," David answered. "I just thought, since I'm here, I should have you demonstrate your progress in operating Hindsight's mobility."

"Umm, I've got something I need to do," she answered unconvincingly. Beth knew that if Hall insisted on going into the lab, the gig was up.

"You go ahead and do what you need to," David said. "I'll wait for you in the lab."

Beth gently took hold of David's arm to stop him, then immediately let go. "Mr. Hall, I hate being put in the middle of whatever is going on here, but Dr. Knab is in the lab and doesn't want anyone in there with him. I don't know how much I should say, but he told me he just wanted to understand Hindsight better. He didn't want anyone to know I was training him."

"I see," David answered. "I appreciate the awkward position this put you in. Thank you for telling me. I won't let on to him that I know." With that, Hall returned to his office.

* * *

Later that day, Knab confronted Hall in the break room. "Marjorie says you're not signed up for this trip."

"I told you I needed to stay home in case Katy delivers early," David reminded his boss. "Her doctor says that's a real possibility."

"I don't remember that conversation. I need you on this trip." When David resisted again, the usually mild-mannered leader lost his cool and threatened to fire David.

David wouldn't back down. "I'm sorry, but I can't. Katy is more important than this project...or my job."

Jacob stormed off, leaving several witnesses aghast in his wake.

* * *

"I can't believe how prevalent this cult is," Jacob exclaimed. He was researching the young earth theory from his home computer.

"What's that, dear?" Kathleen asked.

"I found out that David Hall is not just a Christian. He's part of a fringe group that believes the earth is only a few thousand years old."

"That's bizarre," his wife said. "Is that new, or has he always believed that?"

"I don't know," Jacob answered. "I get the impression he has always believed it. He says that's how the Bible describes creation."

"Is it affecting his work?" Kathleen asked. "I mean, does it really matter?"

"It might. I'm afraid that Hindsight has been compromised."

"What do you mean?" his wife asked.

Jacob explained, "Hindsight doesn't show any images older than seven thousand years. At first, I thought the meteoric window just didn't work any further back. Now, I'm convinced the programming has been tampered with to confirm that the earth is young. Only David or Jonathan would have done that."

Kathleen sought clarification. "Jonathan Daniels?"

"Yes. Maybe that's why he died. He spent too much time with Hindsight, tampering with the programming."

"That just seems so out of character for him…for them," she stated.

"Blind faith can lead you to do almost anything," he said. "They might rather hide the truth than let Hindsight prove that their faith was based on a lie."

"That's so sad," Kathleen said. "Katy is so sweet. I'd hate to think she has been blinded by that thinking too. I remember telling some ladies about Ginger's miscarriage at the last Christmas party."

"Our daughter Ginger? I didn't know she was even pregnant."

Kathleen combined a sigh with a huff. "I told you. Don't you remember?"

He didn't, but chose to tell a white lie. "Oh, yeah, vaguely."

"Anyway, Katy offered to pray for her. I didn't know she meant right then. We just bowed our heads, and she prayed like she was talking to a God she really knew. It was…calming. I never heard anyone pray like that in my four years at Catholic school."

"I don't doubt their sincerity," Jacob said. "But you can be sincerely wrong. Anyway, I've got to deal with this in as discreet a way as possible. I have to find the truth."

Chapter 24 - Déjà Vu

Dr. Knab called The Sycra Foundation and obtained permission to make an offer to their best programmer. He needed someone who could find and correct any bugs in Hindsight's computer code. After almost a minute of waiting on hold, there was a click on the phone line, followed by a woman's voice.

"This is Marty."

Jacob was disappointed that the wrong Marty was on the line. "I'm calling for Marty Rollins," he said.

"This is Marty Rollins." When Jacob didn't immediately respond, she asked, "You were expecting a man, weren't you?"

"I'm sorry. No, I was just distracted." Knab's answer was unconvincing, and he knew it. So, he tried to move on. "I've been told you are the best programmer at Sycra."

"What can I do for you?" the woman asked bluntly.

"I have a delicate situation. Do you know anything about the Hindsight project?" Jacob asked.

"Not much. I know that the man I replaced worked on your project. He died recently, didn't he?"

"Yes, that was Jonathan Daniels," Knab stated. "We think there is a problem with his coding."

"That would surprise me," Marty said. "Everything he did here was top notch."

"Well, it's possible somebody messed with his code." Jacob explained, "The reason for my call is to ask you to come check it out for bugs or viruses or whatever might make it function improperly."

"My boss told me he's agreed to lend me to you, short term. Your offer is quite generous. I'd be happy to look over it remotely in my spare time."

"I'm afraid I need you on site. I don't want to have the code floating around the internet," said Knab.

"I'm tied to a project here right now. I can't leave for two weeks."

Jacob thought for a moment. "Just a second." He looked at his calendar. "Would you be interested in joining me in Israel at that time?"

"Sure, as long as you foot the bill."

"Oh, we will. Give me your email address so we can communicate that way from now on."

The director's plan would fall into place if his next call was as successful. This one was to one of Hindsight's beneficiaries, Gavi Braum. It took three attempts to get the multi-millionaire on the line.

"Director Knab, a pleasure to speak with you," came Braum's greeting.

"You, as well."

"What can I do for you, my friend?" Gavi asked.

"I was wondering if you ever acquired the buildings you needed to tear down, in order to view the inside of Solomon's Temple with Hindsight."

"No, I'm afraid not." Gavi answered, disappointment in his voice. "Why do you ask?"

"Well, I have a proposition for you. I need a favor, and I was going to put you at the top of our list if you can help me."

"I'm listening," the interested Jew answered.

"I need to talk to you face to face about the details, but in general..."

* * *

The next morning, Dr. Knab met with several key employees.

"I've decided to record the Asian continent first," Jacob announced to the confused gathering.

"But why?" Darren asked, bewildered.

"That's going to require a lot of changes," the new administrative assistant commented. "We just got confirmations for our previous adjustments."

"What's going on...sir?" David asked. "Won't that put us right where China wants us?"

"I got to thinking. The Chinese want to steal Hindsight, right? So, I figured, if we do their continent first, they won't have as much time to make a plan and try again. If we do it later, it gives them more time to figure something out."

"Makes sense...I guess," Oats reluctantly agreed.

"Okay," David interjected, "we need to start making arrangements."

"I'll take care of it," Knab offered. "I want to start over the Mediterranean Sea. So, I'm going to Israel personally, and make arrangements.

"Is Israel in Asia?" Marjorie asked sheepishly. As the director's new executive assistant, she felt like she should know the answer.

"Technically, on the far western side," David answered.

As they left the meeting, Darren questioned David, "Why would he start on the west side of Asia if he wants to surprise China? Won't that just telegraph our intentions?"

Hall answered simply, "I don't know. None of this makes sense. All these changes are bound to increase our costs significantly. Dr. Knab has never been careless with money."

Jacob left for Israel alone, leaving David and Marjorie to field questions they couldn't answer. Nevertheless, plans were made and employees were told about the changes. Schedules were adjusted, and the first group of project witnesses was eagerly, if not cautiously, anticipating their trip. Counting family members, there were only seventeen in this first group, besides the actual work team and security forces.

* * *

In Israel, Jacob met with Gavi Braum, who was eager to help. "I've secured a hangar at a small airport not far from here," Gavi told the director. "Your programmer can work there and stay in a nice hotel nearby."

"Excellent," Jacob said. "I really appreciate the help."

"If you don't mind me asking, what is this all about? You didn't say much on the phone."

Knab was hesitant to explain, but decided his benefactor deserved to know. Before going into detail, he thought he'd better ask, "Are you a religious man?"

"I respect the Torah, even if I don't wholeheartedly follow it," came the cushioned answer.

"Do you believe the earth is millions of years old?" Knab asked directly.

"Of course."

"Well, someone has messed with my machine, and made it appear that the earth is only a few thousand years old," Jacob explained.

Braum laughed. "Wouldn't that cause a paradigm shift in the scientific community!"

"Exactly," Jacob agreed. "I need an outsider to find the corrupt coding and correct it before we do a geological project that's planned. My programmer needs time to work. What I couldn't tell you on the phone is that I need an event or threat that will cause the government to shut down the airport for a little while."

"You want a terrorist attack?" Gavi questioned.

"No, nothing serious. Just some leaked intel or other reason for the government to act out of caution." The director began to opine. "Hindsight may well be man's greatest discovery. Even if we are never able to build more machines, in a few decades, we will have recorded countless historical events and objects. Soon, perfectly recorded history will be commonplace. It will be a whole new world."

"Don't move too fast," Gavi protested in jest. "My video of Solomon's Temple is bringing in lots of money from people eager to see it. I hear the same is true of the Greek Wonders. We don't want too much competition so soon."

Jacob smiled. "Someday, there will be so much recorded history, that it will be in the public domain—and free." Gavi smiled back, but it seemed forced.

"I can't help personally, of course," Braum said. "However, I think I can put you in contact with the right people. They will require payment in advance."

"No doubt," Jacob answered. "I came prepared."

A clandestine meeting was arranged, instructions given, and payment made. Jacob returned home satisfied that the attack on Hindsight's integrity would soon be thwarted.

* * *

"Are you sure it's wise to have our staging area in the same country where our first Hindsight was destroyed?" several concerned employees asked the director upon his return.

"Israel is the safest country on the planet," Jacob insisted. "I've been assured nothing will happen. The government is eager to save face after our loss. If anything, they will be overprotective."

Hindsight was sent several days early, ostensibly to make necessary arrangements for using it on the new high-altitude airship that the team rented. The real reason was so the Sycra programmer could begin examining computer code. Jacob's plan was in place for Gavi's security detail to guard Hindsight while Marty worked in secret. Knab didn't want anyone from Hindsight involved, in case the conspiracy was larger than he suspected. This paranoia was particularly irrational considering David Hall was the only other person on staff who espoused the young earth theory.

Anticipation grew as the travel day approached. Jacob's level of involvement in this project surprised many. More concerning was a change in his demeanor that was obvious to more than just the team.

* * *

"What's up with Dr. Knab?" a very pregnant Katy asked as she shuffled to the dining room table. She placed a casserole on its hot pad and rubbed her protruding belly with both hands.

"What do you mean?" David responded as Reese bounded in and took his place at the table.

"Kathleen says he's been acting funny at home. And you said the same about work."

"I'm not sure," David answered. "I'm sure he's under a lot of pressure. I asked him again about testing Hindsight's range, but he said it was taken care of."

"What did he mean? Didn't you say it didn't show images back some thousands of years?"

"Yup," David answered. "I asked Beth and she said they hadn't run it back more than four thousand years. I don't understand why he didn't make sure it will do what he wants before spending all this money on a massive project."

"Maybe he's having a nervous breakdown?" Katy proposed. "Or a mid-life crisis."

David rolled his eyes and changed the subject. "Supper smells good. Let's eat."

"Finally," Reese stated. "Me pray."

* * *

The travel day finally arrived, and more than forty people from Hindsight flew to Israel. The large group packed into several vans and headed toward their hotel. While on the way, city-wide sirens began blaring. The passengers reacted nervously, but local van drivers calmly changed the radio station from music to a frequency dedicated to emergency announcements.

"Good thing you didn't fly into that private airstrip," one driver commented after listening to the announcement in Hebrew.

Darren asked, "Why? What airstrip?"

"There is a large fire blazing sixty kilometers from here."

"To the east?" Darren pressed.

"Yes, do you know that airport?" the driver asked.

"I think that is where our equipment and the airship are," Oats replied, forgetting that he was in a van loaded with frightened people.

As the group entered their hotel, they stopped to watch a video of the fire's aftermath on a lobby television. It was indeed the small airport Darren mentioned. He was soon on the phone trying to determine if Hindsight was safe.

It was not.

"How could this happen again?" Darren wondered. They took every precaution. The equipment was stored, even hidden, in the very hangar that received the bulk of the damage. Non-essential personnel waited in their hotel rooms as Darren's crew set out for the airstrip.

Hindsight representatives were turned away long before they reached the location, but Darren soon received confirmation that the second Hindsight was a total loss. Those who made the trip were stuck in Israel for several days. It was the most subdued vacation any of them ever experienced.

* * *

The incident made international news. David and Katy watched the TV footage in horror and disbelief. Amazingly, only four people were killed, including the Sycra programmer. Autopsies revealed that the two guards died from bullet wounds before the fire was started. A dozen others were injured. It was pretty obvious that Hindsight was the target, even though its storage place was supposed to be secret. Everyone wondered if the same party was responsible for both attacks.

Something that never came to light was Gavi Braum's involvement. In selfish genius, he determined that the absence of Hindsight would make his images of the ancient temple Solomon built more valuable. The more images of the past that existed, the less each would be worth. The value of his collection would be second only to the Greek billionaire. For this reason, he double-crossed Jacob and gave new instructions to the men hired to cause enough trouble to get the airport shut down temporarily. They were tasked with targeting Hindsight directly. Director Knab assumed he had been duped but couldn't inform authorities without implicating himself.

Before the travelers could return to the U.S., the FBI arrived at the base once again. Two agents made their way to Dr. Knab's office. Jacob stood at his opened door, having been advised of their arrival by the front gate.

"Dr. Knab, I'm special Agent Carter with the FBI."

"I remember," Jacob replied. "No offense, but I'm sorry to see you again."

The second agent scoffed. That's when Knab suspected that this wasn't a routine visit. "What can I do for you?" he asked.

Several employees made excuses for being around the office area to see what was going on. David didn't need an excuse, but his motivation for being there was the same.

"Even the way those agents walked in suggested something was up," one employee commented.

"I'd love to hear what's going on in there," said another.

Soon, the two agents exited the office with the director between them— in handcuffs. Other agents interviewed relevant employees without divulging the reason for Dr. Knab's arrest.

Chapter 25 - Onward

"Katy…Katy?" David called out as he opened their front door. She appeared at the top of the stairs.

"Up here…what's wrong?"

"Jacob's been arrested," he answered.

"What for?" Katy asked as she started down the stairs, cradling her protruding belly.

"Don't know, but it's the FBI, so it must be serious," David speculated. "I think we will have to skip date night." He looked around. "Where's Reese?"

"At preschool."

"Oh yeah."

"That's okay. I haven't felt well today, anyway." Just then, a cell phone rang from the bedroom. Katy hurried back up the stairs to answer it. David sighed at the interruption of their conversation. Katy reappeared, pointing to the phone, and mouthed, "It's Kathleen." She then put the phone to her ear.

"Yes, I just heard," she said to Jacob's distraught wife. "I don't know… he doesn't know either." Katy looked at David with pleading eyes. He understood and nodded. "We'll be right over," she said before ending the call.

Kathleen was beside herself when the Halls arrived. Katy called Denise Oats to ask her to come wait for Reese to get home and bring him to Kathleen's. She grabbed a coloring book and some crayons to give to her son once he arrived. Kathleen and the Halls talked among themselves for a while, but nothing of consequence was said—because nothing of consequence was known. They just sat quietly most of the time, but the couple's presence was some comfort to Jacob's distraught wife. Finally, David promised to let Jacob's wife know if he learned anything. She reciprocated.

Reese hopped onto his car booster seat and buckled himself in. As Katy took her place in the front of their car, David noticed her squirm. Then she exclaimed, "Oh, no."

"What, hun?" he asked.

"My water broke."

While David drove to the house, Katy called Denise again, since she had volunteered to watch Reese when the time came. Katy had already prepared two overnight bags, one to take to the hospital, and another to send with Reese. David rushed in to grab them, then raced to get their son to his sitter.

"You don't have to hurry," Katy said, encouraging him to drive more carefully.

Denise was at her front door with their oldest daughter ready to take the child and his belongings at record speed. They moved as quickly and confidently as a race car pit crew. David wasn't sure he had even come to a complete stop before they were waving goodbye. Katy took a pained breath as he backed out of the drive.

"Okay," she said, "now you can hurry...I mean HURRY!"

* * *

Jacob Knab sat alone in the interrogation room for several minutes before two agents he'd never met entered. He was handcuffed to a metal ring on top of a table so his hands were visible at all times.

"Mr. Knab."

"Dr. Knab...if you please," the director said, then closed his eyes in remorse for foolishly correcting the agent.

"Dr. Knab, I just have one question," the agent promised. "Why?"

"Why, what?" Jacob replied, playing dumb.

"Why did you destroy your machine and kill those people?"

"I don't know what you're talking about," Knab claimed.

"Would it help you to know that you've been under surveillance ever since a spy infiltrated your facility and almost stole your equipment?"

Jacob lowered his head onto the table.

The agent continued, "We know you met with people with connections to a terrorist organization outside of Jerusalem. We know you paid them a large sum of money. We know the terrorists they are sympathetic to killed several people while starting a fire in the airplane hangar your equipment was stored in." Some incriminating pictures were flung across the table. Jacob glanced at them without picking them up. "Need I go on?"

Knab refused to speak without an attorney. He didn't have a criminal lawyer of his own, so he called a friend in Washington D.C. to get a recommendation. Once Kathleen was made aware that the case against her husband was "open and shut," she pestered him with the same question the agent asked, "Why?"

* * *

At the hospital, Katy delivered a healthy girl. Neither suffered ill effects from coming a little early. David became the acting director at Hindsight, but all there was to direct was the process of closing down operations. That was a bigger job than he expected. It took three months to tie everything in a bow.

By then, Knab had taken a plea deal that would make him eligible for parole in twenty-four years. When Kathleen visited him, Jacob finally told her the story, a story she later related to the few key people still on the base, David, Katy, Darren, Destiny, Marjorie, and Debra, the attorney.

"David, you told my husband that Hindsight couldn't be used to view history more than a few thousand years ago?"

"That's right. We hadn't tested it beyond that—officially, that is."

"I didn't know that," Darren commented.

"That was disappointing to him, but he could have accepted it," Kathleen continued. "At least until you suggested that the reason was that the earth itself is only a few thousand years old.

"As far as he is concerned, the earth's age is settled science. Anything to the contrary is religious foolishness. He knew that if Hindsight balked during the geological study, it would cause confusion. There are crazies out there who think the earth is very young, but he didn't know you and Jonathan were among them until you told him."

Before David could defend himself, Kathleen clarified, "His words—not mine."

"No offense taken," David responded.

"Do you honestly believe the earth is just a few thousand years old?" Destiny asked.

"I do."

"No wonder you freaked Dr. Knab out," Marjorie said.

"I was just suggesting to him that we test the equipment before taking it on the next mission."

"Well, Jacob did test it and found what you said to be true. It didn't work past a few thousand years, I think he said. He didn't know if the machine just doesn't work any further back or if someone tampered with the programming. Jacob became convinced you or Mr. Daniels messed with the equipment to make it appear to confirm that the earth is very young. He wanted to bring in some unbiased expert to examine the program."

"How does blowing the machine up fit into that plan?" Debra asked.

Darren interrupted. "Technically, nothing was blown up. A small explosion started an intense fire, but Hindsight's screen was really destroyed by firefighters putting out the blaze."

Kathleen continued. "As Jacob became more obsessed with his dilemma, he started making irrational decisions that even he doesn't now understand. He felt like he needed to have the equipment recalibrated and reprogrammed. But David, you would be involved in that, and he was afraid you might be part of the conspiracy. He said he couldn't postpone the project again.

"Nor could he let compromised equipment call settled science into question. He never wanted anything to threaten the equipment, or people. He loved Hindsight, and its potential. He said he ask that Jewish man, Braum, to arrange for a mild threat that would lock down the airport. He thought that would be good reason to cancel the trip but leave the equipment in Israel for continued evaluation. Then he could work with people he trusted to get Hindsight functioning properly."

Darren interrupted again. "You mean he trusted terrorists more than he trusted us?"

"It was just David he lost faith in," she explained. "But he wasn't sure who to trust. He did give the FBI all the information he could about those he hired, but they already knew more than he did about them."

Kathleen hated retelling Jacob's explanation but felt that the others deserved to know the truth. She especially regretted having to share her husband's distrust of David. The story was so strange that the group sat dumbfounded.

"That's just so bizarre," Minx said.

"True that," Darren agreed.

"I'm still confused about this young earth thing," Destiny admitted.

Katy looked at her husband and smiled. She knew this was the kind of opportunity he relished, even if the timing wasn't perfect. David never pressed others to listen to the gospel, but he rarely missed an invitation.

"As a Bible-believer, we trust God's Word to be correct in everything it asserts," David began. "God made a perfect world and placed a unique creature in it. While He created spiritual creatures like angels and physical ones like animals, mankind is of a different sort. We are spiritual beings in physical bodies.

"When the first man sinned—disbelieved and disobeyed God—his spirit, or soul, died. The eternal part of him became separated from God. As fallen man's offspring, we are born with a living body, but a dead soul. The Bible says we are naturally enemies of God, separated from Him.

"Because God is holy and just, He can't ignore our sin condition. And we are unable to do anything about it ourselves. Jesus, God Himself, became a man and paid the penalty for our sin. Those who believe this good news and depend on Jesus Christ as Savior are made new creatures. Our dead souls are brought to life, and we will exist with God forever."

"That's quite a sermon, bro," Darren said.

"Sorry if I got carried away. It's just that I want you all to know that God loves you and wants you in His family. That only happens by faith."

"But what about the young earth?" Marjorie asked, bringing up the original topic.

David answered, "If God is real and the Bible is His Word, it must be right since He is perfect and cannot lie. How can we claim it to be true in spiritual things if we can't trust it in areas we can corroborate? If the Bible is wrong about what it says about science, how can we believe it at all?"

"Good point," Destiny said. "But why does the earth's age really matter?"

Katy jumped it. "It matters for all eternity. What you believe determines your destiny. God gave us the Bible to lead us to His Son, Jesus. No matter how long you live on this earth, it is not even a drop in the ocean compared to where you will spend eternity."

When David recognized that most of the group were losing interest in the subject, he wrapped up the discussion, offering to share more with anyone who wanted. That was Mrs. Knab's opportunity to take her leave.

"I'm going to live with my middle daughter, at least for a while," Kathleen stated when asked about her plans. She said farewell to her friends for the last time and drove away. The others left too. As they headed for the door, both Destiny and Marjorie asked Katy if they could call her and talk more about Bible stuff. She happily encouraged it.

David put his arm around Katy. "How does a man lose his perspective like that?"

"You have to ask, Mr. Workaholic?" Katy answered. "He lost focus on what's truly important."

"He never knew what was really important," David said. "Sometimes I wonder if I don't try enough to share the gospel. I mean, I never really talked to Jacob about it."

"I can't believe he would go to such extremes just to prove you wrong," Katy commented. "Or prove you messed with the machine."

"Being right about his science was more important to him than anything, I guess," David suggested. "A real scientist should want to know the truth, no matter what it is."

* * *

It wasn't long before lab and other equipment was either stored, sold, or returned to the Sycra Foundation. The Hindsight attorney helped David secure generous severance packages for all employees. Most of them found new jobs easily. Nothing says "hire me" like having Hindsight on one's resume. The base closed, and military personnel were reassigned.

David took his wife and two children on a long vacation before opening up his own consulting firm. They visited both sets of grandparents and a few other loved ones. Their time with Trina was especially emotional. She was settling into her new home, job, and life. Despite the tragedy of Jonathan's death, she was maturing as a Christian.

Now that Hindsight was a thing of the past, it was time to look to the future. Even so, David and Katy began writing a memoir together. It focused more on the ups and downs of their walk with Christ than on his Hindsight experiences. That writing project helped David keep his priorities in order.

He was working on that very thing when his phone rang. The caller ID read Darren Oats. He answered.

"Good, you still have this number," Oats said.

"What's up, buddy?" David asked.

"You know who this is?"

"Yup, you're still on my contact list, Darren."

"Cool. I just wanted to thank you for that Bible talk you gave some time ago."

"Really?" David asked in surprise.

"Yeah. You know Destiny and Katy keep in contact, and your wife's been preaching at mine."

Unsure how to respond, David answered, "Is that a good thing?"

"It really is. Destiny tells me what Katy shares. That and what you told us got me thinking."

"Are you sure it wasn't the blow to your head?" David immediately regretted his attempt at humor. He thought to himself, "Here Darren was speaking from his heart, and I have to make a joke. What an idiot."

"Maybe," Darren laughed. "That did wake me up to my mortality. Anyway, we started back to church and finally came to understand that Christianity is not a religion but a relationship with God through Christ."

"That's great!" David exclaimed.

"All of us but my son have trusted Christ as our Savior and are trying to live for the Lord."

"I'm so happy for you. Thanks for letting me know."

"Destiny told your wife already but made her promise not to say anything until I could talk to you myself."

"We'll be praying for Drake," David promised.

"I appreciate that. He's not rebelling. He's just trying to think it through for himself."

David ended the call with a sense of satisfaction. "Hindsight is gone, but more souls are bound for heaven," he thought out loud. "Thank you, Lord, for letting us have a part in the most important work, Your work in saving lost sinners."

* * *

Six months later and six hundred miles away...

A computer screen flickered in a fancy laboratory. A lone figure rose from his desk in a mostly dark room. He opened a safe to reveal four things: a triangular piece of translucent metal, the plate created by remelting broken pieces of the first Hindsight, the sole remaining magical meteorite, and a three-ring binder filled with his findings after thoroughly testing and examining his precious possessions.

He took the triangle out and closed the safe. Then, he returned to his seat and placed the metal under a high-tech device that resembled a microscope. "Once more," he whispered to himself. "Just to be sure."

His attention alternated between that device and his computer. He swiveled back and forth between the two instruments, making a few keystrokes each time he returned to his laptop.

A knock at the door startled him. Quickly recovering, the scientist waved to the custodian he could see looking through the locked door's window.

"Working late again, Dr. Gordman?" the janitor asked, his voice barely audible through the door.

"Yes, Percy, working late again," Carl answered.

"Want me to take your trash?" Percy asked.

Carl responded casually, "I'm good, thanks."

"Good night, then." Percy added, "I doubt that Wentsome pays you enough."

"No, they don't," Carl thought as he stared at the computer screen with great satisfaction. He leaned back in his chair and intertwined his fingers behind his balding head. He smiled, nodding slowly as he read the information on his monitor.

To a layman, and even most scientists, the data on his screen would mean next to nothing. To Carl, it meant a breakthrough. "Finally," he said out loud. "Success!"

The End

Made in the USA
Columbia, SC
26 September 2022